SHADOWS AT MIDNIGHT

ROBERT J. BRADSHAW

Shadows At Midnight

Second Edition

Shadows At Midnight Copyright © 2021 by Robert J. Bradshaw

First Edition: October 2021

ISBN-13: 978-1-7773763-2-1

Dedicated to all those who bought Songs of the Abyss
and believed in me from the beginning

CONTENTS

"The horrors await in halls dressed in white,
Their orderly lapdogs look the same.
But that's all right, because no matter their might,
I won't let this madness take me."

– Korean Steel "Madness Loves Company" 1984
Lyrics written by: N. McCruger and D. Campbell

SIDE ONE

FORGOTTEN RELICS OF THE NEW WORLD

I suppose, like any tale worth telling, one should start at the beginning. My memory leading up to the event is hazy as much uncertainty was in my life, but I shall start with the facts. I was a corporal in the English Army at the time we set sail from Jamaica. I had not been present for the conquest of that island, for when it had been liberated from the Spanish, I was merely a boy.

I was garrisoned out of Port Royal and served my time there for nearly two years. Two years of the sweltering sun beating down on our heavy red coats. Two years of the locals seemingly always nearing a revolt. I do not miss those days.

But I write this journal not to describe the history of Jamaica, nor is it a memoir of my time serving His Majesty. No, it is the events that occurred after I left that island that drives me to action. Events that I will never forget as long as I live.

I am not sure who planned our operation, I only know that Lieutenant Peyton was in charge of our ragged group. His right-hand man was a fellow by the name of Sergeant Hyde. I still remember his duelling scars and that large tobacco pipe he carried around with him. "Old Iron Hyde" the lads had called him.

I received only one briefing before I was ordered onto a ship and informed that I would be heading to the continent. I remember being excited by this prospect. I would finally get to set foot in the New World and its endless mystery.

Our orders were simple: Defend a group of loggers who were stationed along the coast of Yucatan. I had found this to be odd. The Jamaican colony needed every man it could find to assist in its defence from a probable Spanish raid and to quell the local unrest. But there we were, tasked with assisting a band of loggers.

I had heard that many of these men were pirates, thieves, and criminals, the kind of people that did not deserve the assistance of His Majesty's Army. But these men were to send mahogany to Britain, an important resource used in the construction of our vast Navy. At least that's what Lieutenant Peyton had told us as we set sail from Port Royal.

For an officer he was not a bad fellow, just a little high strung and inexperienced. I am still unsure why he lied about our destination and mission. Perhaps he wished to quash any rumours with this ruse before they could arise, or maybe he didn't want us asking questions. Once we reached the shores of the New World, however, the truth came out.

I knew something had gone awry when we appeared to be heading much further south than we should have been. I was no seaman, but I could read a compass and had seen a map in the officer's hut. Yucatan was north of our port, yet our vessel, the *HMS Watchtower*, turned south-west at dawn of the second day.

I remember there being a storm that night, which at the time I found dreadful. I now realize it may have assisted us greatly, for the Spanish did not detect our lonely vessel.

I do not know where we made landfall, but there were no

logging camps or Union Jacks to be seen. Just a lonely beach, crystal blue water, and an endless jungle before us.

As we disembarked our row boats, a certain corporal, Ainsley, I believe, had the realization that we were not where we should have been. That is when Lieutenant Peyton addressed the men, all sixty of us. He said our mission was a unique one. Forty of us were going into the jungle that very evening. Twenty others were staying behind. Commanded by Sergeant Eaton, this smaller group was to set up camp and wait for our vessel to return in one week's time.

Peyton's superiors did not want to risk the boat being sighted by Spanish privateers patrolling the coast, so they ordered her to move out to the open sea. There she would sit until it was time to return and retrieve us.

Peyton then informed us of the particulars of this operation. Command had supposedly obtained knowledge of a lost Mayan City a few days journey from our landing site. They had arranged for a guide to navigate us through the dense jungle and reveal its location. This guide was to be paid quite handsomely for his efforts.

"Pay him with what?" Ainsley asked.

I remember Lieutenant Peyton looking to Iron Hyde and smiling. You should have seen the lads perk up when they told us of what lay ahead in the city.

Gold. An unfathomable amount.

But while that did raise my ears, what the young Lieutenant said next filled me with wonder. Amongst the gold and bounty, a holy relic was to be located. A medallion of sorts, thought to be lost to time.

Peyton's superiors wanted us to return to Jamaica with as much gold as we could fit into our fur packs. They also wanted confirmation of the existence of this relic. If it could be retrieved, then we were to loot it. And if it couldn't? A full expedition force would be dispatched in the coming weeks to excavate it. I wonder now if Peyton had been told of the relic's power, or if he too had been left in the dark.

I remember how I felt as the *HMS Watchtower* raised anchor in the harbour and began to drift away, the wind at her back, taking any memory of comfort along with it. I felt alone, and I'm sure the other fifty-nine lads on that beach felt the same. I didn't have much time to reflect on this, though, as the sounds of the jungle stirring drew my attention back to what lay ahead.

A man emerged from the foliage. With wild eyes and a lean, battle worn figure, he approached. This local showed no fear as sixty muskets and flintlocks were pointed at him.

Peyton stepped forward and addressed the man, asking if he was to be our guide.

The man answered only with a single word, "Si."

Now, to you, that might mean nothing. But to us lads, that was a chilling word. We were fighting the Spaniards and realized our guide could speak that language. Well, that was a terrifying revelation. As my musket was aimed at his boney face, I remember thinking, *Maybe he assumes Spanish is the language of the white man? Maybe he is just as surprised that we can't understand him?*

Peyton and Iron Hyde had a quick conversation over the correct course of action, and it was decided that this local must be our prearranged guide. The order rang out for us to lower our weapons, and while we did comply it was with much unease.

I know the answer to all these questions now, but at the time I had many thoughts swirling through my head. *Could this man be trusted? Is he a Spanish henchman of sorts, luring us into an awaiting garrison? Or is he just a local who stumbled upon a group of lost looking lads in curious uniforms standing on the beach?*

But Peyton did not share my concerns as he counted out forty of us. Before I knew it, we were following this wild looking man into the jungle, leaving twenty men behind to establish a camp. Knowing then what I do now, I would have preferred to tend the fire than venture into those trees.

Forty red coats and one local wandered that jungle for two full days with nothing to report. We slept little at night and took few breaks. Each morning, we marched well before the sun was over the trees, all of us painfully aware that the Spanish menace could be lurking anywhere.

On the third day we arrived at the perimeter of a clearing. I remember it as noteworthy because the guide looked concerned. His calm demeanour vanished, his eyes darting back and forth as he studied that clearing. No matter what Lieutenant Peyton asked, the man uttered the familiar, "Si."

Is that the only word this fellow speaks? I thought as I monitored the gap in the trees, wondering why we had stopped.

A private named Blakemore muttered something about how he thought we were walking into a trap. But Iron Hyde scolded him and said, "You think our guide would look this concerned and be squatting in the bush if he was meaning to trap us? No, he would have led us right into the middle of that clearing with no hesitation."

The sun had moved high overhead before our guide took a step forward. Peyton followed his lead and Iron Hyde sent Blakemore and a Corporal named Ingsly to cover the Lieutenant. As we neared the halfway point of the clearing, time seemed to slow completely.

Vines hung down in the distance and the jungle branches rocked in the breeze. The wind smelled of dew and fruit. I was distracted, not paying as close attention to my surroundings as I should have been. Then I saw a sliver of light pierce the horizon.

I followed it with my eyes, watching as it flew out of the treeline and burrowed into Peyton's breast. He clutched his chest and turned towards us. An arrow stuck out of him, a dark shade of red pooling on his already blood red coat.

A musket fired to the east. While I am not sure who it belonged to, I do know that the savages rushed us a moment after. The jungle came alive as what appeared to be a hundred of them came screaming towards us.

As unheroic as it is to say, I had never been more terrified than at that particular moment. My first taste of real combat was nothing like I thought it would be.

I fired my musket and struck one of the approaching devils. The smoke from my shot blocked my view and before I knew it, the entire clearing was covered in gun smoke and powder residue. Blakemore took an arrow to the eye and Private Darby was hit by a stolen Spanish musket.

Iron Hyde formed a group of fifteen men to the west in a counter march. Two rows of musket balls piercing the jungle leaves put a dent in the barbarian's ranks.

I ran my cutlass through a man's heart and felt an arrow breeze past my ear as I shoved the body to the jungle floor. Corporal Eaton had managed to reload and sent a musket ball into a savage's neck as the brute charged my position. I moved backwards to get closer to Iron Hyde and his firing line.

Another volley was loosed before the sergeant screamed out his cadence, and then, silence. The surviving savages had retreated further into the jungle.

At the time, I feared they would return, or perhaps set another trap for us up ahead. They did neither. I was wrong to fear them, for man was not the horror that lay ahead in the depths of that jungle.

Lieutenant Peyton was dead by the time Ainsley rolled him onto his back. The arrow had pieced his heart. I felt a weight strike me at that moment. Iron Hyde was in command now, and I do not think the old boy was all that eager about the prospect.

Our guide had survived the ambush and stood at the edge

of the jungle, waiting for us to continue. Private Crawford was mumbling and cursing about, "Lynching him by his ankles," and "Cutting out that Spanish tongue."

But Iron Hyde spoke up again. His exact words are lost to me, but the effect of them was clear, "If anyone touches a hair on that local's head, they will answer to me." He raised his cutlass and pointed the blade square into a button on Crawford's uniform. There was a peculiar look in his eyes, like he had gone a touch mad. Perhaps he was worried that all the men would blame the guide for the ambush, just as Crawford had. Iron Hyde had to prevent a potential mutiny before it could fester.

As we marched on, there were rumblings among the ranks that Iron Hyde was losing his thick skin and gaining an affinity for the savages. But I disagreed with the lads then, and still to this day believe Old Iron Hyde was correct in his assessments. No guide who was planning to lure us into a trap would stand directly beside an officer in a bright red coat where a volley of arrows was about to be unleashed. That local had intended to get us through unharmed, for he was our ally, or as much of an ally as payment in stolen gold can make someone.

As the day began to close, it was like we had crossed an invisible line, and I was not the only one to have noticed it. It was like passing a threshold that might exist between the River Styx and Hell itself.

The toucan calls ceased and the monkeys that had been scurrying on the vines behind us stopped. All of them in profile, side by side; those black eyes watching us move deeper into the jungle and farther into the circles described in the *Devine Comedy*. I still see those black eyes in my dreams.

I remember Spooner pointing out a jaguar that was flanking our battered column from the side. Later in the day, he told me that the animal stopped dead in its tracks and just stood there for a moment before turning tail and running off, retreating away from this seemingly unholy barrier.

If even great beasts such as that were afraid of what lay beyond... The thought makes my skin crawl to this day.

It was shortly after the crossing that all of us had removed our heavy coats and had strung them along our waists or shoulders. Even Old Iron Hyde had followed suit. It was devilishly hot, hotter than the rest of the jungle. Never again have I experienced a heat like what moved through those trees.

The sun was low in the sky when our guide pushed aside a set of vines and Iron Hyde stopped marching. His boots were submerged in a mud puddle, but he took little notice. He simply stared off into the distance.

Ainsley moved up to Iron Hyde's position and stopped too, dumbfounded.

I was next. I looked past them and the view was astonishing. We had reached our destination. The Lost City.

Its ruins were overgrown with vines and bush. Like the rainforest had swallowed it up whole. It looked to have been abandoned for over one thousand years. At the far end of the grounds was a tower or temple that rose up to the sky. The stairs to it were battered and broken; the storms of the rainforest having seemingly whittled down the rocks.

The atmosphere this city irradiated was thick with despair. I was starting to think these ruins were not lost at all; they had been forbidden. I could feel the souls of those who had lived there swirling about, warning us not to continue, telling us to flee, and not to enter those cursed ruins. I am not sure how I knew as such, but the air, fraught with sadness, screamed at me to leave.

Orders were orders, though, and I had a duty to the King. At least that's what I believed at the time. We had come to do a job, for England demanded her gold, and by God, we would get it for her. What fools we were then.

To this day, what happened next is seared in my mind's eye like a brand.

Iron Hyde lead us down the slight hill and into the

compound. As our guide scanned the surrounding Mayan structures, he had a look of regret in his eyes, perhaps realizing that no matter how much gold you possess, you cannot spend it if you are dead.

Then I saw it. Several vines and foliage had been cut away and discarded, tossed to the ground.

Our guide whispered something to Iron Hyde, but I have no ghastly idea what language it was. It sounded too harsh to be Spanish, but his tone was clearly one of pure shock.

Someone had been here, and quite recently.

Iron Hyde slapped my shoulder and pointed forward. I could see the sweat pouring down his face. I followed his mosquito bitten hand with my eyes. At the far end of the compound, in front of the stone steps of the temple, I saw it.

A Spanish flag.

It did not ripple in the breeze, as there was no wind. The air was still, and the flag hung like a corpse with its soul stripped away. I didn't believe in omens until that day, but that flag was our last warning.

"This isn't right," Iron Hyde said, as we gazed upon the flag in the distance. His voice was distant but cut through the silence like a razor. "The governor said the Spanish did not know of this place. He was sure of it."

Iron Hyde looked to the guide. The native held out his hands as if to say, "They aren't supposed to be here."

Ainsley snorted and mumbled, "Seems like there's an awful lot this bloke doesn't know." He kicked at a group of weeds as he eyed the guide.

Iron Hyde pointed to Ainsley, Crawford, and myself and selected us as lead scouts, while Spooner and seven other men were ordered to hold this position and watch our rear flank.

I lead our column forward with Crawford on my left and Ainsley behind, the rest of the formation of seventeen red coats trailing by a good distance. I knew what being lead scout meant. I would be the first to take a Spanish musket ball to the heart, or one of those native arrows to the throat.

As I walked, I heard nothing and saw even less. The red of the Spaniards' flag. The green of moss-covered steps of the tower ahead. The brown of the bark. The colours gripped me. No animals, no Spaniards, no savages, just a flag and our formation approaching.

As I neared the site, I saw the remains of a camp. Several fire pits had been dug and sharpened stakes had formed a perimeter. It looked as if this encampment was nearly a fortnight old. Several furs lined the ground, now damp from the rains. I remember thinking, *These Spaniards left in a hurry. No one abandons furs.*

"Where the devil are they?" Ainsley whispered.

I did not answer but I thought, *Perhaps they heard our skirmish with the locals and ran off to a more fortified position.*

Several long pikes were leaning against a hideous statue. A set of conquistador sabres sat on a collection of cut vines, their blades dull and worn from the swath of green they had to clear out of this city. As I looked around the camp, I felt like we were being watched.

Ainsley was busy examining the sculpture, its eyes open wide, and a pair of stone lips peering down at him. The figure almost looked to be gloating in the way the corner of its mouth curled, and how it bore its teeth.

Crawford picked up a water pouch that had been left behind by one of the doused fires and shook it. The water sloshed around inside, a haunting sound to be sure, for no soldier would abandon his water sack in the scorching tropical climate of that rainforest.

I opened my mouth to say something when Iron Hyde cleared his throat and waved at me, asking if he should lead the men into the site. I scanned the surrounding trees and structures again, no one to be seen. I let out a sigh before waving them over. We were committed now, for there was no turning back.

We scouted out the rest of the camp. Other than finding several packs loaded with powder and musket balls, there was not much else to it.

Iron Hyde started to put together a group that would be part of the first excursion into the surrounding buildings, but the scout quickly put a stop to that. He pointed to the low hanging sun and said, "Si."

I'm still not sure if he was actually speaking Spanish or English and using the word "see," but perhaps I was reading into it.

Iron Hyde understood all the same and decided we would hunker down for the night instead. He sent Ainsley to go collect Spooner and the other seven men who were guarding our rear flank and they joined us at the camp just as the sun disappeared into the heart of the jungle.

Iron Hyde ordered that a group of men should climb to the top of the tower to be lookouts. I volunteered, along with Crawford and two other privates whose names time has long taken from me.

As I climbed the steps in the dark night, I noticed several splotches of black that had been sprayed onto the rocks near the top steps. At the time I thought it to be a peculiar looking moss, or perhaps the moonlight playing with my vision. As I reflect on this, I know now that it was dried blood.

I ventured inside the little room that sat on top of the temple. Truth be told, there was not much to it. Just a stone room containing some murals carved into the rock. The Mayan gods' faces beamed at us. Mouths and eyes seeing all. Disgusted by our trespassing.

I looked down at the two fires that our unit had set up in the remains of the Spanish camp. Everyone was huddled up tight around the flames, not wanting to leave the safety of the flickering light. I watched them for a few moments before returning my gaze to the jungle. Time slipped by me as I marvelled at its never-ending majesty. A uniform and constant blackness that swallowed up the earth.

Something caught my eye, at the eastern edge of the tree line. The moonlight had glimpsed the glint of steel.

I watched that line for a long while, thinking my eyes and lack of sleep had betrayed me. Then I saw it again. This time a column of reflective surfaces. At first, I thought them to be sword blades by the way they moved, but I quickly determined they were in fact helmets. I deduced that this column of men must be the Spanish forces, for the local savages never wore such armour.

The Spaniards in their conquistador helmets marched in profile at the perimeter of the forgotten city. Yet they did not enter. I studied them thinking, *Why? Can they not see the fires? Why would they not come in? They should have nothing to fear. If these are reinforcements for the Spanish garrison, then they should assume the fires are friendly.*

It is true, lighting fires such as these in enemy territory was a foolhardy thing to do. Iron Hyde more than anyone knew so. But he was also aware of how the men looked at the structures and statues that closed in on the camp. The fires offered a reprieve for the men's fears, slight that it was.

The helmets continued to march along the eastern perimeter, staying in the treeline.

I wanted to descend the temple and warn the lads of their presence, but the stairs were so steep I would surely fall in the night. In addition, if I attempted to call down to the men below, the Spanish would recognize the King's English and come for us.

So, I stayed and watched the war party patrol, hoping that they would continue to ignore us. If they did start to move in and encircle the camp, then I would have no alternative but to sound the alarm. I realize now why that band of men never entered the camp.

Those men were already dead.

. . .

I awoke the next day with Crawford standing over me. He kicked my boot and said it was time to move. I asked him if he or the other two spotters had seen anything moving in the treeline that night.

"Not a soul," he replied simply. Those words haunt me to this day.

We descended the temple steps just as Iron Hyde said we could eat our rations. I don't remember what I ate, but I can tell you it was salted. We ate in less than half an hour and then it was time for the first expedition. I again volunteered. To this day I don't know why I did so. Perhaps I thought if I ventured into that site willingly, I would be spared the phobias associated with the unknown.

Ainsley pointed out an entrance at the base of the temple and Iron Hyde indicated it to our scout, asking him if that was where the gold was.

Our scout did not answer, instead he walked to the eastern side of the courtyard, towards a set of stone structures that were much less grandiose in scale. I watched the trees carefully, expecting to see a musket barrel trained on my jacket, but only the green of the jungle met my eye.

Our guide was the first to enter. As he did so, he scanned the tight room and nodded at something, his suspicions had been correct, I assume. Iron Hyde and Spooner entered close behind.

I moved in behind a private named Gladwin. I only remember this pour sod's name because of the way this big lumbering fellow carried himself. His rifle jangled as he entered, leaving me on edge.

The air in that room smelled of death. I hate to use such a simple and final word to define a place, but there is no other word that better describes it. The air was heavy and putrid.

The sun from outside offered little illumination to our

surroundings, but my eyes adjusted soon enough. In either direction to our east and west were narrow passageways, but the hallways were not what our leaders were looking at. Their eyes were focused on the wall which lay ahead.

Several stone bricks had been removed to reveal a third corridor, descending deeper into the very bowels of the jungle itself. The Spanish had indeed beaten us to this place and had entered the hidden passage. But where were they now? Still below, too enthralled with their glistening riches to resurface?

Iron Hyde ordered five torches to be assembled. A group marched back to camp and bound together several branches with vines and dried leaves down the centre, a speck of gun powder placed at the top of each. A quick light of flint and the torches lit, creating great hand-carried pyres.

Before we entered the underworld, Hyde ordered for six men to return to camp and stand watch. He gave specific orders that two of our best scouts should remain at the top of the temple to keep an eye out for the Spaniards or savage war parties. He then ordered four men to stand watch at the entrance of the opening. He said it was to warn us if they heard cries from the camp or the spotters on the temple signalled, but I think these men were to cover our retreat. Iron Hyde did not like the smell of this place either.

Eighteen red coats and one guide entered the ramp down to that necropolis, and far fewer would ever return.

The ancient stairs were slick with mildew. The scent of roots and dirt and overripened fruit lingered just ahead of us. Our torches lit the path ahead, showing a narrow passage that moved farther down into the structure.

My eye caught no webs left by spiders or lizards scuttling across the walls. Even the insects knew to stay away. Yet here we were, with such hubris, continuing our descent.

We reached the bottom of the stairs and the passage widened to reveal an open chamber. Mayan sculptures and stone cut-outs littered the walls. The torch light danced across their cold faces. Their demeanour depicted terror in their wandering eyes and fear in their misshapen limbs. Perhaps I was projecting my emotions onto their stone framework, or possibly they served as a final warning from the long-deceased sculptors.

Hyde ordered a torch be placed in the room so we would be able to find our way back in the likely event these catacombs became maze-like and difficult to navigate. Spooner placed his torch into an indentation on the floor so that it stood straight up.

The light reflected off the arched ceiling in such a way that the far side of the room was visible. A single opening cut into the brickwork revealed a misty pathway cloaked in shadow. But while many of the lad's eyes wandered down into its depths, I looked beside the opening. I gasped.

A collection of muskets and cutlasses littered the floor. They were not piled like their placement was deliberate. No, quite the opposite. They had been strewn about as if they had been tossed aside. Red liquid pooled underneath bits of fabrics that sat as rags nearby. A helmet had been discarded to the side with several flintlocks and pikes in the far right corner. It was obvious a battle had occurred.

But what of the bodies? Why were the weapons left where they fell? *The savages have never been known to leave a weapon behind,* I thought. *Especially the superior Spanish muskets.*

I nor any of the other member of our unit saw any evidence of barbarian weapons. No arrows, nor bows, nor clubs. Only Spaniard armaments littered that unholy ground.

Ainsley picked up the dented helmet. "Christ, they must have turned on each other," he muttered.

The boy had only been half right.

Hyde ordered us to group together and leave the armaments where they lay. The way he gripped his musket as he spoke, I think it was the only time someone had seen the old sergeant shake. He ordered us forward in a defensive column and told us to press on.

Some damn fool mumbled about the Spaniards getting greedy and fighting over their golden shares. A few other of the lads nodded. Even at the time I thought that seemed too clean, too human of an emotion. What had occurred in this room looked unnatural, almost animalistic.

As we continued down the narrow hall, I observed that several paths branched off to the side, but again our guide led us straight and true. Forward, always forward. Those black recesses on the eastern and western flanks of our column beckoned us to explore, almost promising spoils beyond our imaginations. But none of us dared venture into their depths.

As I moved by the passage on the right, I heard a sound like a rustling pack or boots on rock. I turned my head, but the torch lights of our unit dared not pierce the darkness either.

I stopped and pointed my musket into its depths. If I were to fire, the void would have swallowed up that shot in an instant. I doubt it would have hit stone or clay or flesh. Just travelling onward into eternity.

My mind told me the truth. Those passageways were made of rock and earth. But my soul knew that the edge our earth existed there. To enter one of those tunnels would lead to an unknown plane far outside of my imagination.

I kept my musket pointed for a long while. Crawford and Gladwin did as well. A few other lads peered past us while the rest of the group continued to trudge on with the torch light, leaving our small group soon to be enveloped in darkness.

Just as the last rays of the hand-carried pyres abandoned us, Gladwin begged me to depart that spot and for us to rejoin the formation. Crawford and the others had already left my side and Gladwin soon turned to leave as well. When he spoke, his words were swallowed up by that eternal void. No echoes or reverberation, just endless silence.

I lowered my musket and pivoted to follow his lead. As I did so, the sound of moving leather fluttered out of the black. Something unseen lay down that passage but I did not have the heart or stomach to venture forth and find out what it was. I sprinted and rejoined my group, keeping an ever-watchful eye on our rear flank and those tunnels that ran in all directions.

Before long, we had reached another chamber that was quite different from the first. Long gullies ran off the sides, leading into a darkness below. It gave the room an appearance like it was floating over an abyss. The walls on the far sides of the trenches were almost indistinguishable as our torch light hardly reached the stone surface. But as the light flickered it revealed a mere glimpse of what was bestowed upon the rock face. I am thankful I could only see a fraction of their depictions. What those murals depicted was unholy.

Countless figures of men and women naked and shivering. Rising upward grabbing at the gods. But below them was what caused my head to look to my boots. A legion of pure terror whose shambling members moved upwards, twisting and without mercy.

The atmosphere of that misty room was of hostile cruelty, but I sensed we were drawing near to our prize. One look at our guide confirmed it. He beckoned for us to continue onward with a confident gesture. But this disguise did not fool me, for his expression was that of a man who wanted to turn back.

We heard it before any of us set eyes upon it. A clanging of iron and dragging of boots.

Then one of our pyres illuminated the shine of a helmet. A conquistador's helmet, moving towards us. The body beneath it was slow, but all the more frightening to behold. The figure moved like he was a marionette operated by a drunken master, for the control of his limbs was lacking and without rhythm. The Spaniard lurched towards our unit, the darkness coating his finer features.

Iron Hyde called out, "Halt." But the figure continued on.

Hyde raised his musket and called out again. "Detente! Stop!" But his command fell on deaf ears as the figure dragged its mud-covered boots towards us.

Iron Hyde's words moved down into the depths below us. The sounds they emitted as they echoed off that dark surface made my skin crawl.

I am not sure who fired first, but it was the final shot that struck the figure in the bridge of the nose, sending its helmet and the back of its head tumbling through the air. The figure crumpled forward in a heap.

It is true that those men should not have fired, the conquistador appeared unarmed, no musket, or flintlock, or sabre in hand. Yet the way he moved, the shambling, the twitching... I shall speak no more of it.

No one spoke as we stared at the corpse that lay ahead. Crawford and the other two shooters reloaded and once they had, we moved on. Iron Hyde didn't say a word.

I looked down at the body as I stepped over it. Its armour was dented, and the gore upon the fabrics of its uniform was peculiar. For the blood was clearly dry. This man had been wounded long before he had his head lightened. The conquistador's mouth was open to reveal brown teeth that looked jagged and shark like, rearranged and pointed. Black goo was splattered upon them. My eyes wandered to where the brain had been but as I glimpsed the splinters of bone and pink mush, I looked away. Despite the man moving mere moments before, it appeared he had been dead for some time.

Our unit exited the chamber and before I knew it, we had marched into another great hall. The air smelled of rot, but I paid it little mind as I was taken aback by the architecture of this crypt. I still have no idea how the Mayan engineers managed to construct it. The walls of the room slanted upwards in perfect lines. Alcoves had been cut away in the stone to reveal passages. The roof was multitiered, cut in a spiralling pattern with several trenches running off into the sides of the upper level, moving to unseen areas deeper in the structure.

As I studied the design, I took a step forward and noticed the floor was uneven and jagged as several murals had been etched there. I stood towards the front of the formation with Crawford, Ainsley, and Spooner. Ainsley's torch revealed that Sergeant Hyde, Gladwin, and two others hovered nearby. The rest of the group were to our backs, including our guide who was studying the swirling ceiling carvings.

Then it happened. All at once and without warning.

The light of our torches revealed movement to the sides of the room. They came out of the sloped wall and moved with obtuse rhythm. Their uniforms tattered and bearing blood, dirt, and mold. Grime covered every inch of them.

The Spaniard soldiers rushed us. A musket was fired, then two, then eight, all our own. A series of flashes and the smell of gunpowder as the smoke from the rifles began to swirl around us. The shots echoed, their sounds moving off into the surrounding tunnels, calling more of the strangers to us. A torch was dropped as a soldier was grabbed and pulled into the dark.

The flashes from the musket fire revealed a second wave slithering out of the crevices. This formation looked older and more decayed than the force prior. Screams filled the air as did the sounds of steel, as men unsheathed their blades.

I fired at a Spaniard who was fast approaching. My musket shot illuminated his face. Those eyes, I will never forget. I had heard that eyes were the windows to the soul. Yes, well what is to say of a man who has no soul for your gaze to meet?

My shot hit him in the intestines, adding a new hole to his ragged uniform. The blood that poured from the wound was rotten and clotted as it leaked onto the stone ground. My shot had little effect on his shambling speed. He kept charging, his tattered boots and rotting teeth moving ever closer.

I retreated and my back ran into something solid but yet alive: a man. I turned and as I went to draw my sabre, Spooner's eyes met mine. His cutlass was held at a position to strike, and the boy nearly ran it through me. He looked into my face and could see the warmth and lack of decay about me. We both still had our souls.

I withdrew my sword from its sheath and watched as the circling figure shifted its focus to an easier target: a lad a few paces from us with his back turned. Whether this beast recognized the steel in our hands or was simply going after the man that was closer, I will never know.

Ainsley, Crawford, Spooner, and I grouped together and backed off towards the far end of the room. The approaching wave of death encircled the surviving members of our group. Crawford was screaming at us to leave, to continue deeper into the tunnels. It was our only chance.

As I turned to depart, I saw Iron Hyde run his cutlass through a conquistador who had several musket wounds. Iron Hyde grimaced as he pierced the decaying man's stomach, no doubt feeling the steel nick rib and slice through rotten muscle. The sergeant only stopped when the hilt of his blade reached the man's tattered uniform. Face to face, one pair of eyes filled with fear, the other glassy and starving.

We turned and fled. I couldn't bear to witness what had happened to our overrun force. We ran deeper into the catacombs, following Ainsley's torch light as it bounded off into the distance. The screams that roared behind me curdled my blood.

Before long the four of us reached a larger room. Crawford entered first and gasped. Spooner swore as he saw the contents and Ainsley swung his torch around wildly. I entered last.

We had found it. The treasure room.

Chests of gold and bronze lined the walls. Clay pots of coin and totems crowned with gems, all spilling onto the floor.

Crawford turned to face the way we had come and began to reload his musket. The poor boy's hands trembled. Spooner moved over to the nearest chest and began shovelling coins into his fur pack. I saw Ainsley raise a brow before continuing through the room.

Despite the horrors we had just witnessed, there was more gold and treasure in that hall than any man could ever hope to see in his short lifetime. It would take a thousand men a fortnight, working all day without reprieve, to move it all, and Spooner wanted to make this mission mean something.

Ainsley continued to scout the room, his torch revealing multiple murals on the wet rocks and several towering statues of curious design. "Spooner," he said after a moment, "help me find the exit."

I watched as Spooner continued to scoop gold into his pack, clearly not hearing Ainsley's order. I moved a step forward and felt water droplets run down my brow. I glanced up to see the condensation was appearing out of the endless black void. My eyes did not linger on the ceiling long, as something in the corner of my eye drew my attention forward.

To call it a podium would be a misnomer. The object I approached was a stone basin that was wide and jutted out of the ground at half a man's height. Before I knew it, I was standing over it, looking down into its depths. I was drawn to it; all other sounds became muffled under cotton as I looked into the waters. The light of Ainsley's torch was the first illumination it had received in ages. *A hundred years or more*, I remember thinking, even though I had no basis for that notion.

The waters were green and soupy with dirt and muck. At the bottom of the shallow basin was a medallion that sat like black obsidian. Its design was similar to the murals we had passed prior and contained holes and ridges upon its face.

I picked it up and lifted it out of its resting waters. It was a mishmash of gold, bronze, and iron, a mirage of colour. Its mural design stared up at me, speaking to me like no object had before. It was larger than one of my hands, and it was heavier than it appeared on the surface. As such, I needed to hold the medallion with both hands.

Ainsley broke my concentration from its alluring call when he said, "Lads, there are no more corridors. But I see a drainage tunnel. If we crawl, we could make it." His voice carried and fluttered around the room, reverberating off the structure's deaf ears and moving upwards to the black ceiling where the droplets rained down.

I looked down at my finding one last time, that slab of gold and bronze and iron. I placed it on the edge of the basin before unslinging my pack and hastily placing the medallion inside it. Ainsley called out again, but Crawford silenced him by saying, "I hear something."

Spooner ceased loading the gold and stood. He hoisted his bulbous fur pack on to his shoulders and drew his cutlass. Crawford took a step back and pointed his musket at the entrance of the room.

Ainsley rushed past me and stood beside Crawford, holding his torch before him in an attempt to illuminate the corridor ahead.

I pulled my pack up and felt the medallion settle to the bottom; it preferred the dark.

I stepped forward as I heard it too. The all too familiar sound of dragging boot heels scuffing their leather against stone. Jostling steel stirred behind.

The lads went to back away, but Ainsley's pyre glimpsed it. A muscular man with a torn red coat stepped forward, using his cutlass as a crutch to assist his walking as he lumbered towards us.

"Sergeant, you've made it!" The glee in Ainsley's voice, the euphoria in his tone, has stuck with me to this day.

Then we all saw the gaping wound bestowed on his neck, the blackened blood clots, and the soulless eyes. All of us stepped back in unison and Ainsley's torch revealed more of them. A mob of redcoats marched behind Iron Hyde's shell.

The horde lurched forward, and I could see conquistador helmets towards the back of the onslaught. All their eyes locked on the torch light. They appeared almost hesitant to approach the fire, but the demons inside them insisted they feed, and that call could not be silenced.

Ainsley and Crawford pushed by me as they pivoted and raced to the drain at the opposite side of the room. Spooner stood there dumbfounded, clearly overtaken by shock. His friends and commander dehumanized and joining ranks with the deceased conquistadors, whose conquest would know no end.

I bounded forward and grabbed Spooner by the pack, pulling him backwards. As we reached the drain Ainsley was already deep inside, crawling horizontally to freedom. His torch light quickly moved away, cloaking us in darkness. The sound of boot leather on wet stone echoed from the black behind us.

Crawford entered the drain, and I watched his coat and trousers disappear into its mass. I followed next, feeling the pull on my pack as I did so. The fur being worn down against the stone as I pushed forward.

Then I heard Spooner grunt from behind. I remember thinking, *They've got him!*

I looked over my shoulder and, to my surprise, Spooner was still there. He grimaced and tugged on his pack as he yelled, "I'm stuck!"

He was the largest of us and his pack was nearly bursting from the Mayan gold and silver. The drain was wide enough that I could turn, and I did so immediately. I moved back to him as he screamed that he could hear them. I would be a liar if I said I did not have visions of Iron Hyde's shell feeding on

Spooner's legs as they kicked out of the drainage tunnel opening.

"Remove your pack," I yelled at him. "The gold's not worth it."

He attempted to throw off the straps, but his hands could not reach around his shoulders. He was packed in too tight.

I reached to my belt and removed my bayonet. I pressed steel to leather and hastily cut the straps. I fear in my haste I may have grazed Spooner, but he did not scream from the wounds. No, his cries were from what approached out of that endless abyss behind him. I could hear them too, the mob endlessly moving towards us masked in the blackness.

With one final cut I removed the straps and pulled Spooner forward. His pack slid behind him and clapped to the stone floor as the deadweight made contact, ten lifetimes of riches contained inside. Spooner and I crawled forward, leaving the shambling wretches and their sounds of death far behind.

We followed the flicker of torch light forward, until we reached the end of the drainage tunnel. I exited and looked about the room. A narrow hallway stood before us. I glanced to my boots and saw that the drainage system continued downward under the stone to an unseen area of the catacombs. The four of us moved through the passageway ahead and before long we reached its end.

The sight at its conclusion was one of the happiest moments of my life. A sliver of light cutting through the darkness. We ran towards it.

The room was small, and the brickwork had been torn away. I looked down as something glimmered in the light. Several steel objects littered the ground beside the discarded stonework. Knives and bayonets. A trail of blood ran from them, moving away from the light.

Seeing the blood, I knew we were not as safe as we

thought. The hoard would continue to follow us through that water tunnel.

Ainsley sensed it too and began to claw away at the rock. Mounds of dirt and brick work folded inward as the four of us scrambled over each other, tearing at the wall, the sounds behind us moving closer and closer.

Crawford slammed his shoulder into the spot we had dug away and we heard the wall shake as rocks slid against one another. We all took to throwing ourselves at the wall and before long it gave way, creating a warm embrace of sunlight.

The three lads pushed past me and up the sloped rocky surface. I began to follow but heard a wet choking sound coming from behind. I looked over my shoulder to see how close they were, but my eyes never glimpsed it.

Before I knew it, I had fallen forward. A searing pain overcame me. My foot had slipped into a crevice in the rocks on the steep incline. I heard the bones in my ankle snap, a sound like dry twigs. I clutched at my wound, thinking of the pain and that frothy gasping moving out of the dark water tunnel towards the light. Towards me.

I must have shouted when I fell. Before I knew it, Spooner was standing over me, and hoisting me up.

In my haste to stand, I put my full weight on the broken ankle and the pain coursed through my entire leg, one hundred-fold. I nearly toppled over but Spooner had a tight grip on my uniform. I put my arm around his shoulder, and he brought me to the top of the incline.

I remember how quiet the jungle was, how not even a breeze stirred. I quickly gathered my bearings and realized we were positioned at the far right side of the compound. The temple was to our west in the distance.

The crack of musket shots cut through the silence, and we knew they were coming from our camp. We all looked at each other and the decision was unanimous. We were leaving and heading for the coast. The same coast that we had not seen since we had arrived.

Perhaps it was wrong of us to abandon our surviving brothers who manned the camp, but there was little we could do. With my ankle, I was in no quarter to fight and by the time we scaled the thick jungle and reached them they would surely have turned. We pivoted and headed back to the ocean as a final flintlock shot rang out through the compound.

It took nearly four days, but finally we reached the shore. Between my wound and the lack of a guide, navigation of the terrain was difficult, but against all odds we made it. Our twenty red coat brothers, Sergeant Eaton among them, greeted us. Ainsley and Crawford did most of the talking. They spoke of the evil we had witnessed and how Hyde and the others had joined their ranks.

My ankle was worse for wear at this point. A ball of swollen black and purple flesh. Keeping my boot on for so many days had caused more harm than good. I knew my foot would have to come off.

That night, as we rested in the camp, I didn't sleep more than an hour at a time. I kept watching the branches sway in the breeze, expecting to see the moonlight reflecting off those soulless eyes once more. But it seemed the Lord saw fit that they should not follow us to the coast, for I did not see those beasts again.

Still, the images remained of the soldiers on an endless march, hunting through the jungle, searching for the treasure I had stolen. Looking for their idol, their life.

The *HMS Watchtower* arrived as the sun rose on our second day at camp. Our group had hoped that other survivors might have fled that accursed city as well and returned to the shore by now. But sadly, no one else returned. Only us four had survived to tell the tale.

Once on board the vessel, the ship's surgeon took one look at my ankle and came to the same conclusion as I. The foot had to come off or the infection would spread. I will spare you the grizzly details of the operation, but the agony was unspeakable, despite the amount of rum I ingested.

At one point in my pain addled stupor, I considered how lucky I was to even feel such discomforts. Unlike Sergeant Hyde and the rest of my brothers who would never feel anything again, except a hunger that would never cease.

After I had lost my leg below the knee and sat in a rum-induced state, Sergeant Eaton approached me in my cot. He talked with me for a long while about that forgotten city. He then went on to say that he had spoken with the rest of the lads, and they had agreed. We should never make mention of that necropolis again. Eaton feared that the commanders would be intrigued by such powers and the wealth that lay under the city. They would likely send another company of men to retrieve it.

I concurred and swore that the secret of the city would never pass my lips again as long as I lived. The thought of other men venturing into that unholy site looking for riches filled me with dread.

Eaton explained that as the highest-ranking man left, he would write a report that would state the city was explored in detail with multiple expeditions and that no gold nor riches were found. He said he would also mention how the locals had attacked our unit continuously, both marching to and from the ruined site, and that, tragically, Lieutenant Peyton and Sergeant Hyde had both perished fighting bravely for King and country.

I assume his report was accepted as truth as, to this day, no officers have ever asked me about the mission.

Upon reaching Jamaica, I was immediately relieved of active duty due to my inability to fight. I was ordered back to

England and that was the last time I ever laid eyes on the New World.

Soon after returning home, I met a woman who's very being was of kindness, optimism, and compassion. Being with her allowed me to forget the things I had seen, and to once again have faith in the world. Despite my wound she loved me for who I was. I married her a short time later.

We had three sons together. It brings me great sadness to report that all of my children died fighting the French in the wars. While my boys were sent to the New World, they thankfully were never ordered as far south as I had been, never having to witness what I had seen.

I am much older now and have not spoken of that unholy city since Sergeant Eaton and I had talked in the bowels of the *HMS Watchtower*. Not a soul.

Upon returning to England, I immediately placed that curious Mayan medallion into a steel case and filled it with gunpowder and several holy relics before planting it under the floorboards. I have always suspected what it was capable of and the power it holds. I know my burial of the relic kept its powers at bay as several neighbours have passed away over the years, but thankfully no one came back. To this day, I know not why I took it from its resting place in that treasure room, but I had no choice. I had to seize it.

I had nearly forgotten about the medallion's existence after all these years until my wife caught an ailment a fortnight ago. It took her relatively quickly and it pains me to say she died last night in her sleep. She was taken from me far too soon and in my rage and grief, my mind turned to the relic. It was like it was calling for me from my memories, from the distant past, from under the floorboards.

I unearthed the medallion once more.

The candlelight basked that horrible mural in a warm glow.

Shortly before I began writing this journal, I placed the

medal on my wife's still chest and left the bed chambers. But now, as I recount that nightmarish voyage to the New World, I realize I've made a deadly mistake. The medallion had tried to hide those memories, to keep them buried in my subconscious like it had been buried in the black powder. But once it sensed my grief, my weakness, it called to me. Pleading to be unearthed.

I ask you not to judge me, nor my actions. For if you had the chance to bring the person you loved most back to this life, even if it was just a fraction of them that remained, would you not take it? Weigh those options carefully before you cast a stone in judgment.

I am not yet willing to let her go. I wish to see her one last time and then I will shatter the medallion into a thousand pieces and scatter the remains into the deepest crevasse. I swear this oath as the Lord himself bearing witness. And I pray he is.

I must go now. I can hear my wife stirring in the next room.

THE TREATMENT PLANT

The siren rang loud and true. It echoed off the road and the chain-link fence. Sailed past the bark of the trees and the greens of the bush. Soared through the rippling stream and the snapped twigs on the forest floor.

The siren rang across the five-acre field and up to the glass table where two men were sitting. They didn't hear it at first, as the hot summer afternoon baked down on them. Beer bottles littered the table and Noah Taylor swatted away a pair of mosquitos.

Brent Stilson looked down at his cards. Not a single hand he could make higher than two pair. A sunburn was forming on his forehead and a pink rose colour had taken to his cheeks.

Noah heard the peculiar noise off in the distance and raised his head. "Shhh. Do you hear that?" he asked, as he put his cards face down on the table.

Brent perked up his ears, the low hum of the siren creeping across the fields of the property. "Ya, I do," he said after a moment. The sun and beer had made him sluggish.

Noah removed his ball cap and ran an oily hand through his greasy brown hair. "Sounds like it's coming from the water treatment plant, don't it?'" He listened closer as the hum continued.

Brent shrugged. "I guess. You would know; it's your house. There ain't no treatment factories out where I live."

Noah emptied a bottle down his throat, the glass had lost most of its chill and left a small puddle around its base. "I know it's my house. That doesn't mean I know what every alarm sounds like," he muttered, as he placed the empty bottle on the table, his eyes moving along the field.

"Mmmhmm," Brent added, as he studied his cards, hoping that the harder he stared at them, the more likely he could conjure up the card he needed to form a full house.

"Let's go have a look," Noah said after a moment as he stared off at the trees on the far side of his property. The wind had picked up and blew hot air around the cool green grass that rippled in the breeze.

"A look at what?'" Brent asked, as he looked at his dwindling number of poker chips scattered around the table.

"At the water treatment plant, you deaf—"

"I know, 'At the water treatment plant,' I'm just saying, at what? You seen one concrete building you've seen 'em all." Brent grabbed the bottle opener from the table and lifted the cap off a fresh beer. "We've been working on your truck all day. I'm beat. Going down the road to look at the grey slab of a building ain't my idea of fun."

"It might be fun if you lose your attitude. We'll go through the woods. It's a short cut. Ten, maybe fifteen-minute walk."

"I just opened this beer," Brent gestured to the bottle in his hand.

"Bring it with ya. I'll grab one and we'll have 'em for the road."

Brent shrugged and lowered his cards to the table. He looked over his shoulder at the woods, the low hum still filtering through. "All right, but buy me a beer when we get back?"

Noah leaned over and opened the small red cooler by his foot. The ice had long since melted, making a lake for the bottles to drown in. "Sure. I've been buying you beers for ten years. What's one more?"

Brent smiled a big toothy grin and stood up, the wave of booze hitting him as he did so.

The two walked off Noah's property and headed into the forest. The alarm continued to grow louder and changed from a hum to a screech. Noah didn't know these woods well enough to form a mental map, but he knew that by following the sound they would eventually get there.

"These mosquitos are murder," Brent said from a few paces behind.

Noah sipped from his beer and tried to listen to the sound of a stream that flowed in the distance. Its finer details were masked by the constant alarm.

Brent swatted at the pests as he looked to the treetops, admiring the rays of sun that glistened through the green canopy. "I haven't been in the sticks in a long time. Pretty stuff," he added after a moment, before downing most of his beer.

Noah again stayed quiet, his mind wondering what had set off the alarm.

Brent turned his gaze to his friend and asked, "What do you think is the matter?"

Noah shook his head as he spoke, "I was just thinkin' the same thing. Chemical spill, maybe? That's the only thing I can think of."

Brent bit his lip and moved over to a thick, aging tree whose trunk was easily triple his size. He knelt down and placed his newly empty beer bottle in the dirt.

"Whatcha doing over there?" Noah asked, stopping to watch Brent. The alarm continued blaring in the distance.

Brent stood up and brushed off his worn jeans. "I didn't want to hold it no more."

"Don't leave it there," Noah snapped.

"It won't be there long, we'll come back for it." Brent walked forward to rejoin Noah. "You know I would never waste a perfectly good bottle." He shook his head. "Returning a case with a missing bottle should be a crime in this state, I reckon."

Noah looked around at the hundreds of trees and short hills that surrounded them. All the trees looked old and mighty. He appreciated Brent's optimism that they would be able to find this exact spot again on the walk back, but he doubted it.

The two men continued on and headed up a steep hill. A single boulder jutting out of the ground at half their height served as the only marker they had seen so far.

As they marched to the top of the hill, the alarm reached its crescendo. The unnerving wail flooded through the low hanging branches. Noah pointed forward, as he could just make out the cream coloured concrete structure. A vine-ridden chain-link fence separated them from their destination. "There she be," he added.

Brent thrust a finger into his ears and rotated them to stop the ringing. "What now?" he said, as he leaned to the right, attempting to get a better look at the buildings beyond.

"Let's head to the fence. Maybe we'll see something worth seeing," Noah said, as he stepped down the hill, the rotting leaves making the descent slippery.

Brent watched as Noah reached the bottom of the hill and studied the fence. After a moment, Noah turned and waved him down, beckoning him to follow.

Brent looked at the small section of the treatment plant he could see through the chain-links. A calm, concrete slab, the sound of rushing water, and the alarm blaring. No employees scurried about, no security roaming the perimeter.

Where is everyone? he thought. While he was no expert on water treatment facilities and was unsure how many people worked at one, he knew someone should be around. Someone, anyone, should be investigating the alarm. *Unless they were evacuated,* his mind said as he studied the still structure ahead. Only the alarm signalled something was amiss behind the calm veneer of the structure.

"Hey Noah," he said as he watched his companion start to walk along the perimeter.

"What?" Noah shouted as he turned.

Brent rubbed his forehead. The sun seemed to be getting hotter and the humidity surrounding the plant was causing him to sweat even more. "I think we should get going," he called down. "Maybe there's a gas leak or something? I don't see no people about." He felt the heat sobering him up with every passing second.

Noah didn't reply. He simply shrugged his shoulders and continued to walk along the fence line. Brent swallowed and adjusted his stained T-shirt as it clung to his back. He shook his head and headed down the hill, smelling the air as he did so. It smelled of crisp water with a soft mix of chemicals. Nothing much alarming or out of the ordinary. But still, he couldn't shake the feeling that something was off.

He looked through the chain-links again. Still no one.

They followed the barbed wire fence for a few minutes until they came to an area where a path had been dug under the chain-links. The burrows under the fence were wide enough for them to squeeze through.

"Well?" Noah said, looking at Brent and then the dugout, "You comin'?"

"Uhhh," Brent hesitated, as he looked through the fence towards the rear of the facility.

"Well, I'm going. Might never get another chance," Noah said as he got down on his knees and removed a small section of dirt to make the hole bigger.

"Why ain't nobody here?" Brent asked, rubbing his fore-head. His burn was beginning to bother him.

"It's Saturday. Maybe that has something to do with it. Or maybe they are inside tryin' to turn off that goddamn alarm."

Brent didn't find either of those answers particularly pleas-ing. *Where are the fire engines or the helicopters?* he thought. *People should be investigating an alarm like this.*

Noah was under the fence with a grunt and on the other side before Brent knew it.

Noah looked around the complex, noting a few windows on the second story and the weeds that grew in the cracks of the concrete. He turned and headed to the right, nearing the back of the building.

Brent sighed as he realized he would have to follow his companion's lead. He was the smaller of the two and wasn't concerned about getting stuck. He was more worried about what had dug this hole and if it had anything to do with the alarm or lack of people.

He scurried under the fence and pulled his shirt as it snagged on the rusted bottom. He climbed out of the rut and jogged to catch up to his companion, who was just about to turn the corner to approach the back side of the building.

Noah leaned around the corner and looked across the compound. Several tanks and sets of sheds sat at the far side. A second concrete structure was also placed farther away, connected to this building by scaffolding and piping.

Still no one.

Noah stepped from around the corner and heard Brent approaching behind him, out of breath. His breathing was short and ragged. Standing out in the open sun, the heat was unbearable. A short distance away a pipe was leaking a slow, steady stream of water. Noah again checked to ensure the coast was clear before walking towards it. Brent hesitated but after a moment, followed behind.

Noah held his hand under the leaking water. It was cool

and refreshing, nearly ice cold. He brought his face closer to the clear liquid and smelled it.

"Don't drink it," Brent said as he reached out to stop Noah. "Might have chemicals or be the dirty water still."

"I ain't drinking it," he replied, as he looked up at the pipe. "It smells okay though."

Noah knew his friend was right, no sense risking it. Instead, he removed his ball cap and held it under the steady stream. The quick patter of water hitting the upturned hat was replaced by the liquid collecting upon itself. Noah splashed some of the water on his face before placing the hat gingerly on his head. The sudden chill upon his neck and back caused him to stiffen up; it was wonderful.

Brent thought of splashing some water on himself but quickly dismissed the idea. *I'll survive*, he thought, as his mind quickly turned back to the lack of employees roaming about.

Brent turned and walked a few paces away along the back of the building. He marvelled at a set of six large glass windows that led to the top of the structure. As he peered through the humid windows, he admired the blue tanks and the brightly coloured pipes that filled the facility.

A desk sat directly in front of him on the other side of the glass. The computer was old, and the paper files placed on top of the fake wood were ragged and disheveled. A cup of coffee sat next to a half-eaten sandwich. The bread and meat inside looked fresh. *They must have evacuated,* his inner voice said. He could hear the nerves in it as he thought the words.

Brent was about to turn, to tell Noah that he was leaving with or without him, when his eyes caught movement on the scaffolding. High above the tanks on the second story, two men dressed in army fatigues and camouflage walked along the catwalks.

They hoisted a barrel between them, the weight apparent by how they struggled to lift it. They upended the barrel and held it over the open tank. A purple powder tumbled out and landed in the reservoir below. The soldiers shook the container before walking away to the end of the scaffold where an additional six drums waited.

Are they fixing a spill? Brent thought, as he watched the soldiers struggle to lift another barrel. *Why is the Army doing it?*

Brent stepped away from the glass and said, "Hey Noah, let's—" he ceased speaking as he looked to where Noah was standing.

A man in a United States Army uniform stood where they had just come from. Noah was frozen as he eyed this newcomer, who had seemingly appeared out of nowhere.

The soldier took a step forward, his field cap hung down, covering his face in shadow. "What are you doing here?" the soldier said, flexing his hand as he spoke in a distant monotone.

"We—We heard the alarm. Thought we could help," Noah answered. His voice trembled as he took a step back, closer to Brent.

"Alarm?" the soldier said as he slowly looked to the sky. It was as if he was confused by Noah's use of words. "Oh, that? Yes, well everything is under control." He paused and returned his gaze to the two trespassers. His face was dull and lacking emotion. "A-OK, as you might say."

Brent noticed that the soldier had no rifle in his hands. *What kind of an Army man doesn't carry his rifle in the field?* he thought, as he directed his eyes to the man's holster placed on his hip. It too was empty. *What the hell?* Brent's mind raced. *Is this guy even really in the Army? Where's all his gear? What is going on here?*

The soldier sighed after taking a deep inhale. He walked forward with steady determination. "Let me see identification."

Noah nodded. "Um ya—Yes sir," he said, reaching into his beige shorts and removing his wallet.

Brent clapped his chest and jeans, stepping forwards as he

did so. He knew his wallet was in his back pocket but thought, *I ain't showing this guy anything. Not a damned thing.*

Noah handed the soldier his driver's license. The man looked down at it, the same vacant expression plastered on his face as he said, "Noah Taylor. Seventy-two Baker Street." The way he spoke, it was as if the words were foreign to him. Almost like he was attempting to sound them out.

The soldier looked up and held out his hand to receive Brent's identification. Brent shook his head, "Sorry… sir. I think I left it at his house." He pointed a thumb at Noah with one hand and pretended to search his pockets once more with the other.

"Hmm. I see," the guard said, his voice dismissive and oddly calm.

He raised his field cap up on his forehead, revealing piercing green eyes. Brent studied the man; there wasn't a drop of sweat on him. The heatwave was scorching, but yet here was this soldier in an M.P. Sergeant uniform, standing like it was room temperature. His heavy pants and camou-flaged long-sleeved shirt showed no signs of moisture.

The sergeant handed Noah back his driver's license and stared at Brent. "Identification?" he asked after a moment.

Brent looked to Noah with a confused glance before saying, "What? You just asked me that." The soldier nodded but uncertainty filled his face. Brent swallowed and continued, "Like I said, it's at his house."

"Hmm. I see," the sergeant said, again in the same cool tone.

The guard reached into his pocket and pulled out a black strand of plastic. A zip-tie. "Until I know who you——" he stopped speaking and lowered the binding to his side, looking at Noah as he spoke. He stared at him for a long while before taking several shallow breaths. Brent backed away slowly.

The soldier cocked his head and looked back to Brent. "You two should run along now. Nothing to see here."

"Is—Is that all?" Noah asked, his voice quaking.

"Run along now," the soldier said, his voice deeper than it had been a moment before.

Without saying a word, Noah and Brent quickly walked past the soldier who stood rigid, staring at the water tanks and the sheds beyond.

As Brent passed by him, the sergeant cocked his head once more, glaring down at him with intense interest. Those green eyes shimmered, and the soldier blinked, then blinked again. It was the second flicker of the eyes that caused Brent's mouth to hang open.

A sideways film had moved across the soldier's retinas.

Brent swallowed and back peddled away, following Noah as he moved towards the fence. Upon turning the corner of the building, the two men dashed towards the hole under the fence, and upon reaching it, scurried under in a flash.

Brent ran beside Noah as they moved to the top of the hill. He looked back at the plant. The soldier stood at the fence line, arms at his sides, staring at them. Standing perfectly still, watching.

Noah pulled on Brent's shirt and said, "Come on. Go!"

The two ran down the hill leaving the green-eyed guard behind on the far side of the fence. As they ran along Brent said, "Did you see that guy? His eyes. He was like a lizard or something. When he blinked. Did you see?"

"What are you talking about? He was just a creepy G.I.," Noah replied, his voice ragged.

"No, I saw it. He's—"

"You're drunk. Imagining things."

"No, I'm seeing straight. I saw those soldiers dumping something in the water inside. I—"

"You're hallucinating. Sun must be frying your brain. I told you not to drink on an empty stomach," Noah argued, as he stopped running and put his hand out to lean on a tree. He was panting. "Shoot! I think the sun's getting to me too. It's humid in these trees. Lord, it's hot." He wiped a lump of sweat from his forehead and removed his hat. "I think I'm getting a burn just like you. I can feel it coming."

Brent placed his hands on his knees and sucked air as he listened to Noah. He took a few shallow breaths before standing up, recognizing where they were. Brent walked over to a large old tree trunk that sat a few meters away, he picked up the beer bottle and moved back over to Noah.

"But why was the Army there? Why not fire fighters or the health department, or maybe the cops? Why the Army?" Brent asked upon reaching Noah.

Noah looked down at the bottle in Brent's hand. "What's that?"

Brent lowered his eyes to the glass for a moment before saying, "I left it by the tree, remember? I didn't want to carry it anymore."

"Huh? Ya... Ya I—I forgot." Noah's voice was overconfident. He wiped his forehead again and rubbed the back of his neck. "Let's get out of here, before that creep of a G.I. decides to come after us." Noah began running once more.

Brent gripped the beer bottle and followed suit. The alarm still blaring behind them.

The two men reached the end of the forest and bounded across Noah's back field. They stopped when they stumbled onto Noah's patio. Brent plopped down in a chair in front of the glass table. The poker chips still held down the cards that lay across the surface. "I'm beat," he said, exhaling sharply as his pulse pounded in his ears.

Noah rubbed his face one more time. He was as red as a lobster. The sun had been murder on his skin. "I need a drink," he said, after licking his chapped lips.

"How about that beer you owe me?" Brent asked, with a smile on his face as Noah turned to enter the house. "A nice cold beer would do us some good, I think."

"Ya," Noah said in a deadpan tone. He opened the creaky screen door and disappeared inside the house.

Brent listened to the wind on the trees in the distance. The buzz of mosquitos flicked around the roof. He dragged a poker chip along the glass, passing it between his fingers as he waited for Noah to return with his drink.

He waited a long time.

The alarm ceased. Suddenly the countryside lay silent, the sound of cicadas quickly filling the gap. Occasionally a truck bounding down the rural highway out front of the property broke the monotony. *More military trucks?* Brent thought as he listened to the hot dry air swirling about.

Noah appeared in the screen door and opened it with a creak as he approached. In his hand was a glass of water, a single ice cube clinking around the brim. He sat down at the table and extended the glass to Brent. "How about some water?" he said, his voice distant.

Brent reached for the glass, but froze, his hand hovering in the air as he noticed something peculiar about Noah's complexion. "What happened to your sunburn?" His voice shook as he studied his friend's pale skin.

"I'm all better now," Noah replied, pushing the glass across the table.

Brent looked up in time to see Noah blink. A second layer of film covered his piercing green eyes.

WHAT SLITHERS IN THE WIRES?

Seattle, Washington, August 1987

"Well, Maggie, the boy has never been what most would call *normal*," Mrs. Saggolilly said as she sipped her tea, her voice carrying from the parlour and down the hall to Jeremy's room. Despite the hushed voices, Jeremy heard every word they muttered as he lay on the carpeted floor of his bedroom. The sound of clinking china echoed from the parlour and Mrs. Saggolilly continued, "I know he's your son, but—"

"Yes... Yes he is, and I should be defending him," Mother paused, "but, you're not saying anything the doctors haven't said before." Her voice was horse as she had been crying shortly before Mrs. Saggolilly arrived.

"He's what? Seven? He might still grow out of it. Maybe it's just from the stress. Trying to get used to a new living arrangement can't be easy at that age."

"I blame myself," Mother said, though she was quickly shushed by Mrs. Saggolilly. Jeremy pressed his ear to the cold wooden door. "No, I do!" Mother continued, her hushed voice growing louder. "I had him when I was thirty-nine. On top of that, Ben leaving us last year. I shouldn't have waited so long to settle down, but my career. I put so much time into it. Now it seems that was all for nothing."

"Did you take him to the psychiatrist I suggested?" Mrs. Saggolilly said, trying to shift the conversation to less upsetting topics.

"Yes, and he said the same thing as the first doctor. They think he will grow out of it, but I'm not so sure." There was a pause and when mother spoke again, she had hushed her voice once more. "What has me more concerned is that he starts the second grade in September and the teacher, a real choice woman, has already gone to the principal saying that she refuses to teach him. She cites his outbursts last year as disruptive." Mother stopped again as she suppressed the urge to cry. "I was furious at first. I still am. But who am I kidding? She's right, Julia. That awful woman is right."

Mrs. Saggolilly mumbled a few consoling words before Mother spoke again, "I can't stand how she talks about my baby, but if I were the parent of one of those other children, I would have complained too." A long pause and then a whisper, almost at the edge of Jeremy's hearing, "They call him dangerous."

Dangerous? Jeremy thought as he looked under the door and studied the small sliver of hallway that remained unobstructed by the olive-green carpet. He knew what dangerous meant. Mother used it when she talked about crossing the street or when the oven was on.

Me? Dangerous? But I haven't burned anyone, and I always look both ways, he thought as he scratched his face. The carpet fibres were starting to irritate him.

Jeremy thought back to the "incidents" that had occurred earlier that year. At least that's what his teacher, Mrs. Rothchild, had called them. Jeremy remembered the shapes.

The ones that bumbled around in the corners of the room, always watching the children.

When they first appeared, Jeremy had studied them curiously, completely ignoring the reading exercises he was expected to be listening to. They were grey, smoky images of ever-evolving silhouettes, twisting and turning in their constant motion. Once the shapes began to aggressively dart along the ceiling, though, Jeremy screamed.

The next week the shapes appeared again, bigger this time and moving more erratically. Jeremy cried out once more but this time he was swiftly taken to the principal's office. Mother had rushed over from work and Jeremy remembered how happy he was to see her. That was until he noticed how furious she looked. She held a smile while speaking with the principal. The car ride home, however, was anything but smiles.

Jeremy had not been allowed to sit in the principal's office while they discussed the outbursts. "While the big people talk," Mother had said before sitting him on the bench in the secretary's office and closing the frosted glass door. Jeremey watched the young woman behind the stack of paperwork as she made the occasional phone call.

She smelled like cigarettes and new paper, Jeremy thought to himself, as the carpet itched the back of his head, his eyes glued to the ceiling. *Not like the principal. He smelled of perfume and wore a jacket with those patches on the sleeves.*

Despite sitting in the room outside the office, he had been able to hear some of what the principal and Mother talked about. "Jeremy is an attention seeker and is restless," the principal's baritone voice filtered through the frosted glass.

"He's six," Mother had replied. "Aren't they all like that?"

The principal had mumbled something, but Jeremy couldn't make it out. It didn't really matter. He already knew the answer. He knew he wasn't like the other children. They couldn't see the shapes in the corners.

"Aren't you afraid he'll hear us talking about him?" Mrs. Saggolilly said as her cup clanked against the saucer. Her voice was even more hushed now.

"No, I put him down for his nap an hour or so ago," Mother said. "He's a pretty deep sleeper and we had a big morning at the park."

Jeremy kept replaying what she had said to him on the car ride home after the principal's office: "Those shapes aren't real, Jeremy. I'm so disappointed that you would embarrass me like that."

Jeremy stayed quiet after that and simply studied the twisting silhouettes whenever they danced about the room. No matter how aggressive they got, he didn't scream. After a couple of days, they disappeared for a while, having seemingly grown bored by his lack of outbursts. Jeremy had thought he had won.

Until the playground incident.

Jeremy shuddered. That had been the worst one yet.

He listened to the sounds of the kitchen outside his room as Mother poured more tea. His mind quickly retreated to the memory of the playground, a memory that haunted him.

The shapes had come from the far side of the school yard, past the parent drop off zone and through the fence where the bus would arrive to pick up the children. Gone were the grey, smoky images; they had been replaced with menacing black creations. The new horrors rushed the playground. Gone were their erratic and lackadaisical movements. This new breed of shapes lunged towards the playing children; their mission was clear.

Jeremy watched as the black rippling voids got closer, moving across the grass with horrifying speed. As the shapes neared, Jeremy watched them begin to transform. The black smoke fell away like a snakeskin, leaving the true form underneath to emerge. Grotesque slithering eels, their teeth locked on the children building in the sandpit.

Jeremy screamed at the big kids to run and pointed at the approaching monsters. The children stayed put and simply stared back at him. The sand in their shovels retuning to the ground on which they sat. Their mouths open, a confused and disturbed expression on their small faces.

Before Jeremy knew it, he was once again sitting in the principal's office. Shortly after that, he was in the nurse's office as well. He told the nurse about the shapes and how they changed. The nurse simply smiled and gave him an ice pack for his head.

That weekend mother took him to the doctor, followed by the pharmacy immediately after. When Jeremy asked why they had to go, his mother simply said, "To pick up some happy medicine." Her eyes were red that day too.

Jeremy listened to the door once again. Mother and Mrs. Saggolilly were talking about his dad. They sounded aggravated and unpleasant as they usually did whenever he came up. Jeremy rolled onto his side and looked at his bed.

The shapes are real, and they have nothing to do with Dad leaving us, Jeremy thought as he admired his Batman blankets. *And those pills don't help. The eels are still out there. I just can't, can't, can't... what's that word? Prove it! Prove it, that's right. I need to prove it to them.*

"Do you think he's just depressed?" Mother said as she swallowed, trying to stifle the oncoming tears.

"He's a little young for that, don't you think?" Mrs. Saggolilly asked in a less harsh tone than she had been using.

Jeremy fiddled with the carpet fibres as he rolled his palm over them. He sighed. He had heard this conversation many times. Mother asked the principal, the teachers, the doctor, even Grandma, except speaking with her was more often done on the phone—

The phone...

He felt his skin crawl as the thought of that off-white menace sitting on the wall in their kitchen latched onto his mind. Its cord hung down like a viper. Jeremy didn't like the phone and, over the past few months, had developed a severe fear of where those corded tendrils might lead.

Jeremy thought back to the night it happened. The night he heard it, and the last time he had touched a phone. Mother was talking with Grandma and the conversation was fairly typical, that was until Jeremy overheard his mother say, "Can you please talk some sense into him?"

As he took the phone from his mother and put the speaker to his ear, that's when he heard it.

That gut-wrenching sound.

A writhing, wet slithering that was just at the edge of his hearing. At first Jeremy thought it was a problem with the connection or maybe a show Grandma was watching and paid it no mind. But the longer he talked, the closer the sound became.

A moist scraping as the horrifying beast moved down the cables and through the phone lines towards his suburban bungalow, following the sound of his small voice.

"Can you hear that, Grandma?" Jeremy had asked multiple times.

But Grandma's answer was always the same, "No sweetie, I just hear you."

Jeremy's imagination ran wild as he conjured up terrifying images in his mind. A gigantic tentacled beast moving through caves deep in the earth before venturing into the sewers and then finally discovering the phone lines. This creature was not the shapes, nor the eels. No, those were just servants to a larger, more powerful being. For what slithered was much worse.

"If money wasn't so tight," Mother's voice suddenly flooded down the hall, causing Jeremy to snap out of the horrid memory, "maybe I could send him to see someone else. There's a child psychiatrist downstate that—"

"Another one, Maggie? Do you think that they will say

anything different? If Dr. Caruthers couldn't diagnose him then who can?"

"If he were any other doctor? No. But…" Mother sighed, "Well, this one could be different. I looked him up in some of those research journals down at the library and it says he helped children get over divorces, losing a parent, over-coming trauma from abuse. Everything. But he's very expensive."

"Are you asking me for money, Maggie?" Mrs. Saggolilly's voice was compassionate but stern.

"No, Julia. I would never——" a pause and then, "I can make my own money. I could take on some overtime at the store, work till closing each night. If I did that for a month, or maybe six weeks, I could send him to see this doctor for an appointment or two."

Mrs. Saggolilly slurped her tea and offered a simple, "Hmmm," in response.

"The only problem is Jeremy is much too young to fend for himself. I have to make him dinner and put him to bed and lay out his clothes and——"

"You know," Mrs. Saggolilly said, her voice warm, "I can always look after him for a few hours a night. I did raise three children of my own, you know."

"I wouldn't want to impose. I just——"

"I insist. You just leave some options for dinner in the fridge. I'll make him something, put him to bed and wait for you to come home. I'll come over half an hour before you leave for work and help you. Anything you need."

"Julia, you are too kind."

"If taking care of the boy for a few hours a week will help you afford to get him some help, real help, then it's the least I can do." She slurped her tea, "And if this doctor is as good as you claim he is, then it's worth looking into." She paused and it sounded as if Mother had hugged her. A moment passed before she continued, "Besides, maybe having someone new to talk to about the divorce will help him cope. Maybe he will open up to me."

Mrs. Saggolilly had always been nice enough to Jeremy, so when he was told officially by Mother that she would be taking care of him for a few hours a night, he wasn't concerned.

On the first night, Mrs. Saggolilly made a simple dinner and let him watch his regular cartoons. She stayed quiet and read a tatty old paperback book that she brought from home while she rocked in the big rocking chair in the corner.

Once, Mrs. Saggolilly attempted to talk to Jeremy about the previous school year and when that failed to gain any traction, she switched up the conversation to his mom. The moment she accidentally brought up Jeremy's father, he ceased answering questions and turned his attention back to the episode of *The Road Runner Show* that was playing.

The phone rang at ten to eight, shortly before Jeremy's bedtime. The boy shot up from the rug and stared at the wall mounted phone. Its cord swinging, waving at him with each ring. The eggshell hue was ghostly and sinister to Jeremy's young eyes and eager imagination.

Mrs. Saggolilly folded the page in her book and headed over to the kitchen. Her stubby heels clicked across the tile as Jeremy looked on, helplessly. *It won't attack her,* Jeremy thought. *It only wants me. Only I could hear it.*

All the same, Jeremy's eyes were glued to the ringing nightmare as Mrs. Saggolilly picked it up from the receiver. As she offered a curious greeting to whoever awaited on the other end, Jeremy envisioned slithering appendages moving out of the wires and thumping to the floor in wet, slimy, bubbling—

"It's your mom," Mrs. Saggolilly said with a cozy smile, as she covered the bottom speaker with her palm.

Jeremy simply stared at her, his mouth agape. *That's how it will get me. It will use my mommy to lure me to the phone,* Jeremy thought. He imagined the creature stretching its spindly tentacles across the country, using every phone line to search for him.

"Oh yes, things are going well. He ate all his dinner and he's watching his shows," Mrs. Saggolilly said, twirling the wire around her finger. "He's staying quiet. Hmm-hmm. No problems…"

If I look away, they will come and get me. It won't matter if adults don't hear it, it will come. It knows I know about them. Jeremy felt his body begin to shake with nervousness.

Mrs. Saggolilly turned her head and looked to the small boy on the carpet. "Do you want to talk to your mom now, Jeremy?"

He shook his head aggressively back and forth, no. He wanted to talk to his mom, of course he did. More than anything else in the world. To hug her and be showered in kisses. But the phone. The slithering. It stood between them.

Why can't anyone hear them? Jeremy thought. *Why does no one believe me?*

Mrs. Saggolilly frowned and bit her lip as she said, "Sorry, Maggie, he says no." She turned away as she continued, adding a quick nod in reply to something Mother had said. "Yes, I think so. He's been staring at it the entire time I've been chatting with you." She was whispering, but Jeremy's young ears picked up every word.

Mrs. Saggolilly nodded again and added a few vague sounds of agreement to the conversation for good measure before saying, "Well, maybe we will try again tomorrow." She paused and looked to Jeremy, who had begun to rock back and forth in place. "I'll talk to him about it."

I'm not imagining it, Jeremy thought as he kicked over a group of army men that lay in a flanking formation around his room. The green army suffered the most casualties from his devastating attack while the grey troopers watched in stoic postures from their mountain positions upon his dresser.

Over the previous few days, both Mrs. Saggolilly and Mother had talked to him at length about his "phobia of the phone." He hadn't known the word "phobia" until two days ago, but now it seemed to pop up in every conversation, following him around relentlessly.

Jeremy pushed up against his bedroom door and slid down until he was on the carpet. He thought back to the day before when his mother was dressing him in his raincoat.

"Why don't you believe me?" Jeremy had shouted at her, as she held the coat up for him to put an arm into the sleeve.

"Oh, honey, I do. The shapes in the walls," she replied as she looked out the living room window. The rain was beading down the glass. "I wish it was nicer, but we have to go shopping," she mumbled to herself.

"They aren't in the walls. They're in the corners, but those are gone now! And I haven't seen the eels either. They ran away, because of the thing in the phone."

"I know they have sweetie," Mother said while zipping up Jeremy's blue raincoat.

"Then why do you and Mrs. Saggolilly talk about me? Why do I hear you talking to my next year teacher telling her to put notes in my agenda when I'm bad? I'm not bad. I won't be bad. I—I—I just was scared because of the shapes and the eels."

Mother frowned as she grabbed his rain boots and put them on the hardwood floor. She adjusted her sandy blonde hair as she spoke. Jeremy had noticed this nervous tick his mother possessed whenever she was uncomfortable.

"Honey, let's just say that I can't see them because I'm an adult. Children—umm well…" She paused, attempting to think of the right words to use. "Kids have magic in them and when you turn into an adult, you'll lose it. That's why some children have imaginary friends. Well, you have these shapes. That's what you see. But remember, they can't hurt you. Not at all."

"Why do I get stuck with the scary things while others get friends in their—imagin—imager—"

"Imagination," Mother assisted him as he slipped into his boots.

"Well, how come?"

"I'm not sure honey. But it's okay because they are imaginary, and they can't hurt you."

"Even the scary ones?" Jeremy said in a tiny voice as he looked into his mother's deep green eyes.

"Especially the scary ones. They just look tough. But really they know they are nothing. Nothing at all. And that scares them."

"Once I become big, I won't see them?"

"Bingo, my handsome boy," Mother said, kissing Jeremy's forehead.

"Then I want to be big now!" Jeremy shouted, stomping his feet in the hallway.

Mother shook her head and stood up from her crouched position. "Oh sweetie, no you don't." She had a look of tiredness in her eyes, like the whole world had been pressing down on her.

Jeremy didn't remember the rest of the conversation. He just knew that his mother hugged him before they headed off to the store together.

Jeremy stood from the carpet and cleared his mind of the memory. He knelt down and picked up the little green soldiers that he had kicked during his temper tantrum. The sergeant of the fireteam was thankful that all his squad was accounted for with no casualties.

Jeremy had just finished moving a column of grey tanks to

the front when there was a knock on the door. Mrs. Saggolilly opened it. "May I come in?" Her voice was soft.

Jeremy nodded. She took two steps forward and surveyed the advancing Green Armed Forces. "Quite a few army men you've got there."

Jeremy shrugged, as he moved a lieutenant behind a shoe box that served as a war-torn building.

"Can I sit? I promise I won't disturb the German guys."

Jeremy nodded before looking up and replying, "They are the Grey Army. They aren't Germans."

"Oh?" Mrs. Saggolilly said in a surprised manner. "My little Ricky always played Allies vs. Germans when he was a boy, oh twenty-five odd years ago." She looked into the distant past for a moment before adding, "The green guys always won."

Julia Saggolilly moved over to the bed and sat down on the edge. A grey trooper holding onto a sub machine gun toppled over but she stood him upright before the boy could notice. She was deeply concerned for little Jeremy.

Here he is, a normal seven-year-old boy, playing with his army men, Julia thought as she watched him line up a group of soldiers. Her memories took her back to her own children, long since grown up and moved away. *Yet something dark lurks inside him. Those shapes or snakes or centipedes or whatever apparitions he claims to see.*

She looked out the window as the sun began to set behind the trees. *And then there is that nasty business with the phone. His aversion to it and the sounds, the "slithering" as he described it. How he ever heard that word in the first place is a mystery, but yet that's what the boy had said... "Slithering."*

As she watched Jeremy shuffle the tank column around, Julia thought back to when she was just a little girl and had an imaginary friend herself, Christen. Except Christen never really talked much and Julia knew she wasn't real. It was just something she made up to keep her company while she hosted tea parties for her dollies and held theatre for her teddy bear collection.

But Jeremy clearly thinks these visions are real, and he claims they are dangerous, Julia thought to herself. *Could the boy be schizophrenic? No, he's too young for that. But then again, every single one of those poor people was young once.* She continued to watch the back of Jeremy's head as he added a fresh set of soldiers to the fray.

The boy stopped playing and looked up as Mrs. Saggolilly cleared her throat. "Jeremy, I came in here because I wanted to say sorry," she said with a calm tone. "I should have chosen my words more carefully. I know they are real to you. I'm sorry for saying otherwise. But I think I know how to make them go away."

Jeremy put down the sandbag wall in his hand and looked at her with intense interest. He wanted nothing more than for the thing in the phone lines to slither off back to the dark crevice it had come out of.

"How?" he asked after a cautious moment.

"Have you and your mom talked about ignoring them all together?"

Jeremy squinted as he thought back to all the talks he and his mother had over the last year. She had mentioned many times about them not being real, but ignoring them? He hadn't thought about that before. "Ignore them?" he asked, his voice quiet and full of wonder.

"Ya, have you tried that?" she said, and her tone was of a soft kindness. Jeremy shook his head and Mrs. Saggolilly continued, "Just ignore them and they will go away. Like a bully. I promise."

"You think so?" Jeremy asked. A look of hopeful wonder filled his face.

"Yes, just ignore them sweetie," she said, and Julia Saggolilly believed every word. She smiled and added, "Let's see what I can make you for dinner." She leaned forward and rubbed Jeremy's shaggy brown hair before standing up.

She looked down at the child, watching him for a moment before turning and heading towards the kitchen. *He will turn out just fine,* she thought as she rounded the corner. *They aren't real.*

Jeremy heard Mrs. Saggolilly's footsteps move away from his room and enter the kitchen. *"Just ignore them."* The voice in Jeremy's mind echoed her kind words. *"Just ignore them and they will go away. Like a bully."*

Jeremy felt a smile move across his face as he held onto his favourite green army man. He had a plan now. Ignoring them. *Then no more doctors, no more pills, no more Mommy crying.* That last part was what he wanted more than anything.

Jeremy shifted his weight to his knees as he heard a shattering sound coming from the kitchen. He listened for a moment but heard no, "Oops," or "Sorry," like Mother always said whenever she dropped something. The kitchen stayed silent, and Mrs. Saggolilly said nothing.

Jeremy stood and felt a rush of concern rise up, prompted by the lack of noise that followed. No sounds of clean-up or muttering, just a stone silence that reverberated through the house.

Jeremy exited his room and walked down the hall, wondering to himself what had broken. He turned the corner and noticed a porcelain bowl smashed against the tile. Hundreds of white fragments had been launched in all directions. He looked up and saw Mrs. Saggolilly, leaning against the counter, clutching her chest.

Her eyes met Jeremy's. Her pupils only a pinprick as pain shot through her body. "I—I—I think, I'm—I'm having—having a heart attack," she called out, her voice almost a whisper. She clenched her jaw and grabbed at her blouse before saying, "Get the phone. Call—I need—Call…" Her words slurred.

Jeremy's eyes widened. *The phone!* he thought as he glanced at the off-white menace before quickly directing his gaze back to Mrs. Saggolilly. He didn't know what a heart attack was, but he knew she was in pain. He knew he needed to help her.

But the phone. She said to use the phone... he thought, as time moved at a glacial pace.

Julia felt the icy pain shoot along her torso and down her arms. *Where is this coming from?* she thought as the agony coursed through her. All her weight was placed on the counter. She stared at the boy, her voice fleeting, unable to speak further. *I asked him to use the phone,* she realized. *He's probably terrified, but—I need—need an—ambulance—*

Jeremy stood still, grinding his teeth. "I can't do it," he heard himself say as he stared into Mrs. Saggolilly's minuscule pupils.

She opened her mouth to speak but nothing came out except for a squeak. *"Just ignore them,"* Jeremy's voice whispered to him.

But I can't, he thought in reply. *They will get me.*

"Not if you ignore them. Like a bully, they will leave you alone."

But what if they don't?

Jeremy's inner voice shifted to that of his mother's, *"You have to be a big boy now. Call Nine—One—One, just like we practiced. Help her, Jeremy!"*

Julia Saggolilly felt her world begin to spin faster and her grip loosen on the counter. *He's shaking,* she thought as she attempted to focus on the child in front of her. She could see it in his face, how much he was struggling with the request to use the phone.

Just before she lost consciousness, Julia Saggolilly saw the boy take a step towards the phone. *That's it,* she thought with a glow of pride. That was her last thought before she crumpled to the floor.

Jeremy had never seen an adult fall like that. He yelled in surprise and ran to the phone. *"You're doing it,"* his mother's voice called out from somewhere in his subconscious.

He put the phone to his ear and heard the sound of the dial tone.

"*See, nothing there. Now push the buttons before it's too late.*"

He watched as his finger moved to the pad and pressed "Nine."

The beast stirred.

Its writhing echoed down the wires as it awoke from its slumber.

Hang up now before it gets you! his inner voice yelled.

"*No, Jeremy, don't. You need to help her,*" Mother's voice cried out.

He pressed the "One" next. The tendrils unravelled in sickly chaos as they moved down the wires with haste. *It's coming! It's coming!*

He pressed the "One" again, and the twisting tentacles were nearly on top of him, their ghastly screaming thundering into his ear drum.

Hang up Jeremy! Hang up! his consciousness screamed.

No, I won't let it win, he thought, as his inner voice joined with his mother's. He was filled with a calm confidence. *It isn't real. Just ignore it. Like—Like a bully.*

The dial tone switched to a ringing as the call was sent out, travelling down the wires and away from the house.

"*See, nothing to worry about. It isn't real—It isn't—*"

Lumpy, drooling tentacles sprang forth from the phone, wrapping Jeremy in a suffocating embrace. The boy went to scream, but what filled his lungs was not air.

"Emergency services. Do you require Police, Fire, or Ambulance?" the voice on the other end of the wire asked. "Hello? Hello…"

PILLS

The day the Federal Health Department issued a statement that Falsomine capsules were no longer for sale in the United States, Shamus Walsh cried. The pills that had been mass produced for civilian consumption for nearly two years were now banned.

Shamus scoured the internet looking to find out why. Piecing together press releases and interviews, he discovered that the government had deemed Falsomine—the nectar of the gods that it was—detrimental to the public health.

"Nonsense!" Shamus yelled out to the New York hotel room he found himself in.

How could a drug that does so much good for me possibly be bad? he thought as he studied a webpage. *Pure propaganda nonsense. I feel the best I've ever felt and now they are ripping it away from me.*

Shamus continued to read the statements. Buzzwords like "highly addictive," "acidic membrane increase," and "frontal lobe shifts" made frequent appearances. Shamus threw up his hands. "What? Now it's suddenly killing me?" he said as he rubbed his face. He felt warm as the news boiled his blood.

Shamus reached for a can of beer and, upon realizing it

was empty, grabbed his fifth of the night from the black mini fridge beside the cheap worktable.

He took a long sip and thought back to his life before Falsomine. Sluggish, prone to anger, tired, meals that didn't fill him, and a sex life that suffered greatly. All that changed after a few days of Falsomine. He felt energized, ready to take on the day. He woke up feeling refreshed and his stress was easier to manage. Not only did he noticed better sexual stamina, but he felt younger, too. Those pills had brought him back twenty years, easy.

He was able to satisfy both Patricia in Chicago and his ex-wife Jamie in Boston, who still insisted on seeing him for quickies on occasion. Hell, he was even able to please Stacy in Dallas-Fort Worth, who was extremely difficult.

Now all that was vanishing before his eyes, all because the government had arbitrarily decided to remove the wonder drug from the shelves. Spreading lies, reporting ill effects when just last week he had seen an advertisement talking about its positives.

Shamus stood and took a sip from the chilled beer. He sighed and felt heat run through him, stress and anxiety rushing in his mind.

He ran over to his black pilot's flight bag and fished out the Falsomine box, with its white and olive colouring. He gingerly pulled out the sleeve. Six tablets smiled up at him from their plastic coating. *Three days worth*, he thought, as he popped two of them into his mouth, chasing them down with a swig of beer.

The anxiety lifted immediately. He held his head back as endorphins cruised about his brain. *Why would they take you away?* he thought as he kept his eyes closed and tried to focus on the relief that swirled around.

After a moment he placed the box in his flight bag and sauntered over to the window, the New York skyline calling.

Armed with two tablets of Falsomine in his system, he was ready to tackle any of life's challenges.

They are jealous that guys like me finally found happiness. It goes against their agenda to keep the working class down. I'll fight them, tooth and nail, he thought as he sipped his beer.

Shamus looked at the sky as a Washington Global Airlines passenger jet took off from JFK International Airport. He saluted his colleague aboard and wondered where they were headed. *Memphis? Jacksonville? LAX.?* He looked at the red flashing light on its wing before thinking, *I bet it's L.A., lucky bastards.*

With that thought, his mind filled with Marisa, the brunette personal trainer he'd had several flings with when he had been making frequent trips to Southern California.

Shamus licked his lips. *What if I order it?* He moved over to his computer in a daze. *The F.D.A. said it was not for sale but it's not illegal to own or import. Nothing mentioned about that anywhere.* Shamus smiled at the prospects of his newfound loophole.

He sat down and began scrolling through several medical suppliers in Canada, Mexico, and the European Union. Canada wanted an arm and a leg for a three-month supply, but Mexico? Pennies on the dollar.

Shamus completed a few checks of the company to ensure it was legitimate. After reading a plethora of five-star reviews, he re-entered the site and bought a ninety-day supply. He had attempted to buy more, but three months was the maximum the website would allow to ship internationally.

I bet everyone's doing the same thing, he thought. *Not wanting to go back to the weak, dreary, memory-shot-full-of-holes fools we used to be.*

Shamus quickly inputted the shipping details for his Boston residence and clicked the shipping options. It would cost him more for delivery than the entire order of pills, but he didn't care. Shamus needed his Falsomine, his life saver, his fountain of youth.

He clicked the button to accept his order and thought back to three years ago, when he had first heard on the news that NATO countries were experimenting with a drug to give to their militaries. At the time they called it a "wonder drug." The term "super soldier" had even been thrown around by some third-party hacks on the media outlets. Shamus remembered reading about what the drug did and thinking, *That sounds pretty good.* It listed all the things that he would end up feeling.

After a year of the armed forces having exclusive access, Falsomine was authorized for sale to law enforcement, first responders, and medical staff at hospitals. Six months later and it was available at every pharmacy in America. The demand was so high that pharmacies had a hard time keeping it in stock. A two-box limit per customer was eventually implemented until the demand was able to be met.

In the three years since hearing of it, Shamus had never read one headline nor been privy to one rumour that the drug was harmful. *Now all of a sudden, it's bad for you. Bullshit.*

He finished the beer and received the email that his order would be shipped in the next five to seven business days. He looked over at his flight bag. *If I only take one pill every other day, I can stretch it. I can make it work.*

He rubbed his face and felt the drug move within him. It was nearly ten at night and he was filled with energy. He had a flight to San Francisco tomorrow at one in the afternoon, but he wasn't too worried about that.

He glanced at his Rolex and thought, *Plenty of time.* He knew Leslie still worked at the sports bar down the road and was always there on Fridays. She was easy and Shamus wanted to take full use of this unbeatable feeling. He knew it would be his last night of feeling fully alive for a while.

II.

Shamus sat in the cockpit of Washington Global Airlines Flight 272 from Dallas to Boston. His shipment of Falsomine had arrived a little over two months prior and he was beginning to get nervous again. His supply would run out in the coming weeks, and he would be left stranded on an island of mediocrity with the rest of humanity.

The F.D.A. had announced a "Falsomine substitute" last month that was supposed to work, "just as well, without the egregious health complications." Shamus had tried it. Two yellow tablets in the morning, then two more at night when he felt no rush.

He gave this new drug the old college try for five days but found himself quickly throwing them away and going back to his beautiful Falsomine. He apologized profusely to the drug, sorry he ever desecrated and abandoned her for such a cheap substitute.

Shamus finished running the pre-flight checks and studied the drab grey terminal in front of him, used and discoloured. *How I'll feel when my stash is dry,* he thought as he felt a wave of tiredness wash over him.

He turned and looked at his co-pilot, Hank Ivory, who was sitting in the seat directly beside him. Shamus watched him for a moment, his crewcut blonde hair and small nose, grey eyes studying the glowing lights in front of him. Shamus looked over his shoulder at the closed cockpit door before saying, "Hank, you use Falsomine, right?"

Hank darted his eyes towards Shamus. "Who's asking?" he answered after a noticeable hesitation.

"Have you tried that new stuff? Zalpozamoxide, or something like that?"

Hank licked his lips. "Zalposadrone? Ya, I tried it... why?" His beady greys locked upon Shamus' clean-shaven face.

"Does that shit work for you?" Shamus had never sounded so serious in his life.

"Nah, it did nothing for me. Nothing can replace

Falsomine. The kick it gives my mental health, like nothing else."

"Tell me about it," Shamus said as he fiddled with the headset, placing it over his ear.

Hank looked out the cockpit window for a moment and then said, "I know a guy, Douglas Smyth, newer captain. You know him?" Shamus shook his head no, so Hank continued, "Well he swears that this new stuff works just as good, if not better. He won't shut up about it."

Shamus snorted and said, "Oh ya, how much are they paying him to say that?"

Hank laughed, "I said the same thing." He paused and ran a finger across his eyebrow. "Say, you still got any Falsomine left?"

Shamus bit his lip. "If you are trying to bum one off me, I've got to say—"

"No, not at all. I would never do that. I know that shit is worth more than gold." He stopped talking and looked at the cockpit door once more. He turned back after a moment and looked at Shamus. "Where did you get your last shipment? The Canadians I ordered it from in British Columbia got shut down, and it's been illegal to import or possess as of last month. I had to resort to other methods."

Shamus' eyes were locked on Hank, "My Mexican pharmaceuticals company no longer ships internationally either and their website removed all links to Falsomine." He nibbled on his tongue, realizing what Hank had just said. "What sort of methods?"

Hank leaned in closer, a little too close for comfort. "I got it shipping from Pakistan as we speak. It's labelled as muscle relaxers, no ingredients that are watched or overly controlled. Should slip by those rent-a-cops at Border Control. I'm talking about a year supply. I should get it in the next few days. I'm just saying, if you want to buy some, let me know."

Shamus widened his eyes, *Of course, Pakistan. Why didn't I think of that?*

"Write down that website for me," he replied. "Are they affordable?"

Hank pulled out a piece of gum from his pocket and wrote the address on the inside of the wrapper. "No," he chuckled. "Not at all. But who cares? It's worth it."

Shamus pocketed the wrapper and decided he would buy a bulk order of "muscle relaxants" after he returned from his Dallas-Fort Worth turnaround tomorrow.

III.

"Good afternoon," Shamus said to a flight attendant as he entered the aircraft. She smiled and adjusted her deep blue uniform. Shamus took a quick left and passed through first class on his way to the cockpit. He was still mulling over the conversation he had with Hank the day prior. In fact, he hadn't stopped thinking about it. *Pakistan as the source country and the trickery of the shipping, he's a genius.*

He waved at another flight attendant who was storing something in one of the overhead compartments. *A quick turnaround to Dallas-Fort Worth and then back to Boston tonight. Then I'll order myself a year supply... hell, make it a two-year supply.*

He reached the cockpit door and entered. *Don't get greedy now. Those bastards at the postal screening will surely open it if I ship too many and then—*

His eyes narrowed as he looked around the cockpit. *Who the hell is that?*

His gaze was locked on the man sitting in the co-pilot's chair. He was in his early thirties and had shaggy black hair sticking out from under his uniform flight hat.

The man turned, "Good afternoon, Captain. Weather is supposed to be good today."

"Where's the other guy? Where's Hank?" Shamus said as he shook his head, trying to make sense of the situation. Hank was scheduled to fly with him the entire week. *He couldn't have called in sick. He looked fine yesterday.*

The co-pilot stared at Shamus for a moment, before gesturing for him to step out of the doorway and come closer. Shamus closed the door behind him and approached the faded blue captain's chair.

The co-pilot took a moment to collect his thoughts before whispering, "I've only heard rumours but…" He looked over Shamus' shoulder to ensure the door had been fully closed. The co-pilot swallowed before continuing, "A friend of his wife said he's been arrested. Something about importing drugs. Falsomine or something like that." The co-pilot shrugged and made an expression of indifference, "Some people, huh? Just can't listen when the health department outlaws something. They think they are indestructible." He sucked his teeth with disgust.

"Ya, some people," Shamus retorted as he rolled his eyes, a thin layer of sweat forming under his flight cap. He cleared his throat and sat down, extending his hand as he did so. "Shamus," he said.

The co-pilot returned the shake and replied, "Terrance. But Terry is fine too."

Arrested. That means they searched his shipment… because they knew. Muscle relaxers. Pakistan. Of course they knew something was up. How am I going to get my year supply? Think, Shamus, think. You've got—

"So how long you've been doing the Boston Logan to Dallas-Fort Worth turn?" Terrance asked as he adjusted something in his flight bag.

"Hmm? What's that? Oh, umm. Just started really. I used to do the New York turn a bit and before that was a lot of LAX. I wanted something new."

"I hear you. I did the Chicago turn for a six-month stint

there. I liked it but I got family in Texas so…" He trailed off as he looked out the cockpit window.

"Oh ya? I got a girl in Chicago."

"Most guys do," Terrance retorted with a sly smile.

If I can't buy it here and can't ship it, then how the hell am I going to get it? Shamus thought as Terrance continued his pre-flight check. Shamus opened his phone and pretended to look at an article. *I have to go to the source. I'll jump on the international roster. The bid is coming up soon and with my seniority I should get a regular Pakistan rotation with no trouble.* A smile spread across his face as he scrolled listlessly through his phone. *Yes, Shamus, you have a plan. A good plan.*

He inhaled a calm breath. Now he just had to pray his dwindling pill count would last until he could get to Pakistan and buy the drug where it hadn't been outlawed yet.

IV.

Shamus' first flight to Pakistan was nearly two months later aboard Washington Global Airlines Flight 1302. His sacred drug supply had been completely exhausted for over a week and he felt absolutely dreadful. Even after heavy rationing— sometimes only a half pill every other day—he had still run out.

Shamus had thought of speeding up the process and flying to Pakistan as a tourist but quickly dismissed the idea once the paranoia set in. He was convinced that a quick trip there would be flagged by Homeland Security, as he had no ties to the country and the tickets would have been purchased very last minute. He would have to explain himself and upon inspection the contraband would be revealed.

Shamus landed the aircraft at 14:52 local time and was out of the airport and in his hotel room by 18:01. In the months he'd spent waiting to bid on the international destinations, he was able to piece together a network of phar-macies and other small businesses that dispensed Falsomine. Shamus was delighted to discover that the hotel was not only close to the airport but located near a store that was on the receiving list. Everything was coming up roses.

Despite his meticulous planning, Shamus was still nervous. *Why haven't the police or FBI or whoever come knocking since I ordered that shipment from Mexico? Sure, it was legal to import then, but you would think they would have kept a record and paid me a visit to see if I was hoarding the pills.*

He paused as he looked to the hotel room door. The voices of a group walking down the hallway carried in a strange way. Shamus waited until they were gone before he continued his train of thought, *Unless they are so busy cracking down on the actual black-market sellers and people like Hank who bought it after the cut-off date. Ya, that's it. I'm small potatoes. Low hanging fruit. They want the big fish.*

Shamus ground his teeth, wishing he could pop a Falsomine tablet to get an edge and lift his spirits. He wanted to pay a visit to the flight attendant who had taken to making subtle advances at him in the baggage hall. He knew she was staying on the floor below him, but he was worried his perfor-mance would be lacklustre.

I'll give her a good time after I get the pills, he thought as he sat on the side of the bed, slowly building up the courage to go to the pharmacy down the block. *A lot. I have a lot of American dollars in my wallet.*

He visualized paying the person behind the counter and adding in a tip to sell him more than they would usually allow. He stared at the brown leather wallet sitting peacefully on the dresser, the money bulging out of it waiting to be spent. *Why are you so worried? It's legal here—*

"*What if they are watching?*" a voice of paranoia spoke from deep inside him.

Who? Who's watching? Pakistani Intelligence? Why would they care about—

"No. The FBI or Homeland Security. U.S. Customs Border Protection and their watchful eyes."

Those Customs guys? Shit.

Shamus had completely forgotten about running into USCBP officers when he returned to Boston tomorrow. *I am so used to flying domestic—how could I have forgotten?*

"I know. But what if they are watching?"

I can't turn back now. I need it. Besides, they never check pilots. Never, never, never.

Shamus licked his lips and reassured himself. *They never check pilots,* he thought again, this time with more confidence. Shamus picked at the skin of his palm thinking of all the Falsomine that waited just down the road.

"I've come this far," he said aloud, his voice moving around the calm room. "I need it, and those rent-a-cop stamp jockeys aren't going to scare me."

V.

The pills came in a bottle. Not the aluminum foil and cardboard box Shamus was used to, but he had shrugged and chalked that up to a regional difference. The label was clear: FALSOMINE. The rest of the writing was in Urdu, but Shamus paid that little mind. He had bought seven bottles, sixty pills a bottle, a bottle per month. Cost him nearly every dollar he brought, but it was worth it.

He had hidden the plastic bottles in socks and shoes in his checked bag before the flight. *Nothing suspicious about pills in checked baggage from Pakistan,* he had thought as he zipped up his suitcase. *Every passenger had bags full of medication.*

After landing at Boston Logan, he headed to the customs hall and stood in line behind several other crew members from various flights who waited to make their declaration. Upon reaching the front of the line Shamus nodded at the burley officer who scanned his passport. The battered officer only asked one question, "Food?" His voice sounding like his soul had left his body years ago.

Shamus shook his head "no" but thought, *Nothing like that, officer. Just four hundred and twenty pills of pure bliss. You know, nothing too serious.*

The officer handed him back his documents and shouted, "Next!"

Nothing to be worried about, Shamus thought as he picked up his checked bag from the belt. He smiled at Francesca, the flight attendant who fancied him. She was thirty-five, unmarried, and they had arranged to meet at his house at 9 p.m. that very evening.

The digital display on top of the baggage belt stated it was 5:44 p.m. *Enough time to eat, freshen up and get energized to give this blonde a good time,* he thought as he stared at her short blue uniform skirt.

Shamus left the baggage carrousel and imagined getting into his car, windows rolled down, spring air racing past. *Finally, some freedom*, he thought as a subtle smile moved across his face. But as he approached the exit of the baggage hall his smile vanished.

Shamus watched as crew members in Washington Global uniforms entered customs secondary for baggage inspection. It would appear the officers were completing a referral of the entire flight. *Shit. Shit. Shit! Why now? Why today? Of all days?* He swallowed. He was mere meters from the exit line. *What am I going to do? Dump it in the bathroom? Flush it?*

"No! They might notice. Eyes everywhere, you know. Always watching."

And I paid so much. I need it, I can't let it go to waste. These uneducated, minimum wage, security theatre hacks! I'm so close. I'm—

"*Wait, look again!*" the voice from deep inside shifted its tone.

Shamus looked at the crew members entering secondary. He didn't recognize a single one of them. They weren't from his flight. Shamus breathed a sigh of relief and joined the line. *Thank Christ, it's not us. They are from another flight. Yes!*

"*I'm saved. Saved! Saved! Saved!*"

Shamus watched as a group of travellers approached the exit officer. They handed the officer their Trinidadian passports along with their declaration cards. The thin officer nodded before handing back their documents and pointing to secondary.

Of course, the islands. That's who they're checking so intensely. Not Pakistan! The islands, Trinidad or Jamaica or St. Lucia, some place like that, he thought as he queued up in the line, four people away from the officer.

"*Keep on looking for that cocaine boys. Nothing to see here. Nothing at all,*" his inner voice laughed with glee, but still the sweat continued to pool under his white uniform shirt, his tie suddenly feeling increasingly tight.

As Shamus moved up in the line, the bag in his hands felt heavier than it had a moment ago. *Be calm, Shamus. You've been through customs before. Maybe a hundred times over the years. The daily Montreal turn, the six weeks you covered Hans and did his Calgary trips for him. Plus, the vacations to Mexico and Dominican. Flying to London as a co-pilot. Act natural, this officer has no reason—*

"Officer," he said in a cool tone as he handed the man his declaration card. He insured he came to a complete stop. Shamus knew from his younger days that to breeze past the officers was a sure-fire way to get a secondary inspection for "attitude."

Shamus' eyes wandered to the officer's hip as the Glock sat in its holster, its grip beaming up at him, seemingly aware of what was in his bag. Knowing the crime that was occurring just a few feet below it.

Time stood still as the officer looked at the declaration card and Shamus felt like his heart was going to beat right out of his chest. *I should just turn myself in. Save myself the torment of waiting in secondary and the officers swarming me when they find the seven bottles. Laughing, handcuffs, jail. Maybe I can—*

"Thanks," the officer said. He took the card, waving forward the next person in line.

Shamus nodded politely but inside his head he screamed with joy. He was free. Why did he ever doubt his plan? His perfect plan. Why had his confidence ever been shaken? He was a free man with seven months on top of the world ahead of him. Seven months until he would have to be a mule for his own interests again.

Shamus stepped through the sliding glass doors and out into the international arrivals waiting area. A coffee shop lay ahead, and he decided he would get one. He had earned it.

VI.

Shamus looked to the glass table where two white, unassuming pills sat patiently. He had finished a relaxing shower and dressed in clothes appropriate for his date that evening. He wanted to feel his absolute best before taking the tablets. Wanted to feel perfect. He grabbed them from the table and could feel himself shaking with excitement. He popped the duo into his mouth and chased them down with a splash of whiskey.

A moment passed before he exhaled. His brain released the endorphins and he felt like a prized fighter. "Better than I remember," he said to his living room with a calm tranquility.

Shamus placed a record on the turntable and listened to the opening notes of the song as they blasted throughout his house. The baseline complimenting the high he was feeling perfectly. He grabbed the pill bottle from the table, "Tonight's the big night," he said to the inanimate plastic, the green and white sticker staring back. "Got to impress this man killer when she comes. It's been a while and I need my stamina."

Shamus winked at the stoic bottle and grabbed two more pills. Whiskey followed a moment later. The rush, exquisite. He let the rhythm of the song rattle through him. "This is living!" he said as he moved to the kitchen to make himself another drink. He flexed his hands and felt stronger than he had in years. "And they wanted to take this away."

He opened his freezer and grabbed a tray of ice. *This drink is going to be better than the first,* he thought as he grabbed the half full whiskey bottle from the counter. Shamus unscrewed the cap and poured a double shot into his cup. The ice cubes cracked as they warmed against the liquid.

He grabbed the glass and was just about to return the ice tray to the freezer when suddenly he saw an afterimage appear in the left peripheral of his vision. He blinked and moved his head around, but the oily ripple remained.

Shamus closed his eyes. He felt his mouth fill with saliva, the same feeling he always got just before he was going to vomit. His stomach twisted into a knot a moment later.

"What the hell?" he said to the empty kitchen, though he wasn't aware that he had spoken.

Then he heard the sound of glass shattering. He looked down at the smashed whiskey glass, its remnants scattered across the floor. Shamus attempted to put his hands out to steady himself, but they did not respond to his orders. The muscles in his legs cramped and a searing pain appeared above his right eye, burrowing a hole deep into his skull.

"What did those... those... those..." His voice was garbled and distant as he fumbled over his words. "...those camel jockeys give me?"

He fell forward as his hands failed to grasp the side of the stove. His head hit the tile and he heard the crunch of glass under him. He pushed his head from the ground and saw a thick red blob had appeared where his forehead had been. Droplets of blood fell to the floor as he attempted to raise himself up.

Shamus crawled forward in a heap, a stream of incoherent nonsense moving past his lips. The entire world spun. The bass of the turning record grew louder as he entered the living room. His ears warped the music, making it sound like it was moving at a snail's pace.

"It's—just, just… Falsasho… Falzalzo… Falsomine." He called to the bottle as it looked down on him from its perch.

Shamus grabbed the coffee table and pulled himself up. He focused his twisted vision and seized the bottle. He closed his left eye in an attempt to steady himself and read the label. It was no use; the centre of his view was still clouded by afterimage.

He ignored the Urdu on the sticker and read the big green word in the middle of the label, "Falsomine."

"What's the… problem?!" he yelled at the bottle.

"I can't read… read… the—" He grabbed his phone from his pocket, his hands flopping around as his digits went numb. After several painstaking seconds he managed to open an app that offered live translations based on the image shown to the camera.

In a shaking daze he gripped the bottle in a clawed hand and placed it in front of his phone's camera for the app to translate the Urdu to English. His twitching mouth opened in shock as the English translation filled the screen: *EXTRA STRENGTH FALSOMINE.*

"Extra strength?" Shamus said as his tongue filled with saliva.

He turned the bottle around, and the app translated again: *AGES EIGHTEEN AND UP. DOSAGE: TAKE ONE TABLET EVERY OTHER DAY. DO NOT MIX WITH ALCOHOL. NEVER EXCEED DOSAGE UNLESS RECOMMENDED BY A DOCTOR. CAUTION: DO NOT EXCEED ONE TABLET PER DAY. SIDE EFFECTS MAY INCLUDE—*

"But I had four. I had—"

Shamus' open eye couldn't focus any longer and the English on the screen melted into a sea of shapes. His phone thumped to the carpet and his sweat riddled head followed immediately after. The bottle of pills clattered nearby and rolled several feet away. Distancing itself from the scene.

Foam pooled next to Shamus' cheek. The spinning record was all that moved.

VICTORIAN LOVE

I walked down the alley, the neighing and clip-clopping of horse-drawn carriages moving down the street behind me. I felt the wind rustle my top hat and swirl my cloak. The moon was full in the sky, offering plenty of light upon the cobblestone walkway. I gave a town drunk a wide berth as he sat in his own filth, muttering to himself about the end of times.

I reached the end of the alley and saw the mist flick along the grass moving towards the bridge that passed over the ravine. A small body of water separated the wealthy southern part of the city and the slums to the north. I pulled out my pocket watch, holding it in a way that caught the light from the houses behind. It was nine fifty-eight in the evening. I was early.

I pocketed my timepiece and smiled as I thought, *I have made it, after all, even if I had to distract the wife.*

I looked down the road to my right. With the exception of one man walking in the opposite direction, the street was empty. I looked to the left, not a soul.

Excellent.

I moved towards the bridge and felt the grass brush

against my trousers. *Victor picked a good spot, as per usual. A jolly good spot, indeed.*

As I neared the bridge, I heard some laughter from the far embankment. The voices carried across the chain barriers and rolled over the water. I listened for a moment before realizing it was coming from the brothels that were further up the boulevard. The laughing and calling continued as I moved under the bridge to our meeting spot.

Three figures stood there in a half-moon formation, facing the water. A small lantern in the middle provided a soft glow to the bridge's cobblestone underside. The group turned as I lifted my cloak to avoid it touching the mud.

"Stewart! you made it," Victor said with his booming baritone.

"It's been a while, Stew," Angie added. She took a step forward and smiled. "How have you been, you old sod?" She wrapped her arms around me in a warm embrace.

"All is well," I replied, and Angie let the hug slip as she stepped back. "You look healthy. Much better than when I saw you last."

Angie curtsied. "Fit as a fiddle," she said.

I looked to the third figure, "Arthur, you're awfully quiet this fine evening."

The thin man in the bowler hat glanced at me and nodded before licking his lips, saying, "I wasn't expecting to get the correspondence so soon. I had plans this evening, you know. Big plans."

"Oh, didn't we all," I replied, a grin on my face as I spoke.

"You are forgetting your place, Arthur old boy," Victor said as he tapped his walking stick into the mud. "The mission is the priority. Not your hobbies, not your extracurricular activities. The mission!" He adjusted his black hat. "You are becoming attached."

Angie flicked her dress and scoffed. "You told us to become attached. To set up an entire life. Or have you forgotten?" She looked to me for reassurance before continuing, "Five years ago at a spot not far from here you said—"

"I know what I bloody well said," Victor scowled. "You think this is easy for me? Hmm?" He brushed his arm out of his cloak and pointed at his chest. "I love my wife. I love this city. The smells, the colours. But I have never forgotten why we came here."

Angie looked at the rippling waters under the bridge, "But Victor, to say in your letter that this was the final meeting, that our mission has come to an end?" She paused, rolling her eyes as tears welled up inside them. "My husband and I were planning to have a baby and—"

"What? Are you daft, woman?" Victor said, stepping forward, his voice a whirlwind of emotion as he pointed a finger at Angie. "No one ordered you to do that. Not a blasted soul."

"Calm down, old man," I said, removing Victor's finger from Angie's trembling chest.

"I am calm," he snapped, stepping back and giving his head a shake. "Why, Stewart? Why must you always ride to her aid? Hmm? She's older than both of us, she can defend herself."

Angie dabbed at her eyes with a handkerchief before looking to me, "Stew, I know you've wanted kids for a while now. Do you understand me? What I'm going through?"

I nodded but did not reply. *I've wanted to be a father for a long time,* I thought. *A long time indeed.* I felt the warmth of her hand as she squeezed mine.

Victor scoffed, "This whole childbearing notion is nonsense. Absolut—"

"It isn't nonsense," I said, cutting Victor off, his face growing red with fury.

He dismissed my comment and continued, "How would that work, Angie? Hmm? Did you think about the repercussions?" He threw up his arms with exasperation. "No, of course not. Only I do the thinking when it comes to matters of importance." He shook his head and rubbed his forehead.

"I had two more years, and it meant so much to my husband," Angie said in defiance as she stared at Victor, her lips curled in a mixture of sadness and scorn.

"We all thought we had more time," I added. Arthur let out an exasperated sigh as he nodded in agreement.

Victor took a series of long, deep breaths before saying, "Where is Isaac? I would like to get down to the actual business and not keep discussing…" He trailed off and eyed the ravine with impatience.

"Who cares?" Arthur replied with his arms crossed over his jacket. "He always reports the same. Fun times all round, the drinking and the women and—"

"Someone's jealous," Angie piped up.

"Oh?" Arthur replied as he gestured towards himself. "I'm not jealous. I just don't think he takes his assignments as seriously as the rest of us."

"Who ain't?" A voice from behind caused us all to jump. We turned and saw the small, thin frame of Isaac, the youngest of us. As he stepped into the lamp light, I observed that his cloak was torn, and his pants were caked with mud.

"What happened to you, old bean?" Victor asked, as Isaac stood before us, clutching his thigh.

"Oh, a spot of bother on the main road. Nothing I couldn't handle," he smiled. "And those two ruffians will think twice before jumping a stranger in the night again, I can tell you that with certainty." He removed his hat and slicked his hair to the side. "But enough about me, let's get this meeting started. I've got a few dates I'd like to attend this evening with several lucky women." He nudged Arthur before twisting his waxed moustache.

"Not bloody likely," Angie snorted.

Isaac looked hurt by the comment. "What's that supposed to mean, Angie? I—"

"When I said in the letter that tonight was the last meeting," Victor growled. "I meant it."

"No," Isaac said, his eyes wide as saucers. "I assumed you misspoke, or that it was our—Well, I didn't know what you meant. We still have two more years. I still have so much to see and do. Oh, lots to do I assure you!"

Victor put a hand out to comfort the boy, but Isaac shook his head. Victor cleared his throat before saying, "I'm afraid our handlers have cut the mission short." He looked around at the group of curious eyes before continuing, "They've asked me to forward along our assessments immediately so they will know how to act. The other two groups have reported in, they are just waiting on our review."

"Well, I vote an overwhelming no," Isaac said. "Same thing I said when we first arrived. I think we shouldn't change a thing. So again, I say no."

Victor nodded and looked to Angie. She removed a tear from her eye, still the thought of leaving troubled her. "It's a no for me as well. The people here... so much potential, and love. My husband has shown me how good they can truly be."

Arthur spoke next as Victor's eyes locked onto his face. "No. We don't touch it," he said. He folded his arms and gave a nod in confidence.

The group looked to me.

Victor licked his lips, "Well, Stewart, it all comes down to you," he said, and I felt Angie grip my hand once again.

I took a long breath. "No," I said. Angie gasped with glee and squeezed my hand tighter in her fingers.

Arthur cocked his head and Victor bit his lip saying, "Oh, changed your mind since the last assessment?" A sly smile crossed his lips.

I nodded slowly. "I stand by what I said, this place is dirty and unsanitary, and the people are capable of such violence like we haven't seen in a millennium. But there is beauty here and like Angie said, some are capable of love." I paused and thought about my words. "Perhaps even more than *some*, maybe most of them are capable of it in some capacity. My wife is perfect and if there are even a handful like her then this is a place worth keeping intact, left alone to its own devices to thrive."

"All right then," Victor said. "I have the vote as four negative actions and zero on positive action." He paused. "Good, good, when we arrive at our carrier we will see what the others have voted. We will know in a few hours."

"I've been thinking," Angie said, her face pale as she swallowed hard before continuing, the words clearly weighing heavily on her conscience, "I want to stay."

I looked at her and saw the sadness in her eyes. Victor clicked his walking stick on the ground. "No, not possible."

"He's right, Angie," I said. "The injections will only last another month before we need more, and we'll be gone by then."

"So leave me with all the vials that we have on board. Should be enough to last me, what? Ten years? Right?"

"And then what?" Victor said. "After ten years you'll go back to your original form, your true form. Do you think they will accept you then?"

"My husband would still love me. I know he would. I—"

"Don't be so sure. Think of the repercussions he would have to face, and how he would feel." Victor shook his head. "You would have been lying about who you are for fifteen years at that point." He paused, taking a gentle step forward as Angie began to sob. "I know you want children," he whispered, "but we are completely different from them. We forget that. Just because we look like them does not make it so."

I stiffened up and felt a tear as well. *I understand you, Angie. I do. I thought of staying as well.* She looked into my blue eyes, and I continued to think. *The moment I got his letter I thought of tossing it in the fire, running away with my wife, going far away. But we can't, Angie. No matter what we think, we are not them. Once the injections run out, the charade is over.* I know she heard me; we'd always had a special bond.

Victor continued, "Please come back with us, Angie. I know it hurts. But it will hurt more if you stay. What if you can't get pregnant at all because we aren't compatible? Think of the toll that will bring to you and your husband. Or what if they are birthed as some sort of half breed or abomin—"

"Don't you talk about my children like that. Don't you dare, Victor!" Angie snapped, and the tears came rushing back.

"Easy, Victor, you don't have to go into so much detail," Arthur said as he looked to Angie with sympathy.

I stroked her back and whispered, "Victor's right though, there are risks. Too many to count." I watched her nod and thought, *But still I've thought about it. I've thought about it so much.*

Angie shook her head. "I know. I know."

Isaac stepped forward and stroked his moustache, "Hell, Angie. If you want children, I'll do it."

"Christ," I said, and watched Arthur shoot an elbow into Issacs's ribs.

"What?" he said, gasping for breath. "I was just saying— trying to— giving her options," he sputtered as he stared at Arthur, his real eyes springing forth for a moment.

"So that's it then?" I said, as I turned to face Victor. "We leave tonight? A note in the mail with no time the get our things in order? Nothing?"

"I'm sorry. I know how short notice this is, but I only found out about the change in policy yesterday morning. We are being reassigned as well."

Arthur groaned and I replied, "All over again? A whole new life?"

Victor nodded; I could tell he too was not thrilled about the idea.

Isaac was grinning ear to ear, "I think it's an adventure. I'll gladly take another posting. The women around here are getting a bit boring anyway." He looked over his shoulder at the brothel district before adding, "Where is the next assignment?"

I shook my head. *Twenty years ago, I was just like that,* I thought. *But integrating into so many societies, I'm tired. Spending more time in a body that takes months to recognize. I only took this assignment because it was meant to be double the length of most. I could have actually built a bit of a life for myself.*

Angie ran her hands up my arm with a soft caress, for she was still listening.

Victor shrugged, "They don't tell me where we'll be sent off to. But we must depart soon. They will want our assessment."

Angie sniffled, "Can't I say goodbye? I mean, I've been married to the man for over three years and I—"

She was cut off as a lamp light appeared beside the bridge and the sound of heavy footsteps followed. We faced the noise and watched as a patrol man rounded the corner. "You lot," the officer called. "What are you doin' there? Come on out, now!" He waved at us to step forward.

The five of us stood perfectly still and stared at the lawman with intensity. He opened his mouth to shout another order when suddenly he stiffened up. I continued to look into his dark eyes, letting my true lenses shine through. I could see Isaac cock his head. He was having fun with his power.

The patrolman grabbed his forehead with his free hand before pivoting and walking up the hill, mumbling to himself. *He won't remember a thing,* I thought. *But Isaac always over does it.* I blinked and felt my yellow lenses disappear behind my human eyes.

"Woo!" Isaac said with a smile on his face. "It's been a minute since I've done that. Twice in one night, really gets the blood flowing."

"I bet all the ladies you spend the evenings with wish you'd do that to them," Arthur said as he rubbed his eyelids.

"No, I'm a real gentleman to all the ladies about town. They love me."

"Enough," Victor snapped. "We have to get to the carrier and report in."

He departed towards the grass hill with gusto and ducked under the stone archway. We followed his lead, all glum and bitter, except Isaac. Angie let out tears every few minutes and Isaac regaled me with tales of his conquests. He had seemingly taken a new meaning to the phrase "integrate into society" and decided to mingle with any female human that would have him. I don't know why he picked me to unload all of these stories onto, but he did, and I was stuck listening. He kept babbling all the way to the outskirts of town. The streets were still empty, with the only exception being a few stray cats.

We reached a small lake next to a farmer's field and Victor pulled out a pocket-sized remote from his cloak. As he dragged his finger along it, the device began to flash blue. The waters bubbled and our carrier shimmered as it rose from the depths, seaweed and mud sliding off the metallic shell and into the water. Once Victor successfully guided our craft to shore, we all climbed the ramp and stepped in.

"Good to be back," Isaac said as he placed his hat on top of a console by the hatch. "It's like we never left."

We approached the centre console and Victor tapped the screen. He cleared his throat and spoke our mother tongue. The main computer beeped, and Victor called out our non-human names. Upon hearing each of our birth titles, we all took turns approaching the monitor and stating our official decision. After all of us had a turn to speak, Victor imputed several commands and sent the report. He licked his lips and said, "Well, if there's nothing else, let's—"

"There is something," Angie said. Her voice was passive but carried a stern determination just under the surface. "I was hoping I could go back and speak to my husband. Erase his memories of me. I couldn't bear it for him to go on wondering why I left him. Wondering what he did wrong. Please, Victor, I beg you."

Victor sighed. "It's against policy. You know the——"

"Please, Victor, I need this. I will ask for nothing else."

He rubbed his face and looked at her for a long while. "We depart in one hour," he said, as he looked out the open hatch and towards the night sky. "Any longer and the cloaking field will need to charge again."

"That's not enough time to get there and back," I said taking a step forward.

"She'll have to run then, won't she?" Victor turned his eyes to the grassy farmland beyond. "Get going. Don't make me regret this."

"Thank you, Victor! Thank you! Thank you!" Angie cried, as she ran over and kissed his cheek. She smiled at me for a moment before running down the ramp and into the cricket chirping night.

———

Nearly two hours passed and still Angie had not returned. "I knew I should have sent someone with her. Bloody hell, I knew it," Victor mumbled as he paced around the carrier, his shoes clicking on the white metal flooring.

"Don't be hard on yourself," I said. "She knows what she's doing."

Victor snorted in reply. He looked past me and yelled, "Isaac, Arthur, any sign of movement out there?"

Arthur shook his head as he stood on the open ramp, and Isaac called down from the top deck, "Nothing. Everyone's asleep. Just like we should be." His face appeared in the ladder opening above us. "Glass of wine, woman in my arms. That's where I want to be."

Victor ground his teeth and turned to me, eyes intense.

"What order was Angie when we checked in and submitted our verdicts?"

"I'm not sure. Second last, maybe? Why?" I replied as I tried to remember the reporting process.

"I was by the console the whole time to ensure everything was in order. You and Arthur stood by me, and Isaac was there," he said as he pointed to a spot on the floor. "All of us were looking at the console."

I thought back to the event and replied, "Yes, that all sounds right."

"All of us but Angie," he said as he looked around the carrier. "What was she doing when our backs were turned?" I opened my mouth to speak, but Victor immediately jogged to the storage chest and threw it open. He stood straight as he peered inside. "That minx. That filthy little—" He waved me over.

I complied and looked to the bottom of the chest. All the vials of appearance-altering serum were gone.

"She grabbed it all," Victor said, as he held a hand to his head. "Two years' worth for everyone, that's—"

"Ten years, just like she said." A coy smile flashed on my lips, *Good for you, Angie, I'm proud of you. Do what you think is right. Not what I, nor Victor, nor anyone else thinks. Only you know best.*

"She's staying?!" Victor shrieked, tossing his hat to the side. "She lied to me. We have to get her, bring her back—"

"Let her be," I said as calmly as I could muster. I grabbed his arm and continued, "She fulfilled her mission and cast her vote. She's made her choice."

"And what will happen when the serum runs out? What then?"

"She knows the risk, and she's made her choice."

"Gah!" Victor threw his hands in the air. "Arthur, shut the ramp, we're leaving."

"But what about—" Arthur said as he looked to Victor with a confused glance.

"She's staying here," Victor snapped.

Arthur sighed before walking up the ramp and pressing the button that sealed the hatch. Victor moved to the console and activated the carrier's engines. Soon we would be in orbit and off to start a new assignment, a new life.

I watched the marble of a world disappear far behind and thought, *If she did find true love, real love, then I know she made the right choice.*

I knew Angie was listening.

END OF AN ERA

A s we sat on the edge of an uncharted solar system watching the planet slowly orbit in the distance, I knew they had found us. It was only a matter of time. We couldn't hide in the shadow of this globe for long, and the size of our ship made it a burden on the cloaking generators. The device had been broken for two standard rotations now, and it was just a matter of time until the conquering forces probed around the planet again.

The atmosphere was a marvel to look upon. The world's purple storm clouds and eternal acid rain bludgeoning the rock formations far below. Turning end over end, the spinning currents of cool gas rising and falling as if at war. This unnamed world had sheltered us with its bulk, but that too had come to an end.

"Captain, fleet sized movement, approaching from the ruins of Elixtera. You are correct," our technical officer sounded off from the upper deck behind me.

I frowned and felt my nails bite into my palm. We were finished, the last of our race. Pushed away from our homes by this alien menace. Our empire, while far reaching, was relatively unarmed compared to the arsenal packed away on the enemy fleet. They showed no mercy or quarter. Obliterated our outer system observation posts in under a quarter of an orbit. Within a half orbit they had begun shelling our capitals.

I was the last one I expected to be leading this colony ship. A quarter of a million souls, all looking to me for guidance. I was an ambassador before the war. No military experience, no tactical prowess. Yet somehow, I found myself at the helm of this vessel, our last hope at salvation.

"My lord," the technical officer's voice quaked. "They are deactivating their hyperdrives. They will be on our location shortly."

I tensed my jawline and felt my headache return. Even all the way out here, on the tip of the farthest spiral arm, they had found us. I had hoped and worshiped that it would take the hideous onslaught longer to hunt us down. That they'd give us more time to survey the planets of this solar system in search of a home or at least a fighting chance. But it was not to be.

"My lord, shall I sound the alarm? Send the nonessential inhabitants to the life pods?" the technical officer spoke, his breathing giving away how nervous he was. He knew it was the end.

"And where would they go? We are—" I stopped myself. I wanted to say that we were finished, exterminated, our nemesis' great genocide complete. But I didn't say those things.

How would I go out from this life? Grovelling, pleading for mercy? Jaded and bitter and feeling sorry for myself? No, I would go out on my feet; the last of our kind would go out standing, full of pride, taking as many of the beasts with us as possible.

I shook my head and turned to look at the technical officer. "There is no point in sending them away," I said, my eyes locked on his. "The planet closest would melt the pods before they made land fall, and to send them into dark space for them to be target practice and prey? No, we shall not be doing that."

The technical officer hung his head. His spouse and children were among the civilians.

"But there may be a chance," my wife, who was also the navigations officer, said from the seat directly beside me. She blinked rapidly and continued, "To have everyone stay on board is useless. Suicide. Set them free."

"I have made my decision. I will not allow them to float through space, defenceless, with no chance of survival. To fill them with hope would be a lie. I know the outcome." I swallowed and felt how dry my throat was. I continued, "No, we will turn the tides and eliminate as many of our foe as possible."

"You don't mean—" my wife spoke, her voice trembling.

"Oh, my love. I certainly do!" I reached out my hand for her to grasp.

She hesitated, eyeing my outstretched limb with unease. Before seizing my fingers in hers, she said, "But, where will we go? We do not have enough fuel reserves to enter the other dimension, to flee. Our thrusters will not allow us to escape the blast." She looked over her shoulder and glanced at the technical officer, who no doubt shared her opinion.

"I know—" I started to snap, but quickly contained myself. "We will go out staring down our enemy, as we launch the weapon. Our once proud empire will depart with dignity once more. A shining star brighter than a million suns. Just like our ancestors would have wanted."

My wife gripped my hand as hard as she could. She knew there was no other choice, surrender had never been an option. Revenge for the hundreds of billions whose fire had been prematurely extinguished. We would wipe out their entire grand fleet in one fluid motion.

"My lord. They are coming around the far side of the

planet." As the technical officer spoke, a low voice of warning was emitted from his machine.

I knew they would be going for weapons lock momentarily. I swallowed hard. I had but seconds to think of my next course of action. I looked to my wife, "We will let them all come around the planet. Let them lock on to us with all their might. Their admiral has been consistent in his attack. He prefers overwhelming force." I looked to my technical officer. "I want all power sent to shields and forward defensive cannons. Everything else can be deactivated and their currents transferred."

"Yes, but, my lord, what of the life support system?"

"Turn off the generators. We won't need to worry about drawing breath. Keep the viewscreen active. I want to see it when it goes off."

The enemy fleet floated towards our single vessel in a staggered crescent formation. Far off our bow with many moons-lengths between each other, one thousand warships with all their ordinance pointed at our colony ship. War paint and clan banners were etched along the cold grey substance that made up their ships. They were much too far away to make out such details, but I had seen enough footage to know how they looked.

I felt free at that moment. The pieces had been played. Fate decided. I had no worry as the weight of chase left my shoulders. The only thing left to do was put on a good show for the gods. A bright light that might blind them for putting our empire in this dire situation.

"My lord. They're sending a transmission," rage filled the technical officer's voice.

The image of the fur-laden mongoloid filled the view screen. Hideous barbarian scum. How they loved to gloat. The admiral spoke in his guttural language, a savage tongue for a savage race. A complete mockery of what a language could become. "They're firing, my lord."

My wife gripped my hand, and I could feel her nails dig into my soft, political palms.

"Our shields will block the first loose of their weapons," I said as confidently as I could. I was quite sure I was correct— quite sure, but not fully.

The admiral was predictable in his attack. He would fire magnetic tipped explosives to shred our shields and finish us off once we flipped on our back like an animal exposing its soft underbelly.

The weapons collided with our shields and the ship shook and rattled, but she held together. She too wanted to witness the coming fire. Revenge for her dead brothers and sisters.

"Shields are still up, but barely. Another salvo and we are no more, my lord."

"Fire all forward batteries. But keep the device until I say."

"Yes, my lord. Firing weapons."

The admiral's face didn't shift emotion as his machines notified him of our advancing projectiles. The commander looked vaguely amused. *Pompous and overconfident vermin,* I thought. I knew the enemy's defensive nets would blast our projectiles out of the sky, but that would distract them long enough for our outlawed device to go straight down the admiral's throat.

"Aim the device at the capital ship, fire on my command."

I smiled. *An outlawed planet killer. Forbidden by a government that, apart from me, ceases to exist. A government that kept only three of the weapons for research and scattered them across our empire. The same government that refused to use them against an advancing enemy.*

In my last hours on the capital world, as the evacuation was well underway and our home fleet sat in ruins on the edge of our solar system, I acted. I used all my sway and clearance to have a special operations team infiltrate the research facility and transport the device to our colony ship. The last of the three.

I watched as our projectiles were intercepted one by one,

creating tiny flashes in the distance. The admiral gloated and spoke once more before he cut the transmission. As far as he was concerned, he had signed our death warrant. Little did he know that I had signed that same warrant on the day I brought the devil machine aboard.

I gripped my wife's hand and shouted, "Fire the device!"

I watched the view screen as the massive ball of metal raced from our forward launcher and streaked towards the gloating admiral. The device armed itself a half-moon's length off our bow and shot off its protective hull, revealing the red and yellow rotating orbs of energy that circled each other within.

I relaxed my jaw as a wave of calm overcame me. I, a former ambassador, was going to take out more enemy ships with one shot than all our admirals and war captains had managed to.

I looked around the command room. "On our feet!" I shouted, my voice echoing off the quiet bulkheads.

Every officer did as I commanded, their eyes fixed on the glow of the device as it moved further away from our ship.

"This is how our race goes out. On its own terms!" I continued. A few officers cheered as the speck of energy moved off towards the small dots of grey that sat in formation along the view screen.

Even if the enemy defensive nets caught the device, its blast radius would still wipe them all out. Once it had been armed, there was no surviving this. *Shoot it down, admiral. I welcome it. Give me the satisfaction.*

I looked to my wife. In that moment, I could see how much she cared for me. Her double-lensed eyes spoke of a deep, adoring love. She wished to be nowhere else but here with me, looking our enemy in the face, as we took our revenge. She was the most beautiful woman I had ever had the privilege of gazing upon. Her pincers smiled at me as she gripped my webbed hand in a gentle but caring squeeze. Her lower set of arms came to the scales on my back and caressed me.

The device slipped by their defensive nets. The mongrels had never seen a weapon like this before. Their overconfident personnel and had no knowledge of how to track it.

My technical officer laughed as he saw a few ships break formation and attempt to steer clear of the device, but it was all for naught. The weapon collided with the admiral's ship and the explosion was breathtaking.

How beautiful, was all I had time to think before the explosion moved across a hundred million moon-lengths of cold space.

THE TUNNEL

Horace Conrad sat back in his chair and shook out the match, a cigar bobbing between his thick lips. A man stood on the other side of the heavy desk, seething. The man's arms were folded across his thin chest, his hair dishevelled. He had been running.

"I still don't understand what you are so upset about?" Mr. Conrad's booming baritone echoed off the bookshelves and plaques that lined the walls of his office.

The other man raised a finger and leaned on the hard wooden desk. "I've been here for twenty years. Head of maintenance for the last ten. A spot *you* assigned me, Horace."

Conrad batted the finger away from his face delicately. The rings on his hand rattled off each other. "Yes, I did elevate you to that position." He blew a puff of smoke into the air between them and continued, "What other pieces of common knowledge do you bring for me today, Mr. Filborne? Hmm?"

Edward Filborne pushed off from the table. "You know what you did. I don't need to remind you. I just need to know why you wouldn't tell me—" he pointed at himself. "*Your* head of maintenance about it?"

"Why what?" Conrad replied as he pulled the cigar from his face and exhaled. A thick blob of grey smoke circled the ceiling fan. He seemed to love getting under his employees' skin.

Filborne's face became red with fury, and he paced the room. He inhaled once, trying to calm himself, but staring at Conrad's bulbous face and tight tweed jacket enraged him even more. "Bringing in a construction crew to work in the subbasement of the residence without informing me. You know damn well what's down there."

Conrad smirked, "The wires need to be run somehow, Mr. Filborne. The subbasement leads right under the east wing renovations and—"

"I know about the renovations," Filborne growled through gritted teeth. "I've spent weeks of my life on it. Don't talk down to me."

Conrad waved a dismissive hand before continuing, "A few simple drills up into the east wing and the cables are in. Saves us from running them across the grounds, disturbing the soccer pitch or the gardens." He raked his fingers through his thinning black hair. "Besides, there is no crew yet, this is simply an estimate. A preliminary look-see." He exhaled again and a waft of smoke engulfed him. "All that being said, Mr. Filborne, I know nothing about what you are implying. Something being 'down there'? The notion is preposterous."

"Nothing?" Filborne asked, as he shook his head, "You don't have a clue what I'm saying? Really? None at all?"

"Not in the foggiest," Conrad replied. A smirk touched his lips as he eyed his employee arrogantly.

"What about Maze? What about when he went missing in oh nine?"

"Oh yes. I had forgotten about him."

"Spare me, why don't you. How could you forget? We never found him. You seemed pretty alarmed at the time."

Conrad ran a finger across his clean-shaven face and

grunted. "The more I think about it, the more I have come to realize something."

"And what's that?" Filborne asked, as he ceased pacing and eyed the head of the university who sat comfortably before him.

"Mr. Maze was not a reliable employee. You of all people should know that his absentee rate was quite high during the eighteen months he was employed here. He also had a knack for consistently showing up late." Conrad moved a few papers around on his desk as he spoke. "I'm just pulling this from the performance reports you wrote. Here, let me quote one." The university head pulled a yellow shabby looking piece of paper from an open binder and read: "It is in my opinion that Mr. Maze's extracurricular activities are interfering with his work, and unless he straightens up his act immediately, I will be forced to let him go next quarter. Signed—"

"Edward Filborne. Ya, I know who it was signed by, and I know what I said." Filborne eyed the open binder for a moment, wondering when Conrad had gone into his office and removed the performance reviews.

"That was written two months before Mr. Maze went *missing*." Conrad replied, as he held up a hand and bent down two fingers for parenthesis, putting an odd spin on the word. Filborne sighed and Conrad continued, "I think Maze knew he was going to be fired and simply chose to beat you to the punch."

"Halfway through his shift, his lunch bag still in the fridge," Filborne replied as he approached the director's desk one more.

"Yes, he always had a peculiar quality about him, maybe he—"

"No answer on his phone, no one at his apartment."

"You are getting off track!" Mr. Conrad bellowed as he balled his hands into fists. "That company is coming to run those wires and that's the end of it. When I get the estimate, I'm signing off on it."

"Is there any particular reason you set up an appointment to receive a quote the day before I go on my vacation to Miami? You knew I would try to stop you."

"I expected nothing of the sort. The wires need to be—"

"Horace. You want me to give the tour to this contractor guy because you don't want to go down there alone with him." Filborne squinted as he realized just how easy Conrad was to read. "You think I'll just show him around and then I'll be out of your hair for two weeks while the work is done. You knew I would make a fuss during the entire project. You are a terrible liar."

"Oh? How's that?" The smirk left Conrad's lips and he quickly pushed the cigar into his mouth to hide it. His pulse had quickened.

"Why else would you wander all the way down to my office and nick the personnel files out of a locked drawer."

Now the smirk was on Filborne's face. For the first time in Mr. Conrad's professional career at the university, he had no answer for his actions.

Mr. Conrad stood inside the dry entrance of the residence building, watching as the rain thundered down upon the university grounds. "Sure is coming down out there," he said to Filborne, who sat on the foyer steps some distance behind him.

Filborne didn't reply and the dormitory was once again enveloped in a tense calm. Conrad tapped his watch before studying the driveway for a moment. He was about to speak when he saw a Rockwell Construction van pulling up the road. Conrad shifted his weight to his heels as he remembered the uproarious review the company had received from an old drinking friend of his. "They do great work, Horace. Great work! And for the price? Can't be beat. Cheap, cheap, cheap!"

Conrad turned to Filborne who was still seething to himself. "The estimator is here, Mr. Filborne. Try to look presentable."

The head of maintenance got to his feet and wiped a small amount of dust from his worn pair of coveralls. The humid air hung around him and he felt sweat form against the heavy fabric.

Filborne looked to the vent above him and rolled his eyes. He knew no cold air would be flowing through the building for several months. Conrad liked to save money in the summers by turning off all the air conditioning in the dormitory buildings.

Conrad watched a burley foreman exit the van. The rain continued to pour down as the man jogged up the stone path and past the white flagpole. The director opened the door with a grunt, as it had started to stick during the hot Mississippi summer. The foreman entered the dormitory and stamped his feet on the rug, giving his dishevelled hair a shake as he did so.

Conrad held out his hand saying, "Mr. Nellowitz, I presume."

The foreman continued to stare around the foyer. He marvelled at the lacquered floors, the winding staircase that moved upwards to the next floor, and the various paintings that draped the walls.

Conrad cleared his throat and looked down at his outstretched hand. The foreman quickly shook it, but paid Conrad little mind as he said, "Call me Fran. Mr. Nellowitz was my father." His voice was distant as he continued to study the dim light fixtures and red carpets that trailed off into the study hall section of the dormitory. He released Conrad's hand before adding, "Nice place you got here."

"Yes, we make do. Now, about the work," Conrad replied curtly, as he wiped his palm on his pants.

Fran nodded before walking towards a sculpture which rested behind a glass pane.

Filborne smirked as he studied the head of the university. He could tell his boss was fuming. Conrad was accustomed to people hanging off every word he spoke like it was gospel, and this contractor had hardly listened to him. Conrad tugged at the sleeve of his tweed jacket before stepping forward and clearing his throat, "Mr. Nellowitz— Fran…"

The foreman took his eyes from the sculpture and turned, "Oh yes, the work. Sorry. I uh—have a certain affinity for the arts and such."

Filborne felt his head tilt softly. He was not expecting the man to have such an air of mystique about him. A voice that seemed well read and educated. *He speaks well. Maybe he's more sophisticated than he looks*, Filborne thought as he studied Fran's frazzled hair, four-day-old stubble, and wrinkled brown polo. A faded pair of dusty blue jeans and worn work boots completed the ensemble.

Conrad nodded at Fran. "Yes, well, we too enjoy the arts. Don't we, Mr. Filborne?"

The head of maintenance shrugged, "Not really." He thrust his hands in his pockets.

Conrad straightened up. "Don't mind him, he's just eager to get on with his vacation tomorrow. Bright and early." As he spoke, he sent an icy sidewards glance towards Filborne.

"More like dark and really early," Filborne retorted as he felt the heat of the old building swirl once more. The smell of dry lacquered wood fluttered around his nostrils.

"Oh, where are you going?" Fran asked as he scratched at his stubble, "Somewhere with a beach?"

"Miami. My wife has a sister who lives down there. Flight is at 6 a.m. and I'm not looking forward to standing in the security line at four."

Fran whistled, "Good luck with that one." He smiled as he added, "Early bird traveller. But those beaches, those will be worth it. I haven't seen one in years, I'm afraid to say."

"Yes, that's right. We wish Mr. Filborne the best of luck on his trip," Conrad said as he tapped his foot impatiently. "Hopefully he gets some well-deserved rest and comes back ready to work." The calm façade Conrad was portraying had begun to slip on the last few syllables. "Now, gentlemen, let's get to the business at hand. Fran, follow me please."

As they walked down the two flights of stairs to the subbasement, Filborne thought long and hard about how he could warn the fellow in front of him. He knew he wouldn't be able to say much without Conrad shooting him down. Nor could he try to get the contractor alone and explain to him the dangers of the tunnel without coming off as a complete and utter lunatic.

The fact of the matter remains, Filborne thought as he felt the humidity in the air began to dissipate, *even if I scare this guy off, Conrad will just find another company to take his place, and I will find myself without a job.*

Filborne let out a sigh that echoed down the narrow stairwell. "You alright back there?" Fran said from over his shoulder, just three steps ahead.

"Ya, I'm fine. Just hot is all."

"Tell me about it, brother. You guys keep it toasty in here," Fran said, as he pulled at the collar of his shirt.

Conrad ignored the comment. He too felt the heat but was able to look past it. He was saving a lot of money by keeping the air conditioning units silent. They reached the bottom of the stairwell and Conrad fumbled with a set of keys. As he attempted to find the correct one, he said, "As you can see, we don't come down here much."

Fran nodded and Filborne bit his tongue. The basement door swung open after the second key was clumsily thrust into the lock. *Is he shaking?* Filborne thought as he studied his employer. Conrad pocketed the small key ring before switching on the light.

The air was heavy, hot, and stale. The head of the university moved further into the room and studied a collection of worn boxes. An unused set of mouse traps sat between them. Conrad smiled with satisfaction, noticing that no mice had been down here since he had become director. Filborne was worth his pay, it seemed.

Fran stepped one pace into the room before looking at the dusty ceiling. Filborne carefully moved past him, attempting to avoid bumping into the foreman.

Conrad's eyes locked onto the head of maintenance immediately. "Mr. Filborne. When you come back from vacation, see to it that these boxes are labeled, and their contents catalogued. I don't want whatever's in them to go to waste."

"Yes sir," Filborne mumbled with as little enthusiasm as humanly possible.

The basement continued in an *L* shape ahead, leaving the remainder of it unviewable from the doorway.

Fran shook his head. "Is this the only way down here? No elevator?"

"No such luck, no. You will have to hand carry any tools and wires, I'm afraid."

Fran frowned as Conrad spoke. The foremen licked the tips of his fingers before reaching into his back pocket and pulling out a folded sheet of lined paper. He clicked a pen that he had tucked on his belt and scribbled something down. Conrad leaned forward on his toes in an attempt to see what Fran was writing. Fran clicked his pen once more and looked up. "Well, shall we continue?"

"Absolutely. Yes, of course," Conrad replied, his chipper tone echoing down the unseen hall.

That bothered him, Filborne thought, as he let a smile touch his lips. *He's dying to know what the lack of elevator will cost him.* Filborne looked to Conrad, who stood awkwardly before the entrance to the tunnel portion of the subbasement. *I wonder how he is going to handle the next slew of questions this contractor will no doubt ask.*

Conrad gestured to be followed and Fran walked forward. Filborne watched as they entered the hall. The low hum of a dying bulb could be heard flickering above them.

Do I really want to go down there? Even if Conrad won't admit it, I know what waits for us in that tunnel. Filborne felt his pulse quicken. He knew if he didn't follow them, he would risk being fired, or worse, being left alone in this portion of the basement. He trudged forward and joined the two men as a soft cloud of dust rose behind their footfalls.

Filborne turned the corner and saw the chain-link gate that sat roughly thirty feet ahead. He had installed the gate himself, lugging down the required materials three days after Maze went missing. Filborne studied the heavy posts that sat on either side of the gate. Conrad and Fran had stopped and seemed to be looking at the chain-links as well.

Conrad spoke up first. "Using this tunnel will save you a lot of time and labour. No need to dig up all the grounds between the buildings just to run the cables. You can just affix them to the walls down here." He rocked on his heels as he continued, "Yes sir, the renovated building. All new insides, completely rehauled. No more of that ancient infrastructure. We are moving it into the twenty-first century. Only the best for our students." Conrad's voice was full of pride.

Filborne bit his lip. *That sounds almost like a compliment to my services. He must be more shaken than I thought.*

Fran didn't seem to being paying much attention as he stared at the tunnel ahead. "Seems pretty underused," Fran said as he scratched his face.

Conrad ignored Fran's comment and continued, "Internet, telecom, backup generator lines, you can run them all down here. Then you'll connect it all to the main building by drilling a few holes into the basement... Boring holes. That's what I think you call it."

Fran nodded and glanced at the concrete walls before pointing to the chain-link gate, "So, why is this here?"

Conrad swallowed and looked to Filborne, who in turn stared past the director's glasses and into his drooping brown eyes. *I'm not saying a goddamned word*, Filborne thought as he stood perfectly still. *I'm not letting him weasel his way out of this one.*

Fran pulled on the chain-link gate for a moment before turning to ensure his guides had heard him. Conrad continued to stare at Filborne, tilting his head slightly. The head of maintenance simply shrugged. *If Conrad wants workers down here, then he should have the balls to tell him.*

Conrad blinked and his stance weakened. "It's to keep people out of the um—tunnel. Don't want anyone wandering around."

Fran fished a pack of gum from his pants pocket and pushed a piece into his mouth. He chewed it loudly as he replied, "Basement door is locked, seems like a lot of security for an empty hallway." He chuckled and pulled on the fence once more, keeping an eye on his two chaperones.

Conrad opened his mouth to speak, his face turning red as he realized he was caught in a lie. He sputtered for a moment before Fran added, "I get what you mean though," his gum rotating about his mouth, "bored college students wandering around. Maybe you forget to lock the basement door one night. Maybe a devious freshman sneaks down here and... BANG!" He clapped his hands for effect. "The kid pulls down some wires and the whole wing has no internet or something. Can't be too careful, right fellas?"

"Ya—you—um—can't be too careful," Conrad replied with a nervous laugh.

Fran shot him a strange glance: he had answered too quickly. The foreman chewed his gum some more before saying, "Well this is a mighty fine gate, gentleman, but I really want to see where the bulk of the work is. You know, on the *other* side of this."

"Right, um, of course," Conrad started groping at his pocket as he spoke.

What's the matter, Conrad? Filborne thought. *Nerves getting the better of you?*

"Mr. Filborne, here, he has the keys to this particular lock," Conrad said, his voice trying to recover from the shaky phrasing.

Filborne smirked as he held up a single key from his breast pocket. As he held it to the light he thought, *Good save Conrad. Take the attention off yourself.*

Filborne moved to the gate and removed the large padlock from the latch. "Jeez, it's like Fort Knox around here," Fran said as he watched the head of maintenance place the padlock on a chain-link. "You'd need quite the saw to get through that."

"Can't be too careful," Conrad muttered as he watched his head of maintenance open the gate. Filborne waited for Conrad to enter first, but the director stayed perfectly still. He stared at the poorly illuminated hallway ahead.

A moment passed before Fran said, "Well I guess I'll go first." A vague suspicion hung about his words.

Filborne took a deep breath before following the contractor, thinking, *I'm not going to let him wander ahead and have something happen to him just because Conrad's trying to save a dollar.*

Fran ran a finger along the concrete wall as he walked ahead, wiping the dust on his palm. After a moment, Filborne quickened his pace to catch up to the foreman and he heard Conrad trailing behind.

Filborne cleared his throat and spoke as Fran admired the various pipes that were mounted to the celling. "No one should ever work alone down here. There should always be at least two people. For um—health and safety." Filborne hoped his desperate tone didn't come off too strong.

"Health and safety?" Fran said as he looked over his shoulder, narrowing his eyes and chewing his gum slowly.

"Health and safety, yes sir," Filborne repeated with a quick nod of the head. His tone was firm. He was more sure of himself this time.

"He's a worrier," Conrad said, seemingly out of breath from the exertion needed to keep up with the two younger gentlemen.

"Ya, but *we* can't be too careful," Filborne said after a second, a deadpan expression etched upon his face.

The tunnel sat in a stone silence for a moment before Fran chucked, "You fellas are funny guys. Like an old married couple." He shook his head and continued down the hall.

Conrad and Filborne glared at each other before both of them moved forward to join Fran. "So, as I was saying," Conrad said, speaking to the foreman's back, "you could just attach the cables there," he pointed to the ceiling as Fran pulled out his pen and paper. "Right to the water pipes—"

Fran turned and followed Conrad's finger with his eyes before saying, "Nah, that's against code." He chewed on the end of his pen as he looked to the black steel. "We'll just mount it with wall clips right on the concrete."

"Um… Okay, yes." Conrad sputtered as they continued walking.

Filborne followed behind, haunted by the lack of sounds made by the tunnel. The only noise was the group's footsteps and the faint echo of Conrad's words that moved off into eternity.

The group passed a small alcove to the left. Both Fran and Conrad ignored it as they moved along. Filborne knew that the short hallway led to nothing apart from a set of sewage pipes. Yet he turned his head as he felt a sense of paranoia flow through him. He stopped dead in his tracks.

A man was stood at the end of the alcove. He wore the same style blue coveralls as Filborne. His blonde hair was slicked back, and he showed no signs of sweat, nor dust, nor grease. Apart from a strange aura that hovered around him, he looked exactly the same as the day he went missing. "Maze?" Filborne asked the tunnel.

Fran and Conrad looked back. "Did you say something fella?" Fran asked politely, but Conrad's eyes widened. The director knew exactly what Filborne had said. "Hey, brother?" Fran added after a moment. "You all right back there?"

Filborne turned his head to look at his companions, his complexion paler than it had been a moment ago. "No, I—" He looked back down the hall to see nothing but several aging pipes staring back at him.

Fran frowned. He clicked his pen several times before saying, "Gents, maybe I'm off the mark here, but I feel like you've been acting strange." He looked over his shoulder for a moment, studying the tunnel beyond. His chewing slowed as he turned back. "You've been hiding something from me, haven't you?"

The two men of the university looked to one another. A cold panic filled Conrad's face, while Filborne's depicted a stern pleading. A solid moment passed before Conrad opened his mouth to speak, "Yes, well—

"There's asbestos in this building, ain't there?" Fran cut him off immediately.

Conrad looked to the contractor before quickly returning his gaze to Filborne, "Uhh—" was all that escaped his gaping mouth.

"Ya… asbestos. Lots of it," Filborne said as he walked towards the contractor. "Yup. Building's full of the stuff. No sense hiding it from a smart guy like you." Filborne shook his head, a nervous smile flashed upon his face as he motioned for Fran to follow him out of the tunnel. "I guess the estimate is over. What a shame," Filborne concluded as the foreman took an unsure step forward.

"He jests," Conrad spoke up as Fran moved away from

him, the sweat was now beading off his thinning hair. "There's no asbestos here, I assure you."

Fran stopped and chewed his gum loudly as he stared at Conrad. He studied the university director for a moment, "Hmmm," he mumbled under his breath. He wiped his nose as he turned to Filborne, "So, which is it? A maintenance guy tells me there is asbestos, and the boss tells me there's not."

Filborne cocked his head and looked past Fran. *Just tell him already,* he thought as he eyeballed Conrad, who was fumbling with the keys in his pocket in a nervous twitch.

Conrad clicked his teeth and said, "Alright, the truth is—"

"You know, I know a guy that removes asbestos. Competitive rates, too," Fran said, as he moved the gum around his mouth. "Got all the permits the state requires."

The director closed his mouth and rubbed the collar of his dress shirt. Filborne gritted his teeth, realizing he had lost the chance for Conrad to explain the situation. He looked to the concrete ceiling in an attempt to gather himself before saying, "What Mr. Conrad was going to say was… well…" the words were harder to get out then he thought. "There have been a few accidents in these tunnels. That is to say, unexplainable things."

"Oh?" Fran asked. He reached for a cigarette from his pocket, but quickly corrected himself. He could sense that Conrad was not the type to sanction such behaviour indoors.

"Well, I wouldn't say *unexplainable*," Conrad spoke up as he ceased fiddling with his key ring. "They are all *explainable*, but odd... And tragic to say the least."

"We talkin' someone dying or…?" Fran asked as he looked around the tunnel, possibly searching for some evidence to their bizarre claims.

"Well, in a few cases, yes," Filborne answered as he looked to Conrad for assistance.

"Let's keep walking," Conrad said, turning away from

Filborne's gaze. "There's still a while to go before we are under the renovated wing."

Fran nodded, appearing lost in thought. He looked to the pipes overhead once again, his eyes cautious and shifting.

As they continued, Filborne quickly turned his head to look into the alcove again. The hall was calm, but contained a sense of something lurking, watching him just out of view.

"What kind of deaths?" Fran said, after they had walked several paces. "Like smoke inhalation? Something structural, or—"

"Falling," Conrad interrupted as he continued on.

"Falling?" Fran stopped in his tracks. "The ceilings aren't even ten feet high."

"Ya, he... um... Felix," Filborne sputtered as he moved up beside Fran, "fell off the small step ladder as he was replacing a light fixture. Screwdriver ended up—um..."

"Like I said," Conrad added after Filborne trailed off, "tragic, but not unexplainable."

"Oh no?" Filborne protested. "What about Scotty?"

"Hmm, yes. Well like I—" Conrad muttered, but was cut off by Fran who interjected,

"Who's Scotty?"

"Scotty was a cleaner of ours," Filborne replied as they began to walk down the tunnel again. "Back in the day, the cleaners used this tunnel as a way to avoid the rain when they had to move between the dormitories and what was then the old science wing." Filborne cleared his throat. "Scotty was the only one working in this section of the university that night, and, well, we... um... we found him the next morning down here in one of the alcoves. Doctors said it was a brain aneurism."

Fran squinted, "So what I'm gathering is you think there's something down here. A ghost or something, that is causing these deaths."

Conrad let out a humourless chuckle as he attempted to mask his nerves, "Of course not."

"Yes," Filborne said, nodding his head aggressively. "But I don't *think* there is. I know it."

The way Fran carried himself after that comment was vastly different from how he had been acting when the group entered the tunnel. His nerves seemed to be getting the better of him. He rubbed his face as they passed another alcove. He looked down the short hall and said, "Nothing down there."

Both Fran and Conrad walked on, leaving the alcove behind, but Filborne lingered. He sheepishly turned his head down the side passage. An overturned step ladder and a yellow handled screwdriver sitting delicately beside it returned his gaze.

The tunnel was listening.

"So, Mr. Conrad," Fran said as they moved on, leaving Filborne a few paces behind. "I take it that you think it's all a bunch of nonsense?"

"Precisely. A series of unfortunate and untimely deaths. Nothing more."

"Tell him about the voices," Filborne blurted out as he studied the overturned ladder, the screwdriver rolling slightly as he spoke.

Fran perked up an ear and Conrad spoke, "Yes, well a few employees—who are no longer in our employ, I might add—said they heard whispers down here." Conrad ground his teeth before adding, "But I've never heard anything."

That's because you never come down here, Filborne thought as he turned his attention away from the alcove and quickly moved towards his two companions. He looked over his shoulder one more time before saying, "I've heard rattling and the occasional muttering."

Fran swallowed his gum and let out a quick cough. He straightened up and said, "Well fellas, I like a good ghost story as much as the next guy but—"

There was a creaking at the tunnel entrance.

The three men turned around. The chain-link gate was now closed. Fran's mouth was agape, and Conrad began to tremble.

Conrad's breathing become more erratic with every breath before he croaked, "Mr. Fisher, Mr. Tetley?" The names were of the other maintenance workers scheduled that day.

"Let's get to the bottom of this," Fran said as he puffed out his chest and marched forward. "Funny guys you are, having someone stay behind to scare me." But the sounds of his words were peculiar, for they did not echo. Instead, they lay limp in the air like the walls of the tunnel had absorbed them completely.

"It's not us," Filborne huffed as he struggled to keep up with Fran's long strides.

Conrad had remained standing in the same spot they left him, his head shaking in disbelief at the closed gate. "No one else is in the dorm today," the director muttered. "No one's supposed to be here but us."

Fran and Filborne reached the gate. The contractor looked down at the latch with disbelief. He pointed and Filborne saw that the padlock was clamped shut. The gate was locked exactly like it had been when the group first entered the tunnel.

Filborne felt his hands shake as he reached for the key. "Keep an eye on Conrad!" he shouted as he rifled through his pockets, the piece of steel he needed staying just out of grasp. Fran opened his mouth to protest when Filborne ordered, "Just do it!"

Fran looked down the hall. "He's still there," he said and raised his hand, "Conrad. Come on! Let's go!"

Filborne retrieved the key, hearing footfalls approaching as Conrad began to run. Filborne fought to squeeze his fingers through the chain-links, attempting to keep a firm grasp on the steel that would lead to freedom. After several agonizing moments, he inserted the key and twisted it.

There was a soft click as the lock released and Filborne pulled down. Fran sagged his shoulders with relief as Conrad stopped just short of them, letting out a series of sharp breaths. The director placed his hands on his knees and rubbed them vigorously.

Filborne removed the key and took off the padlock from the latch. He dropped it to the ground and brought his hand back through the gap in the links.

Within the blink of an eye Fran had pushed open the gate and run through. Conrad limped past and Filborne followed close behind. The head of maintenance spun around and slammed the gate shut. The chains shuttered and rattled as he bent down and grabbed the padlock from the cold concrete.

Filborne looked over his shoulder to see that his two companions had left him, having already turned the corner. He felt the lock in his hand and stood up, raising it to the latch. As he manipulated the lock around the metal, Filborne saw something flicker at the far end of the tunnel. A whisper just on the cusp of his hearing immediately followed. He shook his head and closed the lock, feeling it clasp in his hand. He pushed off from the gate and dared not look back.

Filborne turned the corner to see Fran moving the pile of boxes away from the wall. "What kind of games are you tryin' to pull, Conrad?" he said as he looked in every corner of the room. "Who locked us in. Where is he, where—"

"It wasn't us. I told you!" Filborne snapped as he stood beside Conrad. "I told you there's something down there. Something—"

"Unexplainable, ya I got that!" Fran barked, throwing open the door leading up to the dormitories. His heavy footsteps ascended the stairs, leaving Conrad and Filborne to look at each other.

Conrad stood up straight as he turned his ear back

towards the tunnel. Filborne listened as well but heard nothing. The director swallowed before moving towards the stairway. Filborne followed close behind.

They marched into the foyer and saw Fran pacing hysterically. "Well, I've had just about enough fun for today. I'm leaving," he said and popped a cigarette into his mouth, the lighter trembling in his hand.

Filborne looked to Conrad, expecting him to speak up, to plead with Fran to stay and take the job. Filborne imagined Conrad saying things like, "It was just the wind" or, "You're right, it was a staff member's prank." And when those thinly veiled excuses didn't work, "I'll add in an extra two thousand dollars on top of the estimate as payment for your trouble. No wait! Five thousand!"

But Conrad didn't say any of those things. He just stood there, panting, the artery in his neck pulsating with every beat of his heart.

Fran shook his head as he pointed at Conrad, the fire in his eyes suggesting he wanted to say one last thing. But instead, he stayed silent and grimaced at the director. He lowered his hand after a moment, then pivoted and marched out the front door. A clap of thunder bellowed across the grounds as he reached his van.

Filborne and Conrad moved to the door and watched as the Rockwell Construction van sped off down the driveway, plowing over speed bumps in its haste. The wipers beat frantically as the rain hammered the windshield.

Filborne let the silence of the building settle. *I have to play this right*, he thought as he studied Conrad's concerned expression. *If I act too quickly, Conrad may try to convince himself that it was all a coincidence or a trick of the mind.*

Filborne could see drops of sweat wetting the university director's greying black hair. "Mr. Conrad..." he said as he treaded lightly with his tone, "Horace. Can we agree to not let anymore contractors down there for—"

Horace Conrad nodded aggressively as he fumbled with the keys in his pocket. He continued to nod for a long time in silence before saying, "Enjoy your vacation, Edward. Take— Take as much time as you need." He nearly whispered the words as he watched the droplets bead down the glass.

"Thank you, sir. I will," Filborne answered. But he wondered if he would ever be back at all.

Mr. Conrad extended a hand as he looked at Filborne. The two men shook before Conrad turned around and headed towards the back entrance of the residence building.

A walk in the rain might do me some good. Ease my mind a bit, the director thought as he walked to the administration building, leaving Filborne to stand alone. The head of maintenance stood in quiet contemplation as he watched the door to the subbasement.

Horace Conrad sat in his office. The ticking grandfather clock in the hallway had chimed out 11 p.m. just moments ago. A bottle of rum sat unopened on his desk. He had considered drinking it but hadn't the nerve. He had been unsure why he had stayed at the university so late in the evening, but even subconsciously he had always felt more comfortable in his office than in his empty house.

The director ran a hand through his hair and studied the estimate quotes he had jotted down on the ruled legal pad in front of him. To have the soccer pitch dug up and then to run the cables underneath was going to cost a pretty sum. That was to say nothing of the sod and seeding expenses. He sighed once more. "I have no choice," he said to his dark office.

The clock ticked outside, and he heard a rustling from the hall a moment later.

He sat up high in his chair and saw that several sheets of

folded paper had been slipped under his door. "Mr. Filborne?" he called, his voice trembling.

It's not him, he thought as he felt his heart race again. *I watched his white car leave the staff parking lot hours ago.*

Conrad got to his feet and moved towards the door. His pulled leg muscles cried out with every step he took, still not forgiving him for running earlier in the day. He stopped and stared down at the six sheets of paper that lay fanned out upon the hardwood floor.

He put his ear to the door and listened. Only the familiar *tick tock, tick tock,* of the grandfather clock echoed through the hall.

A long while passed before he built up the courage to pluck the pages from the ground. He swallowed and carefully piled them together, raising them as he did so. He took a deep breath before flipping them over and taking a step back towards his desk. His lips curled as he read the first page.

It was the resume turned in by Felix Harrison, the man who had fallen off the ladder and impaled himself. The paper was old and wrinkled.

This is the original, Conrad thought as he watched the page tremble in his hands. *How did it get here? The records room is locked and I—*

He looked at the aged ink, the original penned signature at the bottom underneath a date of September 4th, 1988.

It's not a copy. But how?

Conrad flipped to the next page and the resume of Scott Tavers awaited him. It was signed January 18th, 1995. He shook his head as he thought back to the night the body was discovered. *Filborne said he found him curled in a ball. Like no man he'd ever seen before. His body twisted in such a way—*

He shook his head, trying to clear the images that appeared in his mind. The next belonged to Blake Maze, signed October 2nd, 2007. "*We never found him,*" Filborne's voice rang out as Conrad remembered what his head of maintenance had said earlier.

Conrad shuffled to the next page. Walter Zim, dated August 21st, 1975, five years before Conrad had started his job as director of the university. *Could this man have died down there when my predecessor was in charge? I've never heard of it. He never told me—*

He moved on to the next page. Stephen Voit, February 1966. *Did Director Jackson try to cover it up? Was he trying to avoid bringing unwanted attention to the school?*

He reached the last paper in the stack. MAXWELL ST. CLAIRE, the resume read, dated *APRIL 2ND, 1954.*

Conrad stiffened up. "April 1954," he said aloud. *That was the same time the construction of the residence building began.* He felt his hand rush to his forehead. *Could this Maxwell St. Claire have been the first death?*

He looked out the windows that sat behind his desk, the dormitory building looming in the background. *Killed in an accident while the foundation of the tunnel was being laid? Tumbled to his death? Crushed?* Conrad's mind raced with the endless possibilities of a man meeting his demise on a busy construction site. *Was his death ever even reported or had the old director bought their silence to keep construction on track and investigators away?*

Conrad folded the papers and placed them in his jacket. *It was never reported. I would have heard—*

With that he threw open the door and hurried to the library wing.

Conrad shuffled through all the microfilm newspaper catalogues from 1954 and 1955. There was not a single mention of an accident at the university. Not even a footnote belonging to a Maxwell St. Claire. No obituary, no missing person notice, nothing.

Conrad lifted his eyes from the projector. *It's like he never existed. But clearly— The resume— I need more records. I need—*

He snapped his fingers and sat back in his chair. *The hospital. Birth certificates.* He stared at the rows of bookshelves that stood before him. *I can track him and the other missing people that way if they were born in the city. But how can I convince the staff there to let me see their records?*

He took a deep breath and the scent of old paper caused him to relax. He pulled the resumes from his pocket and shuffled through them, only stopping when he reached Maxwell St. Claire's. There was something about that raggedy paper that he found mesmerizing.

An idea erupted in his head like an electric shock. *If he was the first, could he be the one roaming that tunnel? Eternally enraged that his death was covered up. No one brought to justice.*

Conrad shook this notion from his head and moved through the resumes once again.

The more he thought about it, the more it seemed likely. The spirit of Maxwell St. Claire was lurking under the dormitories, lashing out as he searched for peace. To Conrad it seemed like the only logical explanation. *But why show me the resumes? To prove that you had existed?* he thought as he felt his growing headache worsen. *But what would he—*

Conrad heard a slight clatter.

His jaw tightened as he felt a shiver run through him. *No one works this late. I'm the only one here.* His eyes shot up and he stared across the well-lit library, his focus on the dark hallway outside the main door.

Something was there, but he could not see it.

"Maxwell?" he said, his voice hardly more than a squeak.

The hall stayed silent. Conrad looked over his shoulder, but only a wall of shelves was there to greet him. He felt his heart pounding under his shirt as he returned his gaze to the open door. The glass wall surrounding it was completely still.

Get a hold of yourself. You're just working yourself into a mess. That entity is confined to the... basement.

Conrad thought back to the tunnel under the dormitories. Even an entire building away it conjured up a feeling of dread. He thought of the chain-link gate, the massive padlock. *But why would that hold it? A physical lock? It could easily leave there. And perhaps it wanders the grounds so late at night.*

Conrad stared at the void, but nothing moved. After several minutes, he stood. Not taking his eyes from the entrance, he switched off the microfilm projector and gathered up his belongings.

It's time for bed, he thought as he moved to the rear exit of the library. *Time to forget about Maxwell St. Claire and that accursed tunnel.*

Edward Filborne sat on the edge of his hotel room bed, the heat of Miami swirling around him. He hadn't slept much since returning from the university the night before. Knowing how close they had come to becoming another victim of the tunnel crept over him constantly.

The closing moments of the eighth inning flashed across the television screen. He could hear children screaming with glee as they splashed around the pool two stories below. The sound of his wife laughing as she talked with her sister under an afternoon sun followed a moment after.

The apartment his sister-in-law's family lived in was too small to accommodate everyone, so a hotel was the best option. Filborne watched as the Marlins' pitcher threw a curve ball just as the phone rang behind him.

He jumped and let out a curse before turning and reaching for the handheld.

"Hello, this is the front desk calling. Is a Mr. Edward Filborne there?" a young-sounding receptionist asked with a soft voice.

"Yes, this is he."

"Oh, hello there Mr. Filborne. There is a collect call for you from a Horace Conrad. He said it is urgent. Would you like me to connect it to your room?"

"Yes. Yes please. Thank you."

"No trouble at all, sir. Have a great rest of your day." There was a click and Filborne heard the line switch over.

"Mr. Conrad. Are you there?" Filborne asked as he listened intently to the sounds of the telephone line.

"Ed. Ed. The tunnel. I don't think the entity is confined to it anymore."

"What? What happened?"

"Things moved around the library last night after I left. Microfilm. Books. I know I didn't do that. And these resumes appeared under my door and—"

"Resumes? From who?"

"Everyone who—who died down there. Their original resumes from the records room. Last night, after you had left. They were just placed under my door with no explanation. Then, as I walked to my car, I saw shadows in the dark, heard whispers all over the grounds. But that's not important."

"Not important? That sounds pretty impor—"

"No, listen. I figured it out. I figured out what the entity is. *Who* it is, I should say. A Maxwell St. Claire. His resume is the oldest and I can find no record of his death. Mr. Jackson, the previous director must have covered it up to keep construction on track."

"That doesn't make any sense. Why would he cover up a death that he had nothing to do with?" Filborne pressed the receiver closer to his ear, his mind spinning. While he recognized Conrad's voice, he sounded nothing like himself.

"Because I think St. Claire died while the dormitories were being built, and Jackson didn't want investigators snooping around and delaying the project. Maybe there was a safety violation and Jackson was trying to—"

"Horace," Filborne interrupted as his eyes darted between the dresser and the small work desk of his hotel room.

"What?" the director snapped.

"Why do you assume St. Claire is this entity?"

"Well—Um, because he's the first resume. The oldest one."

"Okay, but couldn't it be possible that he was just the first victim? I'm not saying there isn't a cover up by the previous director or even the original builders, but why assume he's the one haunting that tunnel?"

"I don't follow?"

"Couldn't it be that the construction crews disturbed something? Like I don't know, an old cemetery site or something as such, and then the entity claimed its first victim? The first one that we know of at least. This St. Claire guy. Maybe this entity showed you the resumes as a way to brag of its work. Or—"

"Like an Indian burial ground? No, I would have known of such a spot. I know—"

"You're hung up on the wrong thought. It could be anything really. A disturbed grave or a cursed plot of land. Anything. But I wouldn't assume this St. Claire is the spirit. There is no motive."

"He's a ghost, Edward. He doesn't need a motive. He—"

"Then why would he be killing people that enter the tunnel?"

"Because he was never brought peace. His death was covered up and forgotten."

"I'm not sure. I think you'd be better off looking into the other route."

There was a long delay and Filborne thought that Conrad had hung up. The kids laughed outside, and a distant horn of a car echoed past the window. "Horace? Did you hear me?"

"Yes, yes. I heard. I—I just have a lot to think about. More research. Goodbye, Mr. Filborne, enjoy your vacation."

Conrad ran down to the library. *The papers, they must mention when the university bought the land to build the dormitories,* he thought as he headed down the hall from his office. *Maybe it wasn't the entity at all that showed me the resumes, but the souls of the dead. Trying to warn me. The whispers, the footsteps.*

As he turned the corner, his eyes gravitated to a small copper plaque that was mounted low on the wall. The bronze-coloured letters read: *BUILT AS PART OF THE STILHAVEN UNIVERSITY EXPANSION PROJECT. 1955.*

Conrad's eyes widened. *This is on the land, too. It's not just the dormitories but the administration building and the library wing. Christ, more than half the goddamn campus.*

He burst through the library doors, leaving the plaque behind, and moved through the still area. The sun shone brightly through the windows as a cool wind knocked on the glass. Books were strewn across the hardwood floors and microfilm projectors still whirled as their cooling fans turned. The entity had made itself at home last night as Conrad had discovered earlier that very morning.

He sprinted over to the storage room where the microfilm records were kept and hastily grabbed ten years' worth of boxes, starting with 1950. "It's got to be in here," he whispered to the hundreds of reel containers that looked down at him with a glum curiosity.

Conrad moved to a switched-off microfilm reader and placed the first reel into the machine. He pressed his eyes to the viewer and twirled through the pages, looking for anything mentioning the university. Nothing caught his eye. Nothing in fifty-one or fifty-two, either. Not even a minor footnote.

It wasn't until he reached the fall of 1953 that he saw a small headline on the fifth page of the *Mississippi Inquirer* that he stopped his scrolling. The headline read: *STILHAVEN UNIVERSITY PURCHASES ABANDONED TWENTY ACRE PROPERTY.*

Conrad's eyes widened as he continued reading the article.

...THE LOT HAS BEEN VACANT SINCE THE ORIGINAL OWNER WENT MISSING IN LATE NINETEEN THIRTY-FOUR...COUNTY SHER-IFFS INVESTIGATED A SMALL HOUSE LOCATED ON THE SOUTHERN PORTION OF THE PROPERTY SHORTLY AFTER THE OWNER'S DISAP-PEARANCE. REPORTS FROM THE TIME MENTION "STRANGE SYMBOLS" ON THE FLOOR AND "SEVERAL ODD ODOURS COMING FROM THE WALLS." A SMALL FAMILY GRAVEYARD WAS ALSO DISCOV-ERED LESS THAN HALF A MILE NORTH OF THE HOUSE WITH SOME GRAVES REPORTEDLY DATING FROM THE EARLY EIGHTEEN-SIXTIES...

...WHEN THE BANK REPOSSESSED THE PROPERTY THAT SAME YEAR, THEY ORDERED THE HOUSE TO BE DEMOLISHED. NO EVIDENCE OF ANY CRIMES WAS FOUND...

...WHEN ASKED FOR A QUOTE BY THE NEW DIRECTOR OF THE UNIVERSITY, DOCTOR NORMAN JACKSON HAD THIS TO SAY, "I AM PLEASED TO ANNOUNCE THAT ENROLMENT HAS BEEN STEADILY INCREASING AND IT IS TIME TO EXPAND OUR FACILITIES. DUE TO THE GENEROUS DONATIONS BY BOTH PRIVATE AND CORPORATE SPONSORS WE ARE ABLE TO AFFORD THE BEAUTIFUL PIECE OF LAND THAT SITS BEHIND OUR CURRENT PROPERTY. THE BOARD OF DIRECTORS HAVE APPROVED THE PURCHASE AND DEVELOPMENT OF THE LAND IS EXPECTED TO START RELATIVELY SOON...

...WHEN THIS REPORTER ASKED THE DIRECTOR TO COMMENT ON WHETHER HE WAS AWARE OF THE HOUSE THAT HAD BEEN LOCATED SO CLOSE TO THE UNIVERSITY, OR OF THE FAMILY GRAVESITE, HE STATED, "WE WILL WORK WITH THE PROPER AUTHORITIES AND ASSESS OUR OPTIONS. IF POSSIBLE WE WILL LEAVE THE RESTING PLACE OF THE FAMILY UNTOUCHED."

I've never heard of any graves on the property, Conrad thought as he finished reading the last lines of the article. *Filborne might be right. Could the residence be built right over it?*

Conrad shifted the film to the next article, though he wasn't really reading it. *Maybe I can find a blueprint, or a map of the original property, and see if the plot that was purchased matches up to the current building locations. The original bill of sale, the deed to the land, maybe. Perhaps a copy of the original sheriff's report would give me more insight into what they found in that house before it was demolished.*

He raised his eye from the looking glass and realized the library was dark. The only exception was the lamp that sat beside the projector. Conrad had forgotten that he had switched it on nearly five hours ago. *How long have I been looking at the papers? Surely not—*

He glanced down at his watch. 11:58 p.m. *No, not possible I—*

Conrad looked to the open boxes of microfilm beside him and shook his head. He grabbed the reels and began to place them in the corresponding boxes.

"It's late. I should go," he said to the empty library as he fumbled with a reel. *I don't want to be here when this being comes by again. I know it was in the hall last night, and I know what I heard on the grounds.* He shuddered, recalling his hasty walk through the parking lot the night before.

Conrad had just placed the lid on the first box when he heard a sound like radio static. It was low and garbled at first, but by the time his brain processed it, the sound was nearly at the library entrance. Conrad stared at the glass doors as they swung open. He felt no draft and saw no one. The doors had moved on their own.

He looked to the windows on the far side of the library. The dark night moved past in a peaceful bliss. The moonlight was faint, hardly illuminating the grass that swayed in the breeze. Conrad's eyes snapped to the door.

There, a sphere of shadow sat, nearly translucent, hovering in the hall, watching.

It raised and lowered in a rhythmic motion as flashes of colour pulsated inside its depths. A calm mist carried on down the corridor as the orb continued to slowly rise and fall. If Conrad didn't know better, he would have sworn that it was breathing.

"I'm—I'm—I'm sorry," Conrad stuttered. "I—I—I didn't have anything to do with the construction. I didn't know anything about the grave site."

The entity sat in silent contemplation, the colours inside it spinning into a curious orange.

"It was the previous director. It was all him. Not me."

The sphere bobbed up and down. Its mist continued radiating, slowly entering the library.

"Can you answer me?"

Still it sat, emotionless, the crackling static moving this way and that.

"Why now? How have no students seen you? Is it because we—"

Conrad felt himself take a step back, planning to move to the fire exit somewhere behind him.

As his foot hit the hardwood, the orb's light shift to a violent red. The static altered from a low hum to an ear-piercing screech. The entity drifted forward at an alarming but uniform speed.

Conrad shrieked and pivoted, running toward the exit sign that hovered over the door at the back of the library. Within a matter of seconds, the screeching was upon him. He dared not to look back as his feet bolted below him. His heart was pounding in his ears, legs aching and—

A sick heat consumed him.

Every heinous act that was committed inside that horrific house revealed before him. Ripping, tearing, skinning, maiming. The family, long before their burial, smiling at the pain their hands produced upon their copious victims. Lacerations and dissections by candlelight. Joy, so much joy. Death, insignificant to them, for it could not hold their wickedness.

As the images of pure madness pierced him like a searing brand, his hands moved to a pair of scissors kept in a nearby drawer.

SIDE TWO

THE MAN WHO LIVED UPSTAIRS

"There's no one that lives upstairs," the landlady said with the tone of a surly waiter.

"Well, I can hear someone up there. At weird times of the night too," Edgar replied.

"There's no one up there. It's just an attic for storage. Must be the wind," Ms. Donaldson snapped, and Edgar assumed she had always been a Ms.

"Or maybe it's the rats," Edgar retorted with a crooked grin on his face.

"We don't have rats!" she growled, before snatching the rent check from Edgar's hands and storming off down the hall towards the stairwell.

Edgar shook his head and closed the apartment door. *If she would wait a few minutes, she would be able to hear it for herself,* he thought as he moved away from the door.

He walked into the kitchen and headed for the fridge. As he reached out to grab the handle, a thump echoed overhead. "Christ, there it is," he said as his eyes bolted towards his watch. The hands were touching 8 p.m. sharp. "Right on cue."

His mind conjured up images of fifty-pound rats the size

of dumbbells, lumbering from floorboard to floorboard, much too fat to scuttle any longer. He looked at the single electric light that was affixed to the stucco ceiling for a few moments before sighing and opening the fridge.

Edgar lived on the sixth story of a small building and was the only occupant on the floor. Ms. Donaldson lived directly below him and had once mentioned that she preferred a much cozier apartment for herself. Edgar had quipped with his ex-girlfriend that the landlady was taking after her cats, seemingly comfortable in tight spaces.

When he had first heard the sounds, he assumed someone had moved in, but he quickly realized he had never seen anyone unpacking. No moving trucks, nor sweaty people lifting box after box of items they could do without but held on to for sentimental reasons. Edgar also believed that the space above him was an attic, something Ms. Donaldson had just confirmed.

The thumping and other curious noises that Edgar could set a clock by started a few weeks prior. A few at six, some more at eight, and then one at two minutes past eleven. Edgar always assumed the ghost—or rat king—must like to take a nap between eight and eleven. From eleven thirty onward, though, it was like the six-step shuffle up there.

It got so bad one night that Edgar had taken the broom and rattled the ceiling with it. That stopped the thumping for a second, but then Ms. Donaldson was soon thumping the floor beneath him with a broom of her own.

In truth, Edgar wasn't home most of the time to hear the bulk of the sounds. He worked the night shift cleaning an office building in the corporate sector of town. He would get home around 2:20 a.m. every night and just deal with the sounds by tuning them out. The three or four beers also helped.

There was another thump directly overhead. Edgar

shrugged and assumed maybe one of Ms. Donaldson's deranged cats was taking all the boxes out for a test drive.

Monday Night:

Edgar stepped out of his car and locked it behind him as he walked through the building's rear parking lot. The rain poured down as puddles filled the potholed asphalt. As he rounded the corner, his eyes drifted over to a white cat sitting along the chain-link fence. It belonged to Ms. Donaldson and had a ludicrous name, though he couldn't remember it at that moment. It was the only white cat she owned.

The feline sat on its haunches and stared up at the building. Edgar approached the animal and held his hand out to pet it, but it stayed completely still, watching the building with a morbid curiosity. Edgar followed the cat's line of sight and looked to the top of the building. A single light shone from the top floor window.

He blinked and thought, *Did I leave the light on?* But as he counted the floors, he realized his apartment windows were dark. This window was directly above his.

Edgar dropped his hand from the cat and approached the front entrance, taking care not to step in the copious number of puddles. Within a minute, he was through the front door and up the six flights of stairs. He stood in front of his apartment looking to the far end of the hall, towards the door that led to the attic. *I'm getting to the bottom of this,* he thought as he scratched the beginnings of a beard on his face. He was wide awake now.

He approached the door leading to the attic and surveyed the frame for any sign of an alarm system that might be activated if it was opened. He found none. Edgar felt the handle click in his hand and opened it.

Before him was a staircase that went up to a small landing

and turned back around a corner. A single dormant light bulb hung down from the ceiling. Edgar groped the wall beside him and eventually felt a switch against his palm. He flipped it and the light came to life with a tinkling buzz.

Edgar climbed the dusty, antiquated stairs. The plaster was cracked, and the paint had chipped away in large pockets. Edgar reached the landing and continued upwards. He made it to the top of the stairs and put his hand on the door handle that led to the attic. He could see the light shining in the space underneath the door where it met the hard wood steps. Edgar turned the handle but felt it seize in his palm.

It was locked.

The light from underneath the door vanished immediately, leaving the attic cold and dark. Edgar stared at that green door for a long time. The only sounds were the rain and the sputtering of the bulb behind him.

Could it be Ms. Donaldson? he thought as he listened to the wind move through the building. *But then why did she turn off the light? And why is she awake at this time of the morning?*

Edgar swallowed as his mind filled with images of poltergeists or gremlins. *It couldn't be a ghost, could it?* He shook his head. *Get a hold of yourself, Edgar,* he thought.

He lowered his hand and walked down the stairs. He stood on the landing and turned back around, sharing a curious glance with the door, before switching off the light and returning to his apartment.

As he lay in bed, staring at the ceiling, one question remained burrowed in his mind: *Who was up there?*

Wednesday Night:

Edgar turned the key in the doorknob and entered his apartment. He had spent nearly half an hour watching the attic window from his parked car. A few times he thought he saw movement but realized it was just his wishful and eager imagination. This was the second night he had watched the window like a perverted paparazzi. Both nights the window had remained dark, devoid of anything interesting.

Edgar took off his shoes and moved over to the fridge to scan its contents. It was barren except for a bag of apples that looked to be on their last legs and a twelve pack of Coors that had a sizeable dent in their ranks. He looked at the cans for a while before shaking his head. He decided he wouldn't be partaking that night. It had been a good shift and the lead cleaner had been in a fine mood, a rarity to be sure.

As he shut the fridge, a thump sounded off from above. "That bastard," Edgar said to the empty apartment as his eyes studied the ceiling with a damning determination. Even he didn't know what he meant by those words but that's all his brain had managed to form into speech.

He thought about charging up the stairs and throwing open the door but quickly remembered that it had been locked. He doubted knocking would do anything. *Do ghosts even answer doors?* he thought as he returned his gaze to the still apartment. He slowly walked over to his own door and locked it. *Can't be too careful.*

He looked at the fridge once more before his eyes drifted to the ceiling. *A beer wouldn't be too bad right now.*

Friday Night:

Edgar plopped down on his couch and switched on the television. The past shift had been gruelling. The lead cleaner had been out in force, taking his marriage problems out on his poorly paid subordinates. A delicate blend of profanity-ladened ridicule had been bestowed on them all that evening.

Edgar flipped through the channels, stopping momentarily on the weather forecast for Saturday before finally finding his way to the sports highlights. He turned his head to the kitchen and thought about having a beer to get over his terrible shift. He focused on the scores once more and swore at his TV when he realized the Yankees had been swept by the Red Sox.

He pointed an annoyed hand at the television as the score scrolled along the bottom of the screen before muttering to himself and rising from the sofa. If his shift hadn't been bad enough, the Yankees losing had been the final straw. It was time for a beer, and he was sure several more tin soldiers were sure to follow.

Edgar took two steps towards the kitchen. Just as he passed by the counter, however, the power went out. He whacked his hip against the linoleum and cursed under his breath. He rubbed the invisible wound and mumbled, "Great, absolutely typical."

He spun around and looked out his window. The buildings all down the block were blacked out as well, now sleeping giants of steel and concrete. *Power failure again? What do I even pay taxes for?*

Edgar exhaled and collected himself. He was about to move to the window when he heard the thumps above him. He turned his head to look at the ceiling, swallowing as he did so. He felt his pulse quicken and realized that with the lights off, the thumping had taken on a sinister cadence. *Get a grip, you haven't been afraid of the dark since you were five,* he thought.

Despite his stern, self-inflicted orders, the recognition that it was three in the morning and he was in a block without power continued to eat away at his confidence.

There was another thump from above, the loudest one yet. Edgar shrieked.

He gritted his teeth and felt a sudden warmth as adrenaline raced through him. He decided that now was the time he would be getting to the bottom of this. Maybe it was leftover rage from being ridiculed for eight hours, or maybe it was to prove to himself that he was not crazy. Either way, he was ready to storm the attic.

Someone is living up there, he thought as he pushed past the countertop. He still hadn't adjusted to the newfound darkness. *And I'm going to see them for myself.*

Edgar grabbed his flashlight from the kitchen drawer, switched it on, and moved to the entrance of his apartment. He was about to open the door when he heard a scratching coming from the hall. He took as step back and stood perfectly still, frozen as the testosterone and adrenaline disappeared faster than a reluctant ally.

The scratching continued, and then Edgar noticed something peculiar. The sounds were originating from the slit at the bottom of the door.

He took a deep breath. For a moment, he considered running to his bedroom and locking the door behind him. He pushed the thought out of his mind before it had time to take hold. He had to know what was in that attic.

He grabbed the handle and pulled the door open, pushing his flashlight into the hallway. His eyes followed the beam of light as it reflected off the cracked plaster and dusty artificial plants. No one was there. No person, and certainly no ghost. Just a silent hallway. Then he looked down.

A white cat sat on its haunches and stared up at him. It flicked its pink tongue at him before yawning and giving a quick meow. Edgar breathed a sigh of relief and laughed as he clutched his chest. *I almost ran and cowered from a cat. A cat with the name of Mr. Tickles or something like that. Oh, how ferocious.*

Edgar ran a hand through his hair and let out a quick sigh. The white feline meowed again before turning and walking to the end of the hall with a steady determination. It sat at the door leading to the attic and began to scratch away at the wood. The cat looked back at him after a moment and meowed once more. As Edgar approached the animal it turned back to the door and meticulously licked its paws clean.

Another thump from above.

Edgar gulped and opened the door. "Are you coming with me?" he said to the ball of white fur that sat below him.

The cat ignored him and continued to groom itself.

He moved up the dark stairwell and turned the corner to see the green door a few stairs above him. A rustling of boxes could be heard from the other side, followed by the familiar thumping.

Edgar moved up the stairs and put his hand on the knob. Another thump.

He swallowed again and turned the handle. It was locked.

The cat meowed from the landing behind him, and Edgar jumped out of his skin. "Jesus Christ!" he cried.

He glared back at the feline as it looked up at him, studying him. After a moment the cat cocked its head and yawned. It looked past him and was eying the door, its pupils wide, urging him to try again. Edgar looked at the cat for a long while before turning and knocking on the hardwood twice. He stood and waited for several moments but nothing moved, not even the cat.

Edgar shrugged and had pivoted to leave when he heard the door unlock behind him. He stood perfectly still, his eyes locked on the cat below. It stood up and circled the landing once before bounding down the stairs and back to the hallway below. Edgar was all alone. His flashlight jiggled in his sweaty palms, and he felt his muscles shake.

He turned and opened the green door.

The door swung open, revealing a spacious room that appeared to run across the entire length of the building. The area was dark, save for the light coming from Edgar's flashlight and the moonlight that drifted through the sporadically placed windows. The flashlight's beam moved across such artifacts as dusty boxes, broken furniture, bicycles, baskets, and old cookware stacked in crude piles around the attic. Edgar continued to swivel his torch until it settled on the far corner of the room.

A man stood there, gazing out a window.

Edgar's eyes widened as he took a step back. He was seeing a living ghost. *I was—was right. I—* his internal voice quivered as he felt himself move away.

The man turned with a calm grace and looked at the trembling Edgar. "Bonjour," he said simply. His voice carried with it a cool mystique. The man adjusted his three-piece suit and checked his pocket watch.

"Wha— What?" Edgar replied as he was taken aback by the man's tone of voice. It had been fluid and inviting.

"Oh. Right. American. Um—Hello," the man said as he took a step forward. His perfectly polished dress shoes caught the moonlight as he passed by the window.

"Are you a ghost?" Edgar sputtered before realizing how childish he sounded.

"Oh no, my dear boy. I am very much alive," the man replied as he stopped at the centre of the attic.

Despite Edgar's flashlight beaming directly into the man's eyes, he did not look away. He didn't even blink. His skin had a tanned, almost grey twinge to it. His hair was slicked to the side in a style akin to the mid-1940s.

"What are you doing here?" Edgar asked, the trembling in his voice still present. "How—How did you get up here? This is an attic."

The man stiffened up. "Quite so," he said and chuckled to himself. "But more importantly, may I ask what you are doing up here, in my attic?" He spread his arms wide to gesture to his surroundings.

"The door opened and I—"

"You knocked. Of course, it opened! One person knocks, the other person opens the door, or have things changed?" The man shook his head. "I know manners have gone to the wayside but *really*. Basic door knocking etiquette? Colour me surprised."

"Who are you?"

"*Who* is not something that really applies to myself. But if you would like to assign me a name, well, you may call me Charlie. A good name, don't you think?"

"Um—Sure. I—"

"Listen fella, if we are going to continue speaking do you mind turning off that flashlight?" Charlie said as he tapped his foot on the attic floor. His eyes locked on the beam.

"Sure. I—"

"Excellent." Charlie raised a hand and the light ceased. "That's better, isn't it? You were blinding me, boy. Blinding me!" Charlie let out a jovial laugh as a thin smile passed his lips.

Edgar held up the flashlight to his eye, a concerned expression on his face. He toggled the switch on and off, but the beam stayed dormant, dead and unworking.

Charlie spun to face the windows on the far side of the room, "Let's get some light in here," he said as he snapped his fingers. A single lamp to the far side of the attic sprang to life and sent light to every corner.

Edgar looked at the dirty old lamp. The shade was stained and covered with cobwebs. His eyes moved along the wire at its base to see if it was plugged in. He followed the black cord to the wall and—

"That's better, isn't it, laddie?" Charlie asked as he pulled a pipe out of his breast pocket.

"Ya—I guess. I—" Edgar stuttered as he looked around the room, a confused gleam in his eyes. He wondered how this man had controlled not only the flashlight and the lamp but was also able to retrieve a pipe out of a pocket that appeared too small to house such an object.

"My boy, I mean this with the most sensitive politeness, but do you finish sentences when you speak them? So far, it has only been I stringing along a coherent series of words," Charlie said as he lit his pipe with a match that appeared in his hand.

"This is all just so overwhelming," Edgar replied as he attempted to hide his trembling voice. He took several deep breaths to regain his composure.

"Pull up a chair." Charlie gestured to the quaint looking wooden seat that sat across from him. Like the pipe and the match, it had appeared out of thin air.

Charlie took a puff from his pipe and before Edgar knew it, the man was sitting in a similar chair directly in front of the one he was gesturing to.

Edgar cleared his throat, trying to speak plainly and with less jitters. "Are you something like… a god? Or…" he trailed off as he approached the chair.

Charlie sighed and said with a shake of his head, "Why is it that anything your kind can't explain always jumps to the same conclusion and assumes I'm a god." He took a long puff before continuing, "I'm just something different from you. Nothing more."

"Then why are you here?"

"I have to be *somewhere*, don't I?"

Edgar took a seat on the cushion and opened his mouth to speak when Charlie cut him off by saying, "Can you believe I stayed in this very building some eighty years ago. Same attic, but it was more of a drinking and card den in those days. I watched a lot of money change hands, and many a card go in a man's favour. Of course, they never saw me. You can bet on that, my boy."

He took another puff of his pipe and looked at the corner of the room as he reminisced on times long past. "I was also here forty years ago, give or take a few, for a quick spot of business. Ms. Donaldson lived here then too. She helped her mother and father run the building. She was a looker then.

Mid-twenties I believe. Oh, how time changes all. The great constant."

Edgar thought about asking a follow up question regarding Ms. Donaldson but quickly realized such a thing would not be relevant. He looked into the man's bronze-coloured eyes before asking, "How come I can see you if no one else could before?" He felt a lump in his throat. He was suddenly very thirsty.

"My boy. Not the quickest of the bunch it seems. Oh well, no matter." Charlie puffed on his pipe and spoke with it between his lips. "Because I am allowing you to see me." He paused and removed the pipe, blowing a ring into the air. "Here," he said after a moment, "have a drink. Maybe it will loosen up that brain of yours, get the juices flowing and all that." He snapped his fingers and Edgar gasped.

A small end table appeared by Edgar's right hand. A tall glass of water perched on top of it, with two ice cubes clinking around the rim. Edgar hesitated for a moment before taking it from the table. Charlie had a soft grin on his face as he watched from behind his pipe. Smoke fluttering around his eyes. Again, he did not blink.

Edgar tasted the water on his tongue and the feeling of it surprised him. It tasted pure and clean. In fact, it was the best tasting water he had ever had. It was as if it had come from an undiscovered oasis after days of marching through hostile desert sands. Edgar wiped his mouth and asked, "How are you doing all this?"

Charlie chuckled, "All this? What? A couple of chairs, a glass of water? Mere parlour tricks, laddie." He paused as he flattened his suit jacket against his chest. "I'm going to start charging you by the question soon if you keep this up." His face lit up with the puff from his pipe. "Now, do you want to hear what I have to say?"

Edgar nodded and took another sip of water. He then realized just how comfortable the cushioned chair was underneath him. "Excellent, shall we?" Charlie added as he flicked his wrist towards the door.

The door shut without making a sound. Only a slight breeze was any proof that it had moved at all. Edgar looked over his shoulder with a curious bewilderment. He licked his lips and turned around, trying to suppress the panic. "You've locked me in," he said.

"Don't be foolish, boyo. You can leave whenever you like. I just don't want anyone eavesdropping on our conversation." Charlie checked his pocket watch before continuing, "Also, it would appear quite peculiar to any outsider looking in to see a young man such as yourself sitting in an attic talking to an empty chair, wouldn't it?"

He paused, looking to the ceiling. "I've made that mistake a few times too many. Many a good man and woman ended up in some precarious places because of me. I shudder to think about the asylums or those blasted witch trials." Charlie rolled his eyes, "Again, people going to the extreme when they can't explain something. Oh well, ancient history I'm afraid."

Charlie leaned back in his chair and stared at Edgar for a moment, studying him. He took another puff from his pipe and then sat up rather suddenly. "Oh, where are my manners? Do you partake?"

As he spoke, a package of curiously labelled cigarettes and a book of matches appeared on the end table beside Edgar. They were both littered with the same odd symbols, a strange alphabet scattered across a white background. "No—No, thank you. I don't smoke," Edgar said as he looked down at the package of cigarettes, his voice distant.

"Very well. Probably for the best," Charlie replied and snapped his fingers once more. The peculiar packaging and match book accompanying it evaporated as quickly as they had appeared, leaving the white doily barren. "But alas, it isn't the cancer that kills you," Charlie went on to say in a relaxed tone before taking a sip from the frothy pint that materialized in his left hand.

"Wait? What?" Edgar said as he sat up, nearly spilling the glass of water.

"Oh here, one for you as well," Charlie said. Before he finished the sentence a pint glass containing the same light-coloured liquid appeared on the end table.

"No, not that. That part about the cancer. What was—"

"Oh, I've already forgotten," Charlie raised a dismissive hand. "I do love your alcoholic beverages. Particularly what you call 'spirits,' but alas, the area I have just come from was drowning in it so to speak. My associates and I went through several barrels of the stuff. So much that I have decided on a different beverage for this evening's festivities." He paused and took another gulp of the liquid, savouring the taste. "Besides, in my experience there is no better way to get to know someone than over a couple pints."

Edgar took a sip from the perfectly poured beer. The crispness and clean taste of the drink was indescribable, and the perfect temperature as well.

"So, as I was saying," Charlie added after taking another sip of the beverage, "I have recently completed my work and find myself with a few days off, so to speak. I require some sort of *amusement*. Something to pass the time, to keep the mind sharp. I will let you in on the fun."

He smiled and ran a hand through his perfectly parted hair. "I will allow you to ask me for five things. Five." He held up his right hand to distinguish the importance of the number. "I know in your Hollywood talkies that you always use the number three for requests such as these. Three wishes from the old genie in the lamp. Well, I give you five. How about that? Generous, I know, but I like the challenge." He slapped his knee in excitement. "I always thought the number five had more *bite* to it, more so than three, anyhow. But that's just me."

He smiled showing his teeth and leaned back in his chair. "Do you accept my little game?" Charlie asked as the smoke of his pipe hovered around his forehead.

"I uh—What if I refuse?" Edgar asked as he sipped the beer for comfort.

"Nothing, and that's precisely it my boy. You would return home and that would be all. But you would never know what could have been, what could have happened had you taken the offer of my five requests. So, do you accept?"

Edgar ground his teeth for a moment before replying, "I do." He immediately took a sip of beer and watched the foam cling to the lip of the glass.

"Very good, very good indeed." Charlie's smile stretched from ear to ear. "There are some ground rules of course. I know *rules*, who needs them? But they are important." He shifted his weight in his chair and continued, "If you ask me for something I deem idiotic, I will give you a shock like you wouldn't believe. For example, do not ask for more requests. The last bloke to do so couldn't use the toilet properly for a week."

"You've done this before? For others?"

"Oh, please, my boy. You are hardly the first." He shot a quick wink at Edgar before continuing, "I've helped all kinds, given scientists that breakthrough, cured a relative's ailments, even moved a bunch of rocks to help a group of savages in the south of England once. I don't know why they wanted them to be stacked on top of one another like that, but I did it for them. I've even helped what you would call a criminal escape the clutches of the law. The lawmen were oh so close to catching him, and his deeds were oh so heinous indeed."

"But that's immoral, evil, even!" Edgar spat as he put the pint glass down to the table with force.

"I don't see your concept of good, evil, right, or wrong. Morality and ethics are just words to me. Human constructs. Do you consider it evil to give bread to a pigeon one moment while squashing a spider underfoot a moment later? Both living beings, both existing in their own environments. I think not, it just… is." He smiled once more and gestured for Edgar to pick up the pint.

Edgar complied after a moment. His mind raced, thinking of all the possible questions he could ask.

Charlie waited for Edgar to grab the glass before speaking, "I will allow you to ask of me a request and then I will show you a preview of the outcome. I am not some second-rate charlatan, peddling magic tricks. I'm not here to fool you. I am going to show you exactly what you requested and, if you like it, you may keep it. If you don't enjoy the outcome, well, simply tell me and it will not come to pass. But that request will have been used up regardless and cannot be used again. Do you understand?"

Edgar nodded as he studied the man or being or whatever he was across from him. Charlie had clearly demonstrated his mystical prowess, the light, the beer, the table, the cigarettes appearing then disappearing. Was it so hard to imagine he could also grant whatever was asked of him? The possibilities were endless.

"So, I will ask you for something," Edgar said, leaning forward. "And then you will show it to me. Before it comes true?" He was unaware that he was rocking back and forth in his chair from excitement.

Charlie nodded as he took a puff from his pipe. "But just because you don't like what you see… well, it still counts as a request."

Edgar sat and thought long and hard about what he should ask for before finally landing on a solid idea. He had always struggled with relationships in the past and thought that a happier home life should be his first request. *Simple and easy as a test run,* Edgar thought as he licked his lips. *Shouldn't be too hard for this guy to make that one come true.*

Edgar opened his mouth to speak but was cut off as

Charlie said, "Better make it a good one." He winked and sipped his pint.

"I wish... Sorry, I mean *request*," he corrected himself as the man across from him shot a stern glance in his direction, "to have true love," Edgar said as he adjusted himself in the chair, a surge of warmth flowing through him with anticipation.

"Oh—A good one, right off the hop. Okay, lover boy. I'll show you what that means."

Edgar didn't hear the last of the sentence as his mind was taken away, far away. A spinning world of black that rotated endlessly until finally, he could see clearly again. He felt outside himself and the surroundings were milky and translucent, almost ghostly and formless in their depiction. "The future has yet to pass," Charlie's voice slipped around the shadows and shapes. "It is still unfinished until the very moment it becomes the past."

Flashes of people filled Edgar's view, a hundred different realities clashing, blending and bending to form one conformed timeline. Within moments all the images congealed until only one reality remained.

Edgar could see a woman dressed in an expensive business suit, holding a baby in her arms. For a split moment this beautiful woman was a stranger. But as quickly as she appeared, Edgar knew everything about her. It was like he had known her his entire life.

Her name was Trista Dorchester, her favourite colour was orange, she preferred dogs to cats and had two Labradors growing up. She was a lawyer, specializing in contracts. Her auburn hair hung down from a loose bun as she nursed the baby with a bottle, rocking it gently. She had always wanted a child and here it was in her arms, eight months old.

Edgar felt in his heart that he loved this woman, a woman he just met yet had known for a lifetime. And he could feel she loved him too. She was about to head to work, but they had planned that evening to have a candlelit diner. He had already purchased an expensive bottle of wine for such an occasion. The images sat in a rosy blur for several moments before changing.

A dark tone engulfed the mists.

Images of Trista flirting with a man at her firm, a co-worker in the office across the hall. The flirting became more and more serious and then Edgar's heart dropped as his wife of five years, the one who he had proposed to on the beach of her childhood town and the mother of his child, went into this strange man's house, the bedroom door closing behind her. She had told Edgar that she was working late. He sat alone at the table, the dinner he had made them long cold and the wine glasses empty.

Edgar was snapped back to reality like a violent whip.

He was in the attic, Charlie sitting across from him holding a fresh glass of beer. Edgar blinked and felt his stomach twist into knots, his mind and memories covered in the mists as if he had just awoken from a nightmare.

Everything had been ripped away. A lifetime of memories, his first date with Trista, their wedding. The birth of Eric, their son, who took the name of her father. All of these seem-ingly real events swimming in Edgar's mind. He felt light-headed and found the illuminated lamp in the corner to be almost blinding.

"I asked for true love!" he cried. "What was that? That's not what I asked for. You said—" Edgar yelled as he held back tears, the images of his wife entering that bedroom haunting him. She had even bought a special perfume for the evening the night before.

"Oh, on the contrary," Charlie said with an unamused grin, "I gave you exactly what you asked for. You asked for true love and that's what I delivered. But love fades. Of course, she did still love you in a way. She hated to hurt you but she—"

"How could she love me and do that?"

"I'm not sure. Only Trista Henderson knows that." He paused and sipped from his pint. "Or should I say Dorchester. She changes it back to her maiden name after the divorce. Only she knows her own heart. But you loved her truly and that, my boy, is what you asked for. True love," he looked down and studied his pocket watch. "But you can ask her yourself if you would like. You'll bump into her in a little under sixteen months."

"I was right about you. You're evil. A terrible person... or thing... or whatever you are for ripping my heart out like that!"

"I did nothing of the sort. Do not confuse Trista's future actions with my own. Consider yourself lucky, lad. I could have shown you a version where you are someone else's true love, but you don't love them in return. An all too true and common occurrence across the entirety of human history. In that scenario you would feel guilt for breaking their heart. Here I'll show you, this one's on the house—"

"No. No! Don't. I retract that request. I don't want true love, at least not..." he trailed off and muttered, "Well at least not that kind. I wish for something else. I wish—"

"They aren't wishes. I'm not a—"

"Yes request. I know I know, you're not a genie or a monkey paw, I got it."

Edgar's head was still spinning but the memories of Trista had cooled in his brain. They were no longer searing like a brand to scar over. The recollections were real, yet impossible to fathom. His brain struggled to categorize what they were and instead began to discard them like all the dreams one forgets upon waking.

"So, you still have four requests remaining," Charlie said as he looked at the pint with satisfaction. It was empty. He snapped his fingers and it refilled in the blink of an eye.

Edgar thought of standing up and returning to his apartment, but the possibilities were truly endless. Four more chances to change his life forever. He tried to think of something that wouldn't backfire like the previous request. He grabbed the glass from the table, took a sip before pointing at Charlie and said, "I want to be rich and famous."

"Technically that's two things, but I'll allow it. It's little work to combine them and it *is* the most common request I get. I must say, it's still the most fun for me to create. But I digress, let the fun begin."

Thousands of images containing millions of dollars flashed though Edgar's mind. Parties, woman, imported cars, drugs, booze. Every vice conceivable. A life that couldn't be farther removed from his own. Images of movie posters where he was in the lead role, doused in makeup, an expensive haircut, and an even more expensive suit. He looked almost unrecognizably exquisite.

He was an action star, a heart throb, a sex icon, someone that was swooned over. Images of billboards, interviews, red carpet appearances all moving together as one. Edgar was raking it in, and with more money came more excess.

I could get used to this life, he thought, but the idea was immediately lost amongst the ripples of sensory overload.

Then, like clockwork, the tone changed. Flashes of money being thrown away on all sorts of decadent items and possessions. Edgar's drive and focus being tainted by narcotics, each more addicting than the last. Soon he wasn't being offered leading roles any longer as he felt himself spiralling down a path to oblivion. A scene flashed of a frail and nearly unrecognizable Edgar attempting to get a loan from the studio, pleading for money before being rejected and escorted off the premises. A mugging shortly after took the last few dollars he had to his name and resulted in him being stabbed twice in the abdomen.

The white walls of a hospital were next. Not a single one of his countless so called "friends" visited him on his road to recovery. He racked up more debt with expensive treatments and physiotherapy. Images of morphine drips and drugs moving through his system. A different kind of addiction soon followed.

The last image was that of Edgar overdosing on heroin. Dying alone in an apartment that was the only proof that he ever had any glory days behind him. The empty rooms, the hardwood floors and the large windows overlooking the New York City skyline. His body would be found not even two days later as the bank repossessed the penthouse. Life had left him without a friend in the world.

Edgar snapped out of the trance, more alert this time. "Jesus, that was depressing," he said as he rubbed the side of his head, trying to massage the already fleeting memories away.

"I'll take that as a no," Charlie said. "You don't want that request fulfilled?"

"No. Absolutely not. It looks terrible. Heartbreaking, all of it."

"You'd be surprised how many people still take it," Charlie added with a thoughtful nod.

"I'm sure. One life, might as well live it up, even if it's quick. But that's not me, I don't want it."

"Suit yourself. What's the next one going to be, lad?"

Edgar sat back in his chair, trying to relax himself. He cleared his mind and for a brief moment, contemplated asking about eternal life. *But I know this, Charlie will make it look terrible somehow. I'm sure he's got a million ways to ensure that request blows back on me,* Edgar thought as he looked out the window behind the mysterious man across from him.

Watching anyone I've ever loved, all my friends, everyone one I've ever even known, die away. Gone, while I stay here. Seeing thousands of years of death and chaos and war. He felt a chill rise through him as he realized, *I would even see the end of time itself. No one could process that.*

In that moment, Edgar realized what his next request would be. "War," he mumbled to himself, hardly even aware that he had spoken.

"What's that? You want to relive a war?" Charlie paused as he took a puff from his pipe. "I had one bloke who wanted to relive Vietnam once. Now there was a man who was certifiably—"

"No," Edgar snapped. "I want there to be no war. I want world peace. That is my request, world peace!" Edgar nearly shouted the words as he nodded in agreement with himself.

The most noble request of all, Edgar thought as he watched the man across from him lick his lips and study the ceiling. *No way Charlie could find a way to turn this—*

Edgar was surrounded by images of flora and fauna. The rainforest healthier than ever. The oceans clear like sapphires as the waves danced over immaculate beaches. The sky open and pure. Then the images of the overgrown cities, the abandoned skyscrapers, and the rusted, hollowed out cars came next. Empty were the subway tunnels, overtaken by massive roots that scaled the tiled ceilings and slithered under the turnstiles. The dusty ticket booths standing guard like blind sentries, unaware of the intruding plant life.

It was beautiful, in a terrifying way.

Then Edgar's soul noticed something even more off putting: the complete lack of animals. There was no wildlife present. No predators, no prey. No bears or fish. Foxes or racoons. Not even mosquitos or ants. Not a single living thing except for the plants that swallowed up the globe. Mother Earth had reclaimed all that was taken from her, and she had struck with a devastating vengeance.

"Enough!" Edgar yelled from deep within himself. But even with all his strength, the cry was little more than a whimper, "I've seen enough."

Edgar was brought back to the shabby attic, his pulse

pounding. Charlie sat back in his chair and took a long drag from his pipe before saying, "What's the problem?"

"Where was everyone? I said world peace, not a—a—an apocalypse.

"Ah, but are they not mutually exclusive? No people, no conflict. It is again——"

"Exactly what I requested," Edgar said, cutting Charlie off. "I get it," he retorted through gritted teeth as sweat poured down his face. "But where were the animals? Dogs, birds? Anything?"

Charlie smiled a coy smile and sipped his beer. He gave a curious look over the rim of his glass. He waited, raised an eyebrow and said, "Really, my boy? Do I have to spell it out for you?" Charlie's eyes stayed locked on Edgar, and when the young man's demeanour failed to change, he added, "You *said* world peace," he drawled out his words as he spoke them. "Animals by their very nature have conflict. The lions hunt and kill the antelope. Wolves and rabbits, eagles and mice, etcetera, etcetera. Where there is prey there will be predators. Doesn't that sound like conflict to you?"

Edgar opened his mouth to retort when Charlie bit back, "You can argue until you are blue in the face, but it will do you little good. This *is* the reality you would receive with that request. But assuming you don't want it, well," Charlie shrugged, "just two more left boyo." He held up two fingers and wiggled them to highlight his point.

Edgar felt large pools of sweat form on his lower back. Everything he had requested so far had been absolutely dreadful. Edgar's mind churned with some questions that had plagued humanity for years. Popular conspiracy theories crept across his mind and sunk in their talons.

Was Oswald the lone gunman or just a patsy? Was the moon landing staged? Was 9/11 a controlled demolition? Alien life? Is it out there and is it friendly or hostile? Is there a meaning to life? Anything after death? A divine power waiting at the end? Was the—

161

"Two more left. But what to ask for? Hmmm?" Charlie repeated himself, almost taunting Edgar. "So many choices."

All these thoughts tumbled through his brain until he realized having the answer to these questions would do little for him. No one would believe him anyway and his voice would just become one of many vying for position on internet forums.

"I don't know what to request," Edgar said as he anxiously rocked in his chair again. A defeated tone lay on his words. "Everything I can think of would do almost nothing to change the world."

"People always struggle with the last two. I wonder why that is?" Charlie asked under his breath as he studied the grooming of his fingernails.

Edgar thought long and hard about his next request, searching for something that couldn't backfire, something that would help everyone and not just satisfy a simple curiosity. In the time Edgar spent thinking, Charlie downed two more pints. He looked around the attic multiple times and checked his pocket watch on occasion, but his face did not display boredom, quite the opposite. In fact, the longer Edgar took to decide, the more intrigued Charlie seemingly became.

Edgar sat up straight in his chair and said, "I got it! A request that not even you can flip on its head." He smiled with self-satisfaction.

"Well lad, let's hear it."

"I request a world without disease."

Charles squinted and frowned slightly. He sighed and then appeared to think deeply on the topic. A moment passed before he rolled his eyes and flicked his wrist, "Fine."

Edgar saw flashes of the world much as it had been, people going to work, families celebrating holidays, farmers plowing fields. All the same as the world he knew. But when his soul was moved into a hospital, he noticed something odd. The buildings were much smaller, and less staff roamed through the halls. The most populated wings were the maternity wards and the emergency room. Lacerations, broken bones, burns, blunt force trauma, bullet wounds all still rampant. But no diseases. No cancers, or hepatitis, or tuberculosis. No Alzheimer's or malaria, not even the common cold.

Buildings that had been pharmacies were now restaurants, tax service centres, and grocery stores. Factories that made pills in Edgar's current world were now car assembly plants or toy manufacturing lines in this reality. He saw flashes of medications being consumed but they were for headaches or meal supplements, nothing to suggest any illness.

Edgar came out of his trance, the world still spinning. He smiled as he blinked rapidly. "No disease," he said after a moment.

"No disease," Charlie repeated.

"I would like that one to come true."

"I figured you might," Charlie said as he crossed his legs and leaned back. He stared forward, eyeing Edgar.

"So, are you going to do it?" Edgar asked as he studied the man. "Make my request real?"

"I already have. Check your pants pockets. You'll find a sealed deed in there. Your signature upon it," Charlie replied as he gestured to Edgar's jeans.

Edgar felt a lump of a folded letter appear in his right pocket but decided to ignore it. He was too focused on this moment. He then looked down at his hands, flexing them. "That's it? I—I don't feel any different."

"And why should you? You are a perfectly healthy young man. A little soft in the stomach but that has nothing to do with disease and everything to do with diet and exercise."

Edgar stood up and looked outside the window to his left. The dawn was approaching, and he could hear birds chirping in the distance. A lone blue car drove down the block, splashing through puddles as it went off into the distance. The world looked and felt the same, and at first this idea alarmed Edgar greatly. Had Charlie lied and not changed a thing?

Then Edgar's eyes glanced to the billboard across the street. The ad that had once been for a real estate company now advertised cigarettes. A young attractive model smoking to her hearts content.

Edgar turned to speak when Charlie said, "And why shouldn't they? No cancer? Cigarettes never killed anyone with your request." He reached for his beer glass. "Think about how many inventions, art pieces, memories, have all be created because people didn't succumb to their ailments. And further to that," he leaned back in his chair, "how many sons and daughters have been born in this reality who never lived in yours."

"Their parents died too young or never met because of—"

"Precisely."

"What about overpopulation or—"

"I thought of that as well. But it seems your people just created more and more to accommodate each other. Roads, cities, farms, everything."

"Did you expect that?" Edgar asked as he walked back to his seat and sat down.

Charlie hesitated before taking a sip of his pint. "Last request," he replied.

Edgar let a smile move across his face. He had known what he wanted to request the moment he had seen the world from the window. Edgar knew he would not be able to live a peaceful life with the weight of knowing that he had eliminated disease and saved countless lives. Nor would he be able to calm his ever-active mind of the notion that he had been given five requests and used the first three terribly. His subconscious would torture him with hundreds of other possibilities that he could have—no, *should* have asked.

Edgar knew he would slowly drive himself mad wondering what else he could have done. He also thought about how alone he would be in remembering a world where disease had killed billions. A reality no one around him would be able to understand. No, he knew exactly what his last request would be.

Edgar sat back in his chair and raised the pint glass to his lips. He tasted the perfected crisp beer on his tongue one last time before saying, "Charlie, I request that I never remember meeting you."

Charlie smiled and clapped his hands together. He took a long puff from his pipe before pointing it at Edgar, saying, "You know, I've never heard that one before."

THE HORROR

Y ou crouch in the cabin, and you feel your knees burn. The wind howls through the long-shattered windows as you look to the night sky. A hundred thousand stars and the sliver of a pale moon is the only light you are graced with this cold eve.

Tonight is the night.

The ritualistic hunt that the religious tenants demand. The chieftains and priests have ordered you to carry it out. To vanquish a horror. The winged beasts that swim high about the milky sky, only revealing themselves when it is time to strike. Your memories are tainted by these beasts, for they have been a threat for as long as you can remember. Bands of humans moving by day in the safety of the bright star, but by night, camping in ancient relics of the long-forgotten past.

Your father has been dead for five rises of the sun and tonight marks the fifth night. The night the holy texts instruct you to grant your father's soul passage, to join your ancestors in the night sky.

You clasp the rifle in your hands and feel the wooden grip against your palm. You've heard that the weapon is at least two hundred winters old. A reliable weapon, a trustworthy one. It is the only thing that stands between you and the horror.

You feel the five spare bullets jostle in your fur pocket, with five more already loaded into the rifle. You have heard stories that a true marksman only requires one shot to send a horror back from whence it came. The spot between the eyes is the weak point. The red eyes, yes.

You have heard the high priests preach of the horror's visage many times. Tails of sharp barbs and black wings, they have been spawned in the Dark Lord's image. The perfect minion.

You curse your older brother Gabriel, as you think about the winged assassins. *Why did you have to die two winters past? You should be the one out here. Out hunting, to allow father passage to join the stars. Not I.*

You exhale and see frost form on the air; the summer is coming to a close. Winter will again be upon the earth, and the narlocks will awake from hibernation. You know in a matter of weeks these very grounds will be teaming with the Dark One's shock troopers.

You've heard stories of the horrors and narlocks engaging in bloody skirmishes over scraps of food. But you don't believe in that type of tale, for it is impossible for one to witness such an event. No one would be foolish enough to venture into their territory when the winter begins. And if someone was that mad? Well, they would never return to tell the story.

You stick your head up over the windowsill. The rocking chair behind you creaks as the wind picks up. You grip your rifle firmly. "Father, be with me," you whisper, as you stick your rifle out the window, using the crooked iron sights to scan the narrow lake ahead. The water ripples in the breeze, the rocky shore cloaked in black. The dead tree branches swaying in the night. It's time for you to face your fears and complete your task.

You build up the nerve to exit the cabin, for you've not

heard any sound for hours. The horrors are patient, you know this. But they are not *that* patient. You lower your rifle and creep over to the door, stepping over various ancient discards that serve no purpose in the society of today.

You open the damaged cabin door and head out onto the decaying wooden porch. The smell of wet leaves and mould enter your nostrils as the floorboards release their scents beneath your boots.

The chieftains say that cabins like this one were constructed by humans of the past to watch the waters for horrors, but you have never believed that. These structures look to have been dwellings in their time, not observation posts.

You walk down the rotted steps and across the tall grass, moving towards the lake, watching the far side for movement, keeping your eyes wide for a horror moving on the ground or another human scavenging. But possibly, God willing, an animal will be bestowed upon you to feed the tribe.

You quickly rid your mind of this notion. You will not fire at the prey even if it appeared. Firing your weapon would rid yourself of a bullet to smite down the horror, and worse, it would attract the Dark Lord's enforcers before the ritual has been completed. You must perform the customs perfectly or father's spirit will go far below. Down to the land where the horrors dwell. You cannot allow that to happen to him.

You scan the sky, hearing no movement nor the sound of wings flapping over the surrounding hills. Despite this you feel the sting of fear in your stomach. Horrors are known to strike without warning and relish in their role as assassins.

Again, your mind fills with memories of your brother. You have heard many times how he perished. Lifted into the night by one of the winged beasts, for the fool had been scavenging far too late into the evening. You should feel sadness, but Gabriel's fate was his own doing. He had not heeded the church's warnings.

You reach the spot you had set aside earlier in the day. The tepee of wood, dried leaves, and bark shavings. This is the location where you will light the pyre, the blessed flame that will attract the horror.

You listen to the bobbing waves of the lake and the rustle of the wind stirring. You feel like you are being watched, but the priests said that is common. It is Father watching, praying for you to complete the ritual correctly so he may know eternal light.

You crouch down beside the pile of wood and lower your rifle to the ground, hearing it crunch against the dried leaves. You take a deep breath and pick up the twigs you placed beside the pyre site as dusk came upon the sky. The sticks were blessed by the priests to provide a swift flame. You say a hasty prayer to the all-seeing one, hoping it finds you worthy to grant you the miracle of fire. You begin to rub the wood together and after a minute, you feel your forearms ache.

You stop and readjust your grip, beginning the process again. You continue for what seems like an eternity. All the stars in the heavens are looking down and watching you. The wind seems to cease as you attempt to light the pyre. A sliver of calm washes over you.

The sky is still, and no wings can be heard. The burning in your arms is intense and you wish this fire would shift from your muscles to the pyre. Blisters are forming on your palms, and you feel flakes of skin tearing off against the dried wood.

I'm not worthy of the gift, you think as you let out a miserable sigh. *Father is doomed to fall below, all because—*

The sticks catch, and a small yellow flame flashes at the base of the tepee. The sparks rise from the embers and slowly you see the fire spread. You don't celebrate your victory, as you know this is but a single test from the all-seeing one. To birth the flame is one thing; to keep it alive in a world seemingly bent on snuffing it out, that's a different miracle entirely.

You swallow and watch the cradle of fire gently move up

the teepee's base. *I must remain calm,* you think as you wrap your arms around the newly birthed fire. *I shall shield the heart of the flame from the wind until it is a grand flare moving its way into adulthood.*

The teepee catches ablaze, causing one of the legs to topple as its base turns to ash, *Now, it is time,* you think as you see the wood bubble and bark lift from the heat. But the thought doesn't belong to you. It is the voice of your father. He is close now and the priests were right; he is watching, praying that you succeed.

You rise and retrieve your rifle from the dew-covered dried leaves. A soft crunch follows as the weight of your weapon is lifted from the ground.

You quietly jog back to the cabin and are careful not to step on the rotted parts of the steps. You hear a twig snap from the other side of the lake as you are a mere moment away from the open door. You hesitate and think of turning back, but you continue on and move into the cabin.

You are running out of time.

You shut the door behind you and grimace as the hinges creak, sending a siren call across the rippling waters. You move to the window and push the barrel of your rifle through the empty frame. You watch the flames dance as the wind feeds the pyre.

"The all-seeing one is helping you," your father's voice whispers from all around you. You look over your shoulder to answer but only the dark room greets you. You quickly turn your head forward as a new sound emerges through the treeline.

A beating of wings. Heavy and daunting as they draw near.

Your memory shifts to when you were a child, watching from the safety of the manor house you had lived in for a summer. Three black beasts circling in the sky above, looking for holy prey so that they could devour their light. That was the closest you had ever been to one.

Until tonight.

You hear the wings swoop overhead and then you see it, a black figure gliding low over the water.

The horror—the beast out of a devil's nightmare—lands on the rocky shore on the far side of the fire. Your view is obstructed and your heart pounds in your ears.

Your finger moves to the trigger.

Wait, you tell yourself, and your father speaks next, "*You must have the perfect shot!*"

You hear its plodding footsteps move up the rocky slope, the crackling of pebbles tumbling far away from the clawed, webbed feet. Then you see its outline beyond the fire. A silhouette twice your size, wings cupping towards the light of the flame. A hooded head tucked to its chest. Two marbles of white reflecting the light of the flame.

You feel sweat sting your eyes but ignore it, any movement now will have you joining your father and brother.

You stay your trigger, knowing the curved wings might deflect your shot. You must be patient and wait for the beast to open its wings so a holy round will find its way, guided by the divine and into the spawn.

You marvel at its eyes. *They aren't red at all. The fire must be playing tricks. The scriptures are so clear in their description.*

You feel the trigger under your finger, cold steel under the warm flesh. The horror shudders as it relaxes, watching the fire.

Almost.

You know the being will stay a long while, unable to resist the call of the flame. The priests have said that the sights and smells of the pyre remind the creature of home. The fowl crevices in the earth where fire burns eternal.

The fire crackles and the flames rise, illuminating the monstrous face. An image so utterly repulsive that you know it couldn't have been created by the divine. Such a terrifying visage that—

You realize it is the face of a man.

You blink and feel the world slow around you. You recognize the face.

Gabriel. Older. Five seasons older. Scarred and weathered, but still your brother all the same.

Your finger loosens from the trigger as a confusion over comes you.

"No, it's a trick," your father's voice shudders. *"Agents of the Dark One use dissidence and blasphemy to cause the weak to falter."*

But it's Gabriel, don't you see? It's him, you think, as you gaze upon the white eyes that study the flame with a child-like fascination. *I recognize him. I—*

"You are weak. You are letting your emotions get the better of you. Letting the Dark One win. You know Gabriel is dead. Carried off. His cries echoed through the hills as he was brought to the horror's nest to fill their mutated bellies."

Maybe he survived or was transformed, or—

"It's a deception placed upon your fragile mind. They've used his likeness as an abomination. Shoot it so I may live on."

You see the horror with Gabriel's face shutter its wings. It lifts its head, its eyes fixating on the cabin, centering on the gleam of steel that sits on the window frame.

"Fire!" Father screams.

Gabriel lifts a taloned hand, and you feel the rifle recoil into your shoulder. The sound of the shot cracks though the hills and across the lake.

The bullet enters the horror's right shoulder and black blood pours from the wound.

Gabriel peers down at the injury you inflicted. You tremble as you cycle the action on your rifle.

You look down the iron sites and see that Gabriel is looking at you. Eyes of white, pleading. Showing pain and fear, emotions that horrors are supposed to be incapable of possessing.

"A trick!" Father yells. *"Using your weak compassion to draw you in. Finish the abomination off."*

You fire again.

You look on as Gabriel's head flies back. The round enters his skull through the right eye. You hear the massive beast slump back and fall to the water. Sounds of splashing and rocks tumbling follow after. You listen to the echo of the shot move through the trees and the crackle of the pyre still burning strong.

You have completed the ritual. You now feel empty as your father has left you. Gone to join the ancestors among the stars. His passage is clear. All that remains of the sacred act is to take an ear from the horror as proof that the deed is done.

You lower your rifle and pull the knife from your boot. You move out of the cabin and head past the fire. You look at the rocky slope below. The black beast is upon its back, wings outstretched as the waves advance and retreat over its corpse.

You feel an indescribable grief move through you. *Was it a trick played by the Dark One? Or was it actually Gabriel, transformed, but with his memories still? Did he recognize me?*

You grip the hilt of the blade and feel the cool night on your face. *I'll never know. And to speak of this to anyone*—a sadness fills you—*will label me as blasphemous.*

You move down the slope and feel your boots fill with water as you step into the lake. You tremble as you poke the beast with your knife, the body still and rigid after each prod. You relax but take notice of its grey talons and muscular physique. It could split you in half with minimal effort.

You shudder as the wind picks up. Your feet are freezing as the water continues to sway back and forth.

You bring yourself to look at the horror's face, Gabriel's visage is still upon it. The eyes are now black, but the emotion in them clear. Fear and sadness. You know your thoughts are defying the church.

What have I done? This was my brother and I tried so little to help him when he needed me.

You feel tears fill your eyes as you lower the knife towards his elongated ear. "I'm sorry brother," you whisper as the steel touches the flesh.

You feel the knife cut through the moist skin and watch as blood leaks from the severance. While the liquid had appeared black from a distance, the moonlight against the rocks now reveals it to be red. The tears sting your eyes again.

The body twitches.

A webbed hand grabs your ankle.

In an instant you are on your back as the flapping wings beat against the stone. Your eyes widen in shock, and you cough up a spray of blood, offering it towards the night sky. Your vision is filled with the grimacing smile of the horror, any likeness to Gabriel now gone.

AMY TISDALE HAS REINVENTED HERSELF

D ave Willis smirked at his beer as Kurt wrapped up his story. The bar bustled around the group with the familiar sounds of a Friday night in a college town. Glasses clinked, friends laughed, and music played as everyone celebrated the last true weekend before September classes came crashing down upon the summer with one cold swoop.

"Dave, do you remember the look on their faces?" Kurt added after a swig from his pint of Coors, taking his eyes from Eric and Matt.

"Ya, I remember," Dave said with a shrug. "She wasn't impressed with you. But that friend of hers, a hottie if I remember right."

"Hottie?" Kurt looked around at the group of three. "Hottie doesn't even cover it. A piece of tail like you boys ain't even seen. The girls from State Grass High, they build 'em better in that little town, let me tell ya."

"Oh, you have," Eric said with a quick chuckle before his eyes wandered across the bar to a brunette that was chatting up the bartender.

Dave admired Eric for a moment. *I wish I could have continued with ball after high school like him*, he thought, as he felt a wave of self-pity overcome him. The beer wasn't helping. *Getting cut from the team before the first preseason game, what a way to end my football career before it even started.* Dave frowned, what had started off as sorrow was quickly turning to jealousy.

"So," Kurt said, as he nudged Matt with an elbow. "Enough about old times. How's the scrap yard business? Must be making good coin working with your old man."

I was hoping we could reminisce some more. I don't want to talk about work, Dave thought as he stood up. A feeling of annoyance moved through him. *Reminiscing is all I have left. I hate my job. I hate my college program. Highschool was the best years for me and it's all over.*

This past year had not been particularly kind to Dave.

"Hey Willis? Where you going?" Kurt said, hardly taking his eyes from Matt, who was still talking.

Dave waved his empty glass at the group and pivoted, heading to the bar in long strides. He smiled at the bartender as she made eye contact with him. She always liked to wear push up bras and show too much cleavage. The ploy was obvious, but Dave tipped generously every time. She looked better than usual tonight, and Dave realized that the beer might be hitting him harder than he'd thought.

The bartender slid him a fresh glass and smiled once again as Dave placed the money on the wooden bar. He grabbed the pint and as he turned around was stopped in his tracks. A fiery redhead stood directly in front of him.

Her green eyes moved up and down, quickly sizing him up. Dave noticed the girl's leather jacket, torn Motley Crüe *Girls Girls Girls* tour shirt, and heeled ankle boots. A pair of long pale legs stared up at him from beneath an extremely close-cut pair of ripped jean shorts.

David cleared his throat and opened his mouth to flirt with this minx when she spoke first, "Dave? Dave Willis?"

"Ya, I—" he stammered, wondering how she knew him.

Had he already seen underneath that small amount of

fabric and forgotten? Dave would be lying if he said he wasn't expecting a slap or a slosh of beer to the face at any moment. *Wouldn't be the first time,* he thought, and felt himself wince as this mysterious red head adjusted her coat.

"It's me. Amy," she said, flicking her long hair out of her emerald eyes. Her pink chewing gum was visible as she moved it around her mouth.

Dave stared blankly for a moment. "Amy…" he repeated, uttering the name like it was the first time he'd ever heard it. *Was she from the college? No, she would stand out. This girl is a smoke show,* Dave thought as he attempted to place her.

"Amy Tisdale," she said, pointing to her chest as she identified herself.

Dave's eyes followed her finger to the spot on her shirt between Vince Neil and Nikki Sixx, each straddling a Harley. Except he wasn't thinking about motorcycles at that moment.

Dave's face lit up, as he returned his gaze to her pale face. "Amy Tisdale. Of course, I remember." And that was the truth.

She was the freckly faced girl who sat behind him in tenth grade chemistry, and in front of him during English the next year. She was always quiet and dressed in plain, shapeless clothing. In high school, she had been an average looking girl. But now that word couldn't be farther from reality. Amy Tisdale was anything but average.

"You're looking great. Really different… in a good way," Dave stammered, suddenly aware of how hard it was to form sentences. "Not that you didn't always look good, that is."

Amy smiled and giggled just as she did in high school. "You aren't looking too bad yourself. But thank you for noticing." She kicked her right foot out and posed as she adjusted her shorts. "I've reinvented myself."

"That's awesome—I mean—are you still seeing Stan then? He went to Connecticut, right?" Dave asked, as he struggled to remember the guy she had always hung around with in the halls. *Was it Stan?* Dave thought after he spoke. *No, it was Steve. Ya, that's right.*

"Oh, Sven? He's old news, yesterday's clothes and all that stuff. And it was Cincinnati he went to," Amy replied as she licked her lips. She ran a finger through her hair and spun it around before adding, "How about you? Still Mr. Football?"

"Ya, well not anymore, unfortunately. It's hard to play college ball and keep my grades up. I had to pick the books over the sports, you know how it is. Broke my heart, but I had to start taking school seriously for once."

Dave took of a sip of his beer and thought, *Damn I'm a good liar when I want to be. That school crap sounds better than, "Hey baby, I got cut from the team preseason. Never played a game." Oh ya, a real killer line you got there, Davey.*

He lowered his glass and continued speaking as Amy stared at him with a keen interest. "Can't party like I used to. But I miss stiff-arming kids into the dirt. In fact, some of the old teammates are right over—"

"Speaking of parties," Amy replied, cutting him off. Her voice sounded nervous. "I'm having one tomorrow night. You should swing by. That'd be cool. You can bring Jenny along if you want."

"Jenny?" Dave asked. He was confused for a moment before quickly remembering, "Oh right." His mind filled with thoughts of the cheerleader he was shagging at the end of senior year. That had been nothing more than a fling, but poor Jenny had been obsessed with him. *I wouldn't be surprised if she told every girl with ears that we were together,* he thought as he remembered some of the more fun times he'd had with her.

"Yeah," Amy continued. "Are you still seeing her?"

"No. That was just a short-term thing," Dave replied as he rubbed the back of his neck. It was getting hot in the bar.

"Oh, that's a shame. Well, you can bring your current girl-friend then."

"Is it cool if I come solo, unless it's a couples thing?"

Amy bit her ruby red lips, "Oh, ya, that's cool. Handsome guy like you, riding solo. I'm surprised."

Dave shrugged, "You know, haven't found the right girl yet." He sipped his Coors a moment after. *How many girls have you used that line on, eh?*

Amy smiled as she stopped spinning her finger in her fiery hair. "Buy a girl a beer, won't you, stud?" she said with a coy smile.

Dave smiled back and nodded. This girl had confidence.

No shit, little quiet Amy Tisdale has reinvented herself all right, Dave thought as he watched her pass by.

She had gone from being an obscure girl Dave hardly remembered to one of the most attractive girls in town. Not only that, but she was clearly interested in him. He just had to play his cards right and those ripped jean shorts would be on the floor of his apartment in no time.

Dave spun around and signalled to the bartender, but he was quickly ignored as she poured a line of shots for a group of frat-looking guys. A muscular bartender passed by a moment after but didn't pay Dave a second glance.

Amy brushed up beside Dave and rubbed against his arm. He watched as the fit server began to chat up a flock of freshmen girls. He shot off a quick grin at the group before pouring a shot for a tall brunette who wore a "Birthday Girl" tiara.

Dave waited until the man looked up again and waved a five-dollar bill in the air. Although Dave didn't notice, Amy had shot a wink at him. The man strolled over and said, "Another beer, man?"

Dave shook his head and gestured to Amy.

The bartender had hardly even looked at Dave in the first place. His eyes had immediately wandered to his companion's small hips. Amy bent over the bar and yelled over the music, "I'll have a Budweiser."

Dave hardly heard what she ordered. He was distracted by

how her attire shifted as she leaned over. The server nodded and retrieved a glass. Amy waited for the brute to turn his back before she whispered into Dave's ear. "I like my beer just like my men, clean and easy."

Dave nearly choked on his drink and quickly lowered the glass. His mouth was still slightly open. *She's a sweet talker alright.*

Memories of her sitting quietly in the library pouring over Algebra problems or standing awkwardly in the hallway as the football team passed by filled Dave's mind.

"Catching flies there, big shot?" Amy said as she laughed at Dave's open jaw.

"No, I— You *have* reinvented yourself. That's all," Dave sputtered.

The bartender returned with Amy's Budweiser, the condensation running down the glass and the perfect amount of foam floating at the top. Dave, again, left a generous tip.

"Thank you handsome," Amy said and ran her hand over his.

Dave felt several marks on her palm as they slid over his knuckles. Amy grasped his hand, seemingly aware that Dave had noticed the scars. "Biking accident when I was younger," she said. "I always forget they're even there."

Amy retracted her hand and sipped her drink before looking over her shoulder, saying, "Come on, there's someone I want you to meet." She grabbed Dave by the wrist and led him across the bar towards a set of booths near the back.

The jukebox changed tracks from Madonna's "Like A Virgin" to Iron Maiden's "Number of the Beast." Amy and Dave passed by a group who cheered the moment they heard it. One scrawny guy who had the smell of dope clinging to him received a few high-fives for the song choice.

Amy released Dave's wrist and sat down at a corner booth beside a large and imposing fellow. The man had bags under his eyes, and he stared straight forward, right at Dave.

Amy kissed the beast of a man on the cheek as she sat

down. "Dave this is Ted. Ted, Dave." She gestured between the two of them, but Ted just stared, those blue eyes pointed forward. A moment of awkward silence dragged on before Amy added, "He's shy," before nudging him gently in the ribs.

Dave took his eyes from the massive man and looked to Amy. "Is this your boyfriend?"

She laughed and sipped her beer. "No—he's my brother. Right, Ted?" She nudged him again. "He doesn't get out much."

This next nudge seemed to jar something deep inside Ted, who sat up straight and took a deep breath. His eyes left Dave's chest and looked at a spot somewhere in the distance. Dave followed his line of sight and noticed that Ted was staring at the group of Dave's football friends and a blonde that was chatting up Kurt. His friends had seemingly forgotten all about him, but he didn't take it personally. No doubt the pair of glitter covered breasts she was flaunting had launched a thousand ships.

Ted lifted his right hand off the table and cracked every bone in it before running it through his long greasy black hair.

Amy looked to Dave once more, "Sorry about him, he's being no fun tonight. We are gonna head out soon anyway. Here, let me give you my address," she said, as she scribbled a note onto a napkin with a pen from her purse. She quickly lifted the napkin and kissed it, leaving a thin outline of red lipstick behind.

Amy slid it across the table towards Dave and added, "I hope to see you at the house tomorrow. And if I do, you'll be seeing a lot more of me." She ran a finger down her neck as she spoke.

Dave looked to Ted. The stone wall of a man was still watching the blonde who had now wrapped her arm around Kurt. She was laughing at something that Eric had said. Ted's expression was vacant. It was obvious that his ears had not heard any of his little sister's conversation.

"Oh, I'll be there," Dave replied as he looked to Amy, trying to ignore Ted's odd demeanour.

She smiled again and Dave turned to leave. He felt his hand be pulled back and looked down to see Amy peering up at him. "And just bring you," she said, as she glanced to the table of football friends. "I want you all to myself. You know… so we can catch up."

She let go of his hand and sipped her beer, smiling to herself. Dave pivoted and walked back towards the bar.

Jesus, she's forward, Dave thought as he slipped the napkin into the pocket of his jeans. *But what a weird guy that Ted was. They looked nothing alike. Different fathers or something?*

Dave looked over to Kurt and saw the blonde now had her tongue down his throat. The other guys had begun to move to the bar to pick up another round.

But Christ, Amy, who talks like that in front of their older brother? Dave let out a quick laugh as he moved towards the bathroom to relieve his bladder. *She's changed all right.*

Dave thundered down the country road and passed a vineyard to his right. He saw a road sign appear at a gravel intersection ahead that read: *EASKAN STREET.* The same street that was blazed across the lipstick-stained napkin.

Dave let out a smile and took the corner at a reckless speed. The latest L.A. Guns release blared from the speakers of his white Trams-Am. *Number fourteen,* Dave thought as he turned down the stereo to help him focus on the fast-approaching house numbers. He passed a dark farmhouse on the left. *Look for the lit up one. That's where the party is,* Dave's thoughts recited the words that were scribbled down for him the night before.

The road was long and the houses that populated it were few and far between. *Different from the suburbs,* Dave thought as he passed a house with a porch light on, the number thirteen painted on its rusted mailbox.

No wonder Amy was weird in high school. She was a country bumpkin with no one really to hang out with.

Dave saw a house in the distance with multiple lights and cars parked in the driveway. He nodded with assurance that he was in the right spot and quickly rolled down his window. He popped the L.A. Guns tape from the stereo and threw in Ratt's 1985 album.

This oughta wake em' up, Dave thought as he turned the volume dial to the max. He smiled, the people needed to know that Dave Willis, the life of the party, had arrived.

He pulled up the stone driveway and saw the golden *14*, displayed proudly over an off-white door. The curtains swayed as his headlights reflected off the glass. It was as if someone had been watching the street just a moment before.

He parked his car behind a red Pontiac and got out, grabbing his six pack of Pabst Blue Ribbon as he did so. The warm rush of a summer breeze met him as he closed his car door. One of the last of its kind before the autumn came and turned all the bliss to memories.

Crickets chirped in the field behind the farmhouse and the sounds of a distant frog croaking from the bank of a nearby stream echoed around.

Dave looked down at his six pack of Pabst. *Hopefully Amy or her friends will let me bum a few cans off them.* Money had been tight this summer and he had spent more at the bar than he had planned.

Dave started up the driveway and moved past the column of parked cars. He counted five besides his own. *Kind of a slow party,* he thought as he heard his feet shuffle over the stone driveway. *But for Amy this is probably a pretty good turnout.* The car at the front of the convoy was an old Honda with Ohio plates. *Long way to come for a party,* Dave chuckled to himself.

He was a few steps from the sky-blue painted deck when

he heard the opening barrage of a Van Halen track. *Perfect entrance music,* he thought as he walked up the creaking wooden steps. *Whoever's on DJ duty for tonight is on point. I'm gonna have to chat them up. Anyone who digs Van Halen is fine with me.*

He knocked on the door with enough force to ensure that it was heard over the blazing guitar work. A few shouts rang out from inside, "Amy! Your friend is here!"

Amy replied a moment later with a simple, "Coming!"

Dave looked down at the beers in his hand and felt a rush of excitement overwhelm him. *Good tunes, a hot chick soon to be in my arms, decent beer. What else could a guy ask for? Tonight is shaping up to be one hell of a night.*

The door opened and there stood Amy Tisdale, a wall of sound tore over her shoulders. Her hair was done to perfection, and she had on even more make up than the night prior. A blue Scorpions' *Love at First Sting* tour shirt clung to her body. She had tied the sleeves up to show off more skin.

Amy grinned as she sized up Dave once again. "I didn't think you were coming," she said. Dave noticed she had licked her lips as her eyes drifted down to his biceps. "Or are you going for the fashionably late thing?"

"Well, I can leave if you want," Dave retorted with a smirk on his face.

"No, no. Come in," Amy replied quickly and grabbed Dave by the shirt, pulling him forward.

He felt Amy's arms wrap around him and run up and down his back in a tight embrace. She smelled of lilac and perfume. After a moment Amy released him and added, "You brought drinks, I see. No need for that. We got a case rockin' in the fridge."

Dave was led into the house by his wrist. Amy pulled him forward with a strength that her tiny frame failed to reveal. She released him and quickly shut the door as he took a step into the living room. Three people sat on a brown leather couch to the right of the entrance.

A brunette lay with her feet on the lap of a skinny looking guy who had long, dark hair hanging down to his shoulders. He took a sip of his beer as the brunette played with his arm hair. The third person was a blonde who sat on the side of the couch closest to Dave and eyed him eagerly. She looked familiar. *Where have I seen her before? Highschool? College?*

The blonde bit her lip as Dave made eye contact with her piecing blue eyes. Instead of looking away when their eyes met, she continued to stare. A slow creeping smile filled the corners of her mouth.

A small colour TV was perched against the far wall across from the strangers. Dave recognized the movie immediately, *A Nightmare on Elm Street*. The notorious body bag scene was quickly approaching, and he nodded with approval. "Good movie," Dave said as he returned his gaze to the group.

The three sat in stone silence as the blonde rubbed her neck seductively. Dave cleared his throat and became aware that the sound of the television was off. He assumed it was so the movie wouldn't interfere with the music that was blaring out of the speakers, but he found it odd nonetheless.

The brunette and her lanky paramour studied the film with keen interest, seemingly unaware that Dave had even entered. The only indication they gave that they were even alive was when the girl adjusted her feet, and the guy hoisted the beer bottle to his lips.

"Here," Amy said as she appeared from Dave's blind spot, "I got you a beer." She handed him a glass, the golden liquid bubbling to the top.

"Thanks," Dave replied, as he grabbed the chilled glass from her hands. He placed his six pack on a small end table beside him and looked to the far side of the room.

A record player was placed in between a pair of massive speakers and was pointed directly at Dave and the three strangers. A slew of records sat in a glass cabinet underneath and several albums were strewn about across the floor. Dave didn't recognize the cover art of any of them, but the images were littered with satanic pentagrams and sinister men in corpse paint. Dave took a sip of his beer and thought, *Shit, someone likes black metal around here.*

Amy seemed to notice Dave's gaze and quickly shuffled past him. As she did so she ran a hand along his jeans and grabbed his backside with a hard squeeze. "Oh, don't mind those," she said as she moved over to the curious records, quickly gathering them up and placing them in a pile beside a speaker. "Those are Ted's. They're a little too heavy for me. Unless you like them?"

"No, not particularly," Dave replied, more aggressively than he had intended. His eyes wandered over to the images on the TV. The protagonist of the movie was now about to enter the basement of the school which led to the boiler room.

Amy walked back over and grabbed the six pack from the table. "I'll put those in the fridge for you," she said.

She's nice but these three seem weird, he thought, his grasp tightening on the glass of beer. It felt like the only lifeline to the normality that he had left.

"Go on, don't be shy. Make yourself at home. They don't bite," Amy said from the kitchen as she opened the fridge and moved several items around.

"I do," said the blonde from the couch, as she let out a quick giggle.

Dave chuckled politely and took a step into the room. He saw Amy's head peek around the corner from the kitchen in his peripheral. She shot a glance to the blonde girl that screamed, *Don't you dare mess this up for me.*

Dave took another step forward. Despite being told to make himself at home, this house felt strange and foreign. From the two people sitting in stone silence watching a horror movie with the sound off, to the blonde girl that looked like she was about to jump on Dave, nothing seemed normal about this party.

Dave sat down on the couch as the blonde moved closer to the brunette and patted the cushion beside her.

The lanky guy lit a joint and offered it to the brunette, the smell of marijuana filling the room. She held out her hand with a glazed sluggishness before taking a long drag herself. She ran her fingers across her partner's leg as she returned the dope to his outstretched hand.

The brunette held her head back and quickly moved her hand down the shirt of the blonde. The blonde continued to stare at Dave, a look of intrigue etched across her face, seemingly unaware that the other girl was groping her.

Amy moved into the room from the kitchen and said, "I'll introduce you to everyone." Her eyes moved from Dave onto the brunette's hand placement. "They're friendly, I promise." While her tone was lighthearted, her face looked less than amused.

She opened her mouth to speak but quickly closed it as she perked her ear to the record player. "What happened to the music?" She glanced to the lanky guy in the camo jacket, "Harrison," she said and gave him a whack on the arm, "you were on DJ duty. The record stopped."

In truth, Dave hadn't even noticed that the music had ceased playing. The sense of discomfort he felt was taking up all his senses. Dave turned his head and looked at the man who had been identified as Harrison. The guy still continued to gaze forward as he watched the images flash across the screen. He appeared completely oblivious to Amy and her hit on his arm.

Amy frowned and gave him a hard poke in the cheek, a look of anger flashing against her face. "Hey you, change the record."

"What?" Harrison said as he rubbed his hands across his jacket. His tone irritated, his eyes glassy.

"Harrison. The record. It stopped," Amy growled through gritted teeth while quickly pointing to the still turntable.

"So?" he answered with complete disinterest. He quickly turned his attention back to the movie as his hands played with the brunette's feet.

Amy sighed and turned to face Dave. She smiled and clapped her hands together. "Sorry about them," she said. "Any preferences?"

Dave brushed some hair out of his face and shook his head. His eyes were still locked on the three occupants of the couch. The brunette's hand placement on her partner was becoming more sexual with every passing second.

Amy walked over to the record player and opened the glass case. Harrison turned his head to face her and watched her backside as she bent down to fumble through the records. "Put on Rainbow," he mumbled after a moment. His words slurred though his lips. He took another sip from his drink before adding, "I wanna hear Richie Blackmore's Rainbow."

"No, all you do when you're here is listen to Rainbow," Amy replied with a less than amused tone, running her polished nails along the spines of the albums.

Harrison shrugged and turned his head back to face the small television. His hand fumbled along the worn wooden end table next to him. His fingers searched for the joint that burned eagerly in the ashtray.

Amy pulled out an LP. "How about some Doors?" she asked, as she got to her feet and slowly removed the record from its sleeve. "Jim Morrison is a poet. Great lyrics."

Dave took another swig of his drink as he watched Amy lower the needle to the black vinyl. The glass felt light in his hand. He looked down and realized he had downed more than half the beer in the few minutes he had been there. *I always drink when I'm nervous. And I don't think I've been this uncomfortable since prom night.*

Amy placed the record's sleeve on the ground before walking over to a dishevelled rocking chair that sat facing the entrance to the room. She looked at Dave as the opening notes to "Strange Days" played over the speakers and said, "Don't worry, there's more people coming." She gestured around the house as she spoke, "Some are out back getting some fresh air, and Ted will be along shortly. He should be bringing a few more friends with him, too. We will get crazy soon," she snickered to herself, and Dave flinched as he felt the blonde place her hand on his jeans.

Dave straightened up and Amy shot an icy look to the blonde. She spoke immediately. "As I was saying, let's meet everyone." She adjusted her ruby coloured hair and continued, "The blonde one beside you is Lizzy." Lizzy finished her beer in a dramatic gulp and after a moment Amy added, "Lizzy, say hi."

Lizzy lowered her bottle and replied, "Oh, I'll say hi *later*. Trust me." She sized up Dave with eyes that could only mean one thing and preceded to draw circles with her finger on his pants.

Lizzy turned to Amy and made a face. Amy frowned before saying, "The two love birds are Harrison and Willow."

The couple continued to watch the TV for a moment before Willow raised a lazy hand in the air to signal that she had heard her name. Her other hand appeared to be more acquainted with Harrison's belt.

Dave took another sip of his beer and realized that the glass was now empty. Amy was up a moment later and before Dave knew it, his empty glass was replaced with a new one. The liquid smiled up at him.

She returned to her chair as the song changed. "I love this one," Amy said as the music poured through the speaker.

Dave nodded in agreement, but quickly felt a small pain move across his forehead as the room subtly began to spin. *One beer, and I'm already feeling it?* he thought as he rubbed his face. *I know I didn't eat dinner, but I'm a more experienced drinker than that.*

He looked to Amy who rocked slowly in her chair, studying him. The subtle feeling of pain was quickly replaced with an intense sting like his brain was being stabbed with broken glass. Dave coughed as a hot flash moved across his body and black dots filled his vision. The mirages spiralled around his rotating view and the loud music was making the effect worsen.

Dave wanted nothing more than silence and found it difficult to breathe. A moment passed and he lost feeling in his hands. The full glass tumbled to the ground as his spinning world gained more and more momentum.

The trio on the couch turned their heads in unison. Amy was already on her feet. She yelled something, but Dave couldn't understand it. He suddenly realized that he had slumped down to the green carpet. His vision went fuzzy as the room became a mishmash of colours and shapes. He opened his mouth to speak but his tongue felt like it weighed a hundred pounds.

A thundering of heavy footfalls moved across the floor on the level above him, but he quickly forgot about them as he fought to stand.

Every muscle disobeyed him, and he felt drool slip out of the side of his mouth, quickly seeping into the rug. He slipped into a stream of unconsciousness that felt like a warm blanket of jagged diamonds.

Just before he was washed under the waves of sleep, he thought he heard Lizzy yell, "Too strong, Amy! You made it too strong!"

"Let me take him for a spin when he wakes up," a harsh but feminine voice cut through the black. "One last hurrah before we mark him."

"No, we get started now! He will wake up soon," someone replied. The second voice belonged to Amy, no doubt about it. She sounded stern and annoyed. "Besides, I get to be his first when he's turned." she added a moment later. The lust in her voice was clear.

"Harrison," a booming voice rang out immediately after. The man's voice sounded further away than the others. "Give our guest the wake-up call." A moment of silence passed, and the man spoke again. "Harrison!" he barked, before a snapping of fingers echoed through his dissipating words.

"He's totally greened out, man. Look how high he is," the first female voice spoke again. Dave recognized now that it belonged to Lizzy. He was beginning to regain consciousness, but his eyelids felt like bags of cement. "Willow gave him that shit to smoke," Lizzy continued, "I told her not to. And they were drinking too. Mixing!"

"You're such a little—" Harrison's voice lumbered out of the darkness, his speech still slow but the anger clear.

"You got high before the ritual?" the man's voice bellowed. "You're going to miss it. You stupid—"

The thunder of the voice ceased as Dave stirred about, bobbing his head slightly, still in a daze and struggling to remember where he was.

"Get out of here," the man added, hardly able to contain his rage. "Just know that when he turns and The One arrives... Well, you won't like what happens next." The voice moved closer to Dave. "Lizzy. Make sure our friend is really awake and not having a stroke. The amount of shit you fed him, Amy! Really?"

"I did exactly what you said. Exactly!" Amy retorted. "Same amount as you used last time. Not my fault he's a scrawny little fella."

"Little Miss Goody-Goody screwed something up and got called out for it," Lizzy giggled, as her footsteps moved towards Dave.

Dave was gaining more senses by the second and was beginning to pray that this entire experience was simply the most visceral fever dream he had ever experienced. Memories of the drink, the couch full of strangers, and the loss of muscle control all came back to him.

"I thought I told you two burnouts to get out of here!" the male voice roared with venom.

There was movement as footsteps hurried up a flight of stairs before slamming a door behind them.

The sudden racket caused Dave to flitch. He realized that his hands were bound behind his back, and he was in a sitting position on an uncomfortable surface, a chair by the feel of it. His back ached like he had been thrown about, and his wrists felt bruised and battered.

Dave took a deep, deliberate breath and gagged as the air filled his nostrils. The scent it carried was mildew and vomit mixed with iron.

Dave grimaced as he felt something wet move along the side of his neck. He attempted to move his head away, but his reflexes were slow and unorganized.

"Don't worry. sugar. It's just me," Lizzy's voice sprang into his right ear.

Dave felt a hand move along his crotch, followed up by a rough squeeze. Dave mumbled something as he heard an unzipping noise. His jeans. He stirred again and attempted to open his eyes but found it to be impossible. The ache in his head was throbbing and his—

There was a sudden spike of agony coming from his right ear lobe.

His eyes shot open. He looked to his right and saw Lizzy pull away. She smiled at him as blood moved down her lips. She unclenched her teeth and licked them. "Works every time," she said, as she moved her hands into Dave's pants.

"Lizzy! That's enough. He's mine!" Amy's voice echoed around the dark room. "I found him; I get first ride. That's the deal."

"He's awake, isn't he?" Lizzy snickered again and ran her hand across Dave's chest. "He's a sweaty one," she added as she softened her rough grip, moving her fingers across his face. "I like 'em that way." She pushed his head back and continued with a playful ferocity, "And I haven't even gotten started yet, baby." She pivoted and walked into the darkness.

Dave moved his sluggish head around the room in an attempt to see his surroundings. His vision was still cloudy, and the pounding in his skull constant. The only light in the room was a dim flicker coming from somewhere behind him. He saw no one around, but could hear their breathing. One heavier than the other two.

"You had your fun with the girl from Ohio last time. Now back off," Amy snarled from somewhere in the void beyond Dave's limited senses.

There was a moment of silence before Lizzy's voice cut through the dark once more, "Ted didn't say that I couldn't inspect him… Make sure he's got all his…bits. I haven't had a good ride in months," she giggled again and added, "I'll try him out once you're done, which shouldn't take long. No stamina. Let Nys try a real woman, not your scraggly ass."

There was a shrill laugh from Amy's area of the darkness. "Nys won't want a trailer trash whore like you. Trust me!" Amy shrieked. She took a step forward out of the darkness and Dave could see that she had donned a black robe.

"Ladies. We need to focus," the male voice spoke, much calmer this time. "Without Willow or Harrison, I'll need your help setting everything up for the ritual."

Lizzy sighed and moved to the far right side of the room. She entered Dave's sight for only a moment, but he saw that she too wore a black robe. Dave's throat ached and he now tasted vomit as he became more aware of his surroundings.

"Amy? What's—" he mumbled, trying to focus his eyes on the room around him.

"Hey hot stuff, don't worry your pretty little head," Amy said as she stepped beside him and ran a hand through Dave's hair. "We have something to show you. Don't we, Ted?" She moved her hand down the back of Dave's shirt.

"Now that he's awake, let's begin," a man's voice bellowed, no doubt belonging to Ted.

Dave felt his chair spin. A hefty pair of hands grabbed the wooden seat and rotated it around with a single grunt. Dave blinked and attempted to focus his attention on the sight in front of him. The scent of stale cigarettes and day-old sweat filled Dave's nostrils as Ted moved about him. Dave blinked as the beast of a man left his field of vision. The source of that dim light had been revealed.

Before him sat a shrine.

Lit candles, wax trickling down the sides of their slender white bodies, sitting upon a dusty wooden table. A single stone tablet with a pentagram etched upon it was perched at the top of the altar. It looked down at its congregation of burning candles and admired them with pride.

Dave squinted as he felt the throbbing in his head worsen. His eyes locked on three clay bowls. The one farthest left contained a slab of bloody meat. The rhythmic dance of the candles made it impossible to distinguish its origin.

Dave's eyes lazily wandered over to the second bowl that sat in the middle of the altar. The horn of a goat was placed inside, the teeth of a hacksaw marking the base.

Dave swallowed as he looked to the third bowl. It was empty.

Ted emerged from behind Dave. His heavy black boots echoing with each step. "Lizzy, lead us off," he said, the serious tone never leaving him.

Lizzy gracefully moved to the left of the unholy altar and looked to Dave. She flipped strands of hair from her face before moving into a chant that caused Dave's eyes to widen with horror. Her previous playful voice had switched to that of a guttural snarl.

Dave flexed his wrists, attempting to break free from the

bonds. It was no use; Ted had tied the ropes with expert precision.

"Shhh. Don't try it, baby," Amy said, as she pressed her finger into Dave's cheek with a force that caused a dull pain.

"You're… you're… you're Satanists?" Dave said, as he moved his head away from her sharp nails. "A bunch of satanic—"

Amy straightened up, candlelight roaring around her face. She ground her teeth and said, "Satanists?" she let out a long laugh. "No, no, no. Old Beelzebub has got nothing on The One." She glanced at Ted for a moment and added, "I knew he was a dumb jock, but this is too much."

Dave grimaced in pain as Amy grabbed his hair and pulled his head back. She bent down and whispered directly into his ear with glee, "Satan? He doesn't exist. Only Nys." She slapped him across the face and stood up straight. "Now stay quiet and let this happen."

Dave tried once more to loosen the ropes that bound his hands; he could feel his skin growing raw as the ropes began to bite. Amy stepped towards the shrine and joined Lizzy in the chant.

Dave grimaced and let out a shriek as he felt a cold substance splash down over his head and neck. Ted lurched forward and appeared to the left. He held a ceramic bowl in his hand and smiled at Dave who let out a whimper as the last of the fluid ran down his back. Dave felt the liquid enter his mouth, the taste seeping onto his tongue.

Blood.

Copper, laced with fur and manure. Dave gagged, realizing that Ted had wasted no part of the goat that night.

The brute's voice cut through the chanting like a knife. "Let it out. Fear makes the process go faster." He laughed and smeared the blood across Dave's forehead and left ear. Dave screamed.

"Ugh—he screams louder than me," Lizzy said, interrupting her monotonous chant.

"Focus. We need to do this right. We have one shot to turn him. And tonight is special," Ted barked, as he grabbed something from Amy.

"Willow is better at this shit," Lizzy pouted, holding her hand over the flame of a candle, seemingly enjoying the pain it brought her.

Ted turned and struck Lizzy with the back of his hand in one deliberate motion. She moved back and clutched her cheek, her mouth wide as she struggled to find words.

"That will teach you to watch her more closely next time," Ted grunted. "Her and that idiot burn out of a partner she chose." Ted clenched his fists and Dave expected her to be struck again. "I told you not to let them take anything. Fucking degenerates!" Ted yelled, his voice echoing off the wooden support beams.

"At least I wasn't upstairs playing with myself or whatever," Lizzy retorted, finding her voice. She quickly backed away as Ted raised a fist in the air.

Ted let out a deep sigh and said through gritted teeth, "I was preparing."

He ran a hand through his oily hair and seemed to relax his shoulders. He slowly raised his hand to Lizzy's face and Dave could see that the girl was expecting another hit.

Ted opened his hand and moved a thumb down the side of her face, removing the tear that had rolled down from the corner of her heavily mascaraed eye.

Ted's hand stayed on her red cheek for several moments before he turned around in a drastic motion. He must have realized that this small act of compassion might make him appear weak in front of their freshly caught prey. He beamed at Dave once more and said, "If you want something done right, you've got to do it yourself."

Ted moved forward and turned his head to Amy before

nodding. She moved towards the altar and brushed her fiery red hair from her eyes. She began the chant once more and gradually took a knife from her robe.

The chant became louder and louder and before long Lizzy joined, building the piece into a crescendo of horror. Amy held her hands high above the altar. She rolled her head back and moved the knife to the open palm of her opposite hand.

Ted slithered around the candles and began to speak in a dialect that Dave couldn't understand. The unwashed savage reached into his robe and placed something onto the wooden altar.

White rocks scattered across the table with a soft clatter. The soft glow of the candles flickered off the small pebble shaped objects. Dave grimaced, realizing quickly that the white shapes were not stones at all.

They were teeth.

Red specks dribbled down and clashed against the enamel. Dave looked to Amy and watched as blood flowed from her raised hands. The blade looked to have slashed deep across her palm. She continued to chant, despite the pain clearly affecting her.

After a moment she lowered the knife to the altar and placed it directly in front of the stone tablet. She moved her blood-soaked hand across the pentagram and uttered several words in the same tongue as Ted, who had now migrated towards Dave once more.

Dave felt his head jerk to the right as Ted grabbed his hair, pulling his head towards him. Cold steel touched the top of his ear and a sickening pain leapt forth from the side of his head.

Dave squealed, and through his tears he saw Ted walk forward towards the altar, a piece of flesh between his thumb and forefinger.

A human ear.

Dave attempted to grope the bloody wound, but with his hands bound, he felt defenceless. The pain grew worse. His screams were hardly audible over the chanting as a fourth voice joined in.

The new voice spoke with a sharp tongue and while the other three members stumbled through each syllable, this one spoke the words as if it were born to them. The voice was clear in its delivery. It demanded violence.

Dave felt the blood run down his neck and watched as Ted rubbed the piece of skin that had once been an ear against the tablet. He seemed to pay particular attention to the penta-gram and traced it out multiple times. Dave's blood lapped over Amy's and the combined liquids began to bubble. A heat was forming upon blood and stone.

Ted continued his chant and crushed the ear into his massive palm as he balled his fists. He held them forward for a moment, showing the tablet what he had done. He appeared to speak to the new voice before discarding the flesh into the bowl that had previously sat empty.

The fourth voice became louder, and Amy lowered her hands, quickly pivoting towards Dave. Her shoulders slumped, her face tired and worn. Dave could see a sense of fear in her eyes. He wanted to call out, "Why are you doing this? Why? Why?" but the pain was too much and only a muffled moan escaped his lips.

Amy raised her bloody palm to the spot where Dave's ear had been and pressed the two wounds together. There was a sizzling, followed by the smell of burning. Dave cried out as Amy's blood mixed with both his and the goat's.

The blistering continued until the fourth voice screamed.

Every candle extinguished before the might of the voice. The chanting ceased.

Dave froze as he felt a rush of heat flow through him and a tightness in his chest. His heart raced faster than he ever thought possible, and he could feel the blood in his body flowing, tossing and turning through his veins and arteries. His temples ached and his tongue held the flavour of bile.

The basement was still. Only the sounds of a slight breeze could be heard, a breeze that appeared to be originating from the tablet. The pentagram sat cloaked in a blue hue as it pulsed with the drafts of air that flowed through from distant lands.

Ted spoke first, slicing through the silence. "Lizzy! Light the candles. Amy! See if Nys has joined us. Let's not waste its time keeping him trapped in this weak flesh."

Dave thought he heard footsteps move about him in the darkness, but he paid them little mind. All he could focus on was the blue rippling glow and what lay on the other side of it. A world of memories filled his head. He had been to that place. A place not of this earth. He had lived it; he dared to say it had even been home.

The flame of a match sprang forth and Lizzy's full face stood hovering above it. She quickly began to relight the candles and seemed to be keeping her distance from the tablet. The scent of fire and spent matches filled the cold basement.

Dave felt someone pull his face forward and realized Amy was holding his head in her hands. His blood ran down her fingers and he could feel the warmth in her palms. "Nys? Are you there?" she asked in a somber tone. Her face was full of concern, but the tears in her eyes told a different story.

Dave tried to free his head from her grip. "You cut off my fucking ear!" he screamed into her face, though he hardly recognized the voice.

"Go to plan B," Ted's voice sounded off from over her shoulder.

Ted moved over to the tablet and touched the stone, quickly retracting his hand. Dave knew it to still be white hot. *But how do I know that?* he thought as Amy stood up, towering over him.

"Will we have enough time?" Lizzy asked as she struggled to light the last set of candles which sat directly in front of the all-seeing pentagram. "I have so much to ask him, and I ran out of time last go around."

"The girl you brought home was weak," Ted muttered, dismissing her query. "Let's hope this one is stronger. But don't worry, if we did the ritual as he instructed, we will have Nys as our guest for a long time."

A long time indeed, Dave thought, but quickly shook his head, trying to focus his attention away from the tablet and the intruding thoughts. He needed to concentrate on escaping.

Dave heard Amy mumble a series of tongues before slapping Dave across the face with the back of her hand. Dave swore at her through gritted teeth.

"Hit him again," Ted called out as he watched Amy with satisfaction, a bloody blade clutched in his hand. "The One is in there. We just need to let him out. Let him overtake this body."

Ted took a step forward and paced around the room as Amy slammed her fist into Dave's stomach. Dave wheezed as she knocked the wind out of him.

The tightness in his chest was becoming unbearable and his head felt like it was going split in two. Suddenly his voice shouted out unprompted, "What's the matter, Teddy? Got a girl doing your dirty work. Can't hit me yourself?"

Ted ceased pacing and yelled, "No! No! No! Amy. Not like that." He stepped forward. "Like this!"

Dave immediately felt a fist slam into his jaw. Ted let out a loud grunt. "We are running out of time," he panted with exertion, "and I have to ask Nys about the next step of his plan."

Ted grabbed Dave by the top of his head and rammed his fist into the side of his face. This punch was hard enough that it sent Dave and the chair tumbling to the ground.

Dave looked up to see Amy just barely peeking out of the

darkness. Her eyes looked manic as she glared down at Dave laying on the cold concrete of the basement floor. She clutched her bleeding palm as tears of pain seeped from her eyes.

"Use this. Cut him!" Ted shouted as he handed her the blade.

Then Dave felt it. All of it. All at once.

A sudden strength that rose up and up and up, out of the bowels of an unseen parallel. His bonds felt looser. The pain in his wrist, his ear, his body, gone. All of it evaporated. He felt overwhelmingly powerful and all he wanted was to cause violence. He could escape, he just had to—

He felt the knife slide across his left forearm behind his back. Amy had moved around behind him and was starting to carve. Dave flexed his wrists and smiled. The ropes began to give way as he shredded the fibres with newfound strength.

Dave felt himself being turned over and saw Amy's face as she crouched over him, the knife held in front. Her eyes were widened when she saw his toothy grin appear.

Dave pulled his hands apart and the ropes broke free. He seized the knife and plucked it from her shaking hands with ease. Her grip was loose. She had not been expecting him to strike. The knife entered the base of her throat. Panic filled her eyes as her blood seeped onto Dave's arms.

He retracted the steel and tossed the body aside. He could hear Amy gurgling, grasping at the last strands of her life. He bolted to his feet and Lizzy screamed. Ted lunged forward, seizing the hilt of the blade, forcing the knife upwards over their heads.

Dave held the weapon firmly in his grasp, not letting go. He still needed it; he had some carving of his own to do.

He felt a smile form across his lips as he burrowed his left thumb into Ted's eye. The brute released Dave and staggered backwards, a muffled cry of pain escaping through his fingers as he clutched his face.

Lizzy sprinted past Dave toward the stairs that lead out of the unholy basement. Dave turned, before realizing he had even done so, and looked down. He saw the knife plunged deep into her womb.

The cry she made sounded like a dying animal. *And that's exactly what she is,* Dave thought as a voice stirred around his skull.

There was a clatter from behind.

Ted had lost his balance and slammed into the altar. The candles went out as they tumbled to the floor.

The perfect prey, Dave thought as he lurched forward. *Blind and uncoordinated.*

Ted attempted to catch the steel as it descended towards him, but his defence was all for naught. The blade bit him hard in the shoulder and Dave quickly twisted as he stared down at the meat below him. Ted let out a cry, but Dave couldn't hear it over his overwhelming urge. An urge to bite, to sink his teeth into this man's jugular artery.

Where is this coming from? Dave thought as he felt his mouth open and his pupils dilate with pleasure.

The spray of blood was bad, but the screams were worse.

Dave stood in front of the altar and gripped his forehead. The rhythmic pounding felt like his heart was going to beat right out of his skull and drop into one of the clay bowls. He realized he must have blacked out for a moment as the basement now sat silent around him. The last thing he remembered was breaking free from his bonds. Then nothing. Just a black void of memory.

Dave looked down and saw Ted laying at his feet. His vision had become accustomed to the dark and he could see the wounds on the cold body's neck were—

Dave looked away as he felt like he was going to throw up. His entire mouth tasted like copper and iron. He gagged.

Dave turned around to face the steps at the back of the basement and saw Lizzy's corpse several feet away. She had managed to crawl a fair distance, but her soul had left her body long before she could get there.

Did I do that? Dave thought as he traced the trail of her blood along the concrete.

I need to get out of here. I— Dave took a step forward and felt something under his shoe. He looked down and saw Amy Tisdale. Her body still laid where it had been tossed aside. Her throat a gory wound, the look of panic frozen in her glassy eyes. Dave stared at the body for a long while, the same words in his head repeated over and over. *All of this is a blur.*

Dave took a deep breath and wiped the mix of blood and sweat from his forehead before he—

"GaaaAAHHHH!" His scream filled the basement.

He had touched the spot where his ear had been, and the pain was blinding. He looked down at his hand and saw that the blood still flowed freely.

"Son of a bitch!" he cried. "My fucking ear!" He turned around and gave Ted's body a hard kick. The corpse wobbled as his foot struck a spot between the ribs.

While clutching his wound, Dave directed his gaze to the steps that led to freedom. He stepped over Amy's body and moved towards the stairs. The short staircase creaked with every step as he ascended.

Before he knew it, he was standing on the landing, looking down at the silent tomb where he had just been held prisoner. Dave felt his eyes gravitate to the altar once more. The tablet glowed a hot blue and the pentagram emitted a soft draft, a final breath before turning back to the colour of stone. Dave gulped and quickly found the doorknob in his hand. He pushed the door open and moved out of the newly created crypt.

Dave carefully scanned the living room. *There still might be someone here. Harrison or the brunette,* he thought, as he fumbled over a small table, sending a book toppling to the ground.

He looked to the ceiling as he heard a thump. He calmed his breathing and steadied his pounding heart, focusing on the sounds above. There was a great deal of noise coming from the second story of the house. A mix of screaming in pleasure and grunting as a headboard thumped against the wall. A chainsaw like guitar tone serenaded them as they completed their deed. Willow and Harrison were distracted, completely unaware of what had happened only a few feet below them.

Images of him moving upstairs and slaughtering them filled his brain. The thoughts were followed by an unfamiliar voice that lurched around behind his eyes. He pushed the haunting images from his mind and quickly moved to the front door. *I need to go before more of these whack jobs show up, or those two finish upstairs.*

Dave reached the front door. He moved his hand to his pocket and felt his car keys. *A stroke of luck, finally,* he thought as he flung open the off-white door. *I still have them!* He had never felt more relief than in that moment.

The air outside was cold, and a thin mist had engulfed the driveway. As Dave sprinted towards his Trans Am, he could see that the mist was slowly creeping across the surrounding fields.

Dave reached his car and flung open the door. As he threw himself into the driver seat and started the engine, he looked once more to the farmhouse. The old building was black, and the mist seemed to swallow it before his eyes.

Dave put the car in reverse, leaving his lights off as to not alert the couple on the second floor. With luck, Willow and Harrison would not discover their dead friends until the next morning, when he would be far away. Dave looked over his shoulder through the rear window and slowly moved the car onto the road.

Keep the engine quiet. Don't let them hear it.

As Dave shifted the car into drive, he felt a toothy grin fill his face. The pain from his ear fading ever so slightly. He had done it!

He waited until the house was far in his rear-view before stepping on the gas and thundering towards the intersection. As he turned the corner, however, he felt a sudden tightness flood through his chest. Then his head started to ache. A thousand times worse than before. It felt as if his skull was being split into pieces. The taste of ash immediately followed. His eyes burned like funeral pyres.

Dave tried to move his foot to the brake pedal, but his limbs didn't respond. His hands stayed locked on the wheel and his foot stayed pressed to the gas. Dave felt a final stabbing sensation through his chest and then his sight shifted.

He could not see from his eyes any longer.

He found himself drifting upward through a dark silo, moving towards a light source high above him. He became aware that he was weightless, floating. He reached the ceiling of this tunnel and turned towards an opening.

White obelisks hung from both the bottom and top of the entryway. He focused on the light ahead as he drifted closer to these jagged pillars. He could see a road racing towards him, the mist, the dashboard of a vehicle. A pair of hands clutched the steering wheel.

He looked at the white obelisks more closely and realized they were teeth.

His teeth.

Dave squirmed as a cold panic moved around him. He was outside his body now. He turned around to face himself. A face, his face, was smiling at him, a sinister grin beaming down on the small speck of life that he now was. A soul, fleeing from a sinking ship overrun by a parasite.

Dave realized that the body he looked at was no longer

his. Something had taken over. Something from the lands that lay behind the tablet.

Dave tried to escape but he could not move. All he could do was stare at his former self and watch the menacing smile grow. The new inhabitant of his body opened his mouth. His pupils became massive black spots. A blue light appeared in the centre of his throat and then the voice spoke once more. The fourth voice. Dave could hear it ringing through all eternity.

Then he felt the pull.

His soul was moving back towards his former body. Towards the blue hue and back into that gaping maw. He tried to fight, but it was no use. He passed by his teeth, and they closed around him, turning all to black.

What had once been Dave was gone. Only The One remained.

DOCTORAL AFFAIRS

The doctor sat in his red reading chair, listening to the clock that ticked over the fireplace. The embers shot into the air as a knot in the log was consumed by the flame. A distinctive crackle followed after.

The doctor looked to his mug of tea; long cold as it sat perched on the small table beside him. The wind echoed off the windows and the rain pattered along the roof.

A knock on the door caused him to snap from his stupor. He sat up in his chair. "Yes?" he called to the door on the far side of the study.

"I'm sorry to disturb you, sir," Margaret, the house maid, said through the heavy wood, "but Mr. Rothsteen is here to see you."

"Yes, send him in," the doctor replied, as he reached into his jacket and retrieved his pipe and a small box of matches.

The door opened and Vincent Rothsteen entered, carrying with him the same air of importance that he always did. He swung his hand free of his cloak and bowed as he looked at the doctor.

The doctor did not rise or bow. He simply reached for the box of tobacco that sat next to his tea.

Mr. Rothsteen frowned and moved across the room, admiring the stormy night through the window. He stopped beside the red chair nearest to the door, turning his attention to the fireplace as he said, "May I sit?"

"Yes, of course," the doctor replied, his voice distant, his tone peculiar.

Mr. Rothsteen ran a hand through his pointed beard as he sat down. He opened his mouth to speak but the doctor spoke first. "Care for a smoke?"

"If you are offering, old friend, certainly. I'm far too frugal to pass on such amenities." Mr. Rothsteen reached into his breast pocket under his cloak and retrieved a pipe of his own.

"Margaret should have taken your cloak. I apologize. She's been slipping as of late."

"No, no, don't scold the poor girl. She offered, but I'm afraid I've caught a bit of a chill. This damned rain. I prefer to keep the cloak on."

The doctor shrugged as he filled his pipe with tobacco, his eyes never leaving the fire that danced before them.

"Clive," Mr. Rothsteen said as he cleared his throat, "I worry about you."

"Oh? How so?" the doctor muttered as he struck a match. His voice was unassuming, but he knew precisely why Mr. Rothsteen worried, for he worried about it himself.

"Well, I've heard that you haven't left the property grounds for nearly a week. You've missed multiple appointments, both with your patients and ones you've made for yourself." Rothsteen grabbed some tobacco from the wooden box before continuing, "You missed afternoon tea today with me. An appointment we have had for a fortnight. It's not like you." He swallowed as he too looked at the fireplace. "You've never missed such an appointment before."

"Everything has changed," the doctor said, as he lit his pipe.

Mr. Rothsteen sat up slightly, "What? What happened? Is it Helen? Does she have her health?"

"Yes, yes, she's fine," the doctor said as he threw an arm up erratically, brushing away the comment.

"Well, what is it?" Rothsteen pressed, as he lit his pipe, taking several small puffs. He watched the smoke move towards the wooden support beams that sat high above. "It can't be money? The practice has been doing marvellously. Especially with the fever that has been moving across the countryside." Rothsteen was about to continue that train of thought when he noticed the doctor grip the arm rest of his chair with a vice-like strength. "Is it something to do with the fever?"

The doctor relaxed his grip and puffed at his pipe. "She died, Vincent."

"Who died?" Rothsteen said, as he noticed the rain picking up outside.

The doctor visibly hesitated, then muttered, "A patient. The fever took her."

"Oh, that is most unfortunate." Rothsteen licked his lips, trying to keep his voice compassionate, "But these things happen when the fever comes along. People die. But, Clive, you're the best physician in London. You've saved, what? A hundred, two hundred people? And you've lost one—"

"I've lost eighteen," the doctor rumbled as the wind thrashed against the glass of his study.

"Eighteen?" Rothsteen said, as he held his mouth open with bewilderment. "During such a winter as this? That's low. Those numbers are unprecedented. Such a harsh winter it's been."

"It doesn't matter. I could have lost a hundred. But I lost the only one that matters," the doctor said, his voice shifting to a withdrawn tone.

"Who was this patient Clive? Why was she so special?"

"She *is* still special. She…" The doctor trailed off before taking a puff from his pipe. "She was my love. My one true love." He held his head as he felt the grief return all at once.

Rothsteen stayed silent for a long while before saying, "Does Helen know? Does she—"

"Are you daft?" the doctor snapped as his head shot up. "You think I would tell my wife that I've fallen for a woman twenty years younger? Fallen for a woman as immaculate and beautiful as they come? Do you think that wise? Really? What Helen would do—" He paused, his grip on the arm rest shaking. "What her father would do, to know I dishonoured her so."

Rothsteen licked his lips. He shook his head before rising from his seat.

The doctor clenched his fist. "Where are you going? Sit down!" His words hovered in the air for a moment before he took a breath and added, "I'm just distraught. I did not mean to shout."

"I'm not leaving you. I'm helping myself to a drink. Something strong to help with this news."

The doctor turned in his chair to watch his old friend as he moved to the far end of the study. "There's brandy in the bookcase."

"I know where it is," Rothsteen said, as he opened the small doors of the cabinet.

"And pour me a glass too, won't you?"

Rothsteen retrieved two small glasses and uncorked the bottle of aged spirits. He poured the golden liquid as he spoke. "Where is your wife tonight?"

"Oh, who cares? I haven't spoken to her in days. That mousy little woman. She is nothing compared to Virginia. Nothing!"

Rothsteen watched the raindrops race down the glass window before placing the bottle of brandy down and grabbing the half full glasses. "You know, you should be careful. She could hear you."

"Oh, let her. I hate her! She suffocates me. Has for my entire marriage. Thin, sickly, boring, and plain. Only giving me one son who is an ingrate. Fat, no job, no courtship. Both of them spending money faster than a boat load of whores pulling into market. Damn the lot of them."

"You don't mean that, surely you don't. Thomas is a lovely boy. And you said yourself that if Helen's father finds out that he—"

The doctor threw his hands up once more and Rothstein ceased speaking. Instead, he took a sip of brandy and looked at the crackling flames.

"Damn them, I said. I loved her, Vincent. More than anything, and I loved her more than I fear Helen's father and his wrath."

"How long has this been going on for?" Rothsteen asked, as he watched the doctor run a hand through his hair.

"Ten months of serious affair," he replied with an exhale of smoke, his eyes looking to the heavens. "And I loved her more in that short time than the two decades I've spent married to that ball and chain that roams the halls calling itself my wife."

"Ten months? And she was always a patient of yours?"

"I first met her a little over a year ago. She escorted her little brother, who had a touch of a stomach ailment. I fixed him right up, but I noticed her eyeing me then. It took more than four months of running into her at markets or the theatre for me to build up the nerve to take her up on her offers. To break my vows to a woman I loathe." He sipped his drink. "And let me tell you. Once I did, it was like a weight had been lifted," he smiled, "an enormous weight, and I felt young again. By God, I felt young. A teenager in love for the first time." The doctor's smile changed to a frown. "She was my soulmate, Vincent, and now she's gone."

The two sat in silence for a long while as they sipped their brandy.

The doctor escorted Mr. Rothsteen out of the house at the stroke of midnight. Helen sat in the parlour knitting by candlelight. Her usual custom. The frail woman had not gotten a full night's sleep since her wedding night.

As the doctor shut the front door and began to scale the stairs, Helen called out, "Are you going to bed now, or would you like something? I dismissed Margaret for the evening, but I can make you something."

"Brandy," the doctor bellowed. "I'll have it in the library."

"Okay, my love," Helen said with as chipper a tone as she could muster. "I'll get it for you."

The doctor did not reply. He simply trudged up the steps with an aura of contempt about him.

Helen arrived in the library a few minutes later, delivering a glass full of brandy to her husband who sat on a chair with a book upon his lap. The flames of the candle flickered as she entered.

The doctor said nothing as she left the drink on the table in front of him. He was pretending to read, but his mind was occupied. Images of Virginia spiralled around his brain. Her beauty, her laugh, her untimely death. He struggled to keep the tears back as he watched Helen swiftly head towards the door.

The poor girl had so much life left to live. Had so much of the world she needed to show me, he thought, lost in his swirl of grief.

He did not notice that Helen had stopped in the doorway. She wanted to speak, but she held her tongue.

The doctor moved into his bedchambers and stumbled. He was feeling quite drunk from the three additional glasses of brandy he had consumed in the hour prior. Helen had been kinder this evening than she had been in years. Waiting on him hand and foot. Fetching him additional drinks before the glass in his hand had been empty.

He noticed his bed had not been slept in and Helen was absent. The doctor shrugged, that wasn't uncommon; they rarely slept together anymore.

He drew back the covers and saw a folded letter placed upon the pillow. He turned it in his hands and noticed that there was no wax seal. He frowned. *Something from the servants?* he thought as he unfolded the parchment.

Helen's handwriting was immediately recognizable:

CLIVE,

YOU ARE NOT SLY, AND YOU ARE NOT SUBTLE.

I HAVE KNOWN FOR A WHILE ABOUT YOU AND YOUR INFI-DELITY, BUT YOU SHOULD BE AWARE THAT THE FLOORS ARE THIN AND YOUR VOICE CARRIES. I WAS WAITING FOR YOU TO ADMIT IT BEFORE I ACTED. I GUESS SOME PART OF ME WAS HOLDING OUT HOPE THAT IT WAS FALSE, OR THAT I WAS MISTAKEN. JUST A MAD, MAD WOMAN WITH NO BASIS FOR SUCH ACCUSATION.

I HAVE LEARNED NOW TO ALWAYS TRUST MY INSTINCTS.

I WANT YOU TO KNOW THAT I LOVED YOU ONCE, EVEN IF YOU NEVER LOVED ME. EVEN IF YOU ONLY MARRIED ME TO HIDE THE SHAME OF THE PREGNANCY. NOW THAT THE TRUTH IS OUT, I NEED YOU TO KNOW ONE THING...

SHE FREQUENTED THE TAVERN DOWN THE ROAD WITH ANOTHER GENTLEMAN. IT APPEARS YOU WERE JUST A GAME TO HER AFTER ALL. YOU THREW AWAY MY LOVE FOR SOMEONE WHO COULD NOT EVEN COMMIT TO YOU.

I LEAVE YOU WITH THIS ONE PASSING THOUGHT: DO YOU REALLY THINK YOUR WHORE DIED FROM THE FEVER?

— H

The doctor crumpled up the note as he felt his chest begin to tighten. The headache he had been battling for the last quarter of an hour morphed into a seething pain. He went to step forward when his mind filled with the warm memories of Virginia, his vision becoming a narrow tunnel of black.

Helen sighed as she heard his ragged breaths through the floorboards. Then a loud, hollow thump followed a moment later.

"I'm free," she mumbled, setting down her knitting needles on her lap. She stared at the window for a long while, watching the storm move through the property. "I don't feel as if any weight has been lifted," she said to the empty mansion. The crackling fire sent shadows along her pale face. "I don't feel any different at all."

Helen sat up in her chair and listened to the wind howl outside.

AND THE DARKNESS CAME

T he van moved down the long stretch of country road as the gorgeous spring day passed by. Fields of warm grass and blue sky were all there was to see. Lucca held his hand out the window, drumming to the beat of the song that played over the radio. He looked at his co-worker, who sat in the passenger seat, and asked, "Any plans after we get back to the shop?"

Gary adjusted his back in the seat. "I don't know. Sleep? I'm beat. That last tower just took it out of me." He closed his eyes for a moment before adding, "How about you? Gonna take advantage of that new barbecue you were talking about?"

Lucca grinned as he looked at the dusty road ahead, "The Mrs. said she was making steak for dinner. I told her we would be getting home late, just like we have been all week, but she said she would wait." Lucca nodded, licking his lips. "A steak and a cold one. That's my night."

Gary moved his head so that it rested against the window of the truck. "Lucky guy. I think it might be a sandwich or something for me, if I even make anything at all. I'm honestly too tired to eat."

"It's been a long week. But we agreed it will be worth it."

Gary shrugged, "It was easier to think like that on Monday when I was full of energy. Four days of hard climbing, doing almost double our workload, replacing all those bulbs, adding all those components. How could I think this was a good idea?"

"Because once we report that all the jobs are done the boss will be happy. Maybe that raise will be coming our way like the rumour mill said." Lucca nodded in agreement with his statement, picturing the increase of pay appearing in his account. "We do two towers tomorrow and that's it. Finished hours ahead of schedule. It will be like a long weekend."

"Done by noon," Gary replied as he opened his eyes, staring at the ceiling of the truck. "You're right, it'll be worth it. Drinks tomorrow are on me."

Lucca took in a deep breath of the heavenly summer air and watched as a seagull flew off to the right. He followed it with his eyes and that's when their destination emerged from behind a small pocket of trees in the distance. A steel radio tower.

"There's our girl," he said, as he felt the muscles in his legs burn with the anticipation of the climb.

"You said you're doing this one, right?" Gary asked as he lifted his head just enough to look at the tower.

"Yup, it's just the bulb at the top that needs replacing."

"Good. I promise I'll get the next one, first thing tomorrow. I just need some sleep, man."

Lucca listened to the GPS as it instructed him to turn down the road ahead. He completed the turn and said, "You know, if you weren't up till God knows when, burning the candle at both ends—"

"I didn't know you were my mother. I said I would do the tower. I'm just tired now," Gary replied. His tone was pleasant, knowing Lucca well enough to sense he was joking around. He yawned before adding, "Besides, I told you, that girl works late. We can't all go to bed at eight like some people. It's still light out then, how the hell do you do it?"

Lucca shrugged, "I don't know. All I know is four a.m. comes too early no matter when you go to sleep."

"Ain't that the truth."

Lucca finished replacing the red beacon at the top of the radio tower and relaxed in his harness. He watched the light pulse several times before nodding in approval and closing the protective casing. The sun was getting noticeably lower in the sky, and he knew by the time he reached the ground it would be nearly over the horizon.

He felt the wind blow past him, carrying the humidity of mid-May and the soothing scent of the nearby lake.

Lucca started his long two-hundred-meter descent and heard the breeze echo through the tower frame. He felt weary from his long day of tower climbing, but he was in the final stretch now. Soon he would be home, sitting across from his beautiful wife while they ate dinner, and that's all that mattered to him.

He turned to face the farmland behind him and that's when he saw it. The endless black that sat upon the fields several kilometres in the distance, continuing off over the horizon.

Lucca ceased climbing as he attempted to decipher what it was. He gripped the ladder tight and with his free hand rubbed his eyes thinking, *Clouds must be getting thick. Is it going to storm?*

Lucca looked up. Not a cloud in the sky.

What the hell? he thought as he returned his eyes forward and gazed through the rungs of the ladder.

The blue of the nearby lake was still present, the beach-side community glowing bright and true. The forest greens to the east, still radiating life. He looked down to the base of the tower. The gravel and grass sat below him, as did the radio tower building, with its red and white roof. Lucca tied his harness belt to the ladder to steady himself and again looked over his shoulder to the south.

The creeping darkness was still there, and Lucca could have sworn it was moving ever so slightly.

He shook his head, looking to a spot far south where the outskirts of the city should have been. Now only a black void remained. Dead, no emotion, not a ripple or sign of life, just darkness.

Jesus, this is some twilight zone shit, he thought as he remembered Rod Serling acting as his guide through worlds of terror. The only sane man in a colourless realm of madness.

Lucca looked back towards the farmland. A stretch of roadway visible mere moments ago was now gone. The creeping black was definitely moving. The sun offered no solace from its loathing visage. No reflection or light escaped its grasp.

This isn't real. It can't be, Lucca thought as he felt the blood flow through his tired limbs. He uncoupled his lanyards and carabiner and began to descend, faster than he ever had before.

His knees were on fire at the fiftieth rung down. It had been a long week, replacing bulbs all across the southern peninsula. Gary and he had purposely—

Gary, he thought as he tied himself off once more.

Lucca looked down. There was the company van parked next to the chain-link fence at the base of the tower. Gary had said he was going to sleep in the vehicle while Lucca climbed. They had been taking turns scaling towers all day and Lucca couldn't believe he had nearly forgotten about him.

He turned his attention to the south again. The farmland was cloaked in black. The rural streets gone; the darkness had moved all the way to the dirt road where the tower sat at its head, alone. He knew he could never reach the bottom in time with how swiftly the blackness was approaching.

And even if I did, where would I go? It's swallowing up everything, he thought as he looked to the lake, to the cool blue of the waves and the ripple of water. *I have to warn Gary.*

Lucca checked his pants pocket for his phone but stopped as he quickly remembered leaving it in the van to charge. *How can I tell him? I have nothing except—*

He looked to his climbing satchel. The burned-out bulb sat at the bottom of the white material. *It should make a loud enough noise if it hits.*

Lucca also saw his wrench and screwdriver hanging from a carabiner on his belt, but he felt like the bulb was his best bet. He reached his fingers into the pouch and felt the glass in his hand. As he held the bulb, an intruding thought entered his mind. *I'm about to break the golden rule of climbing: Don't drop anything.*

He watched as the blackness crept silently up the dirt road, fast approaching the van and the unaware Gary inside. Lucca thought of how hard he would have to toss the bulb for it to hit its mark. He did a practice toss, still gripping the glass and mentally imagined where the object would hit. Satisfied with the prediction and accounting for the wind, he held his breath and tossed the bulb. He lobbed his arm forward and felt the glass leave his fingers.

Lucca watched as it fell in slow motion. He felt his heart beating in his neck as he hoped his aim was true. A gust of wind flowed around his face, and he looked out past the van. The dirt road was quickly disappearing as the doom approached. It was less than a hundred meters from the base of the tower now, swallowing all in front of it.

The bulb shattered on the roof of the van like a gunshot, the sounds of fractured glass echoing up to him.

He waited with bated breath. *Is he still in there? Am I the last person on Earth? Left behind, forgotten about while the end of the world forms beneath me?* These thoughts and a hundred more moved through Lucca's brain as the wind whipped by his ears and the darkness crept along.

Lucca's eyes widened as he saw the sun glisten off the white of the opening van door. A tanned arm reached out. *Gary,* Lucca thought, *he's still alive. If he hurries, he can—*

The darkness swallowed him and the van in silent majesty.

Lucca felt his heart sink. Gary, his friend for over ten years, best man at his wedding, gone in the blink of an eye.

He watched as the darkness passed the base of the tower. He expected the structure to tip as its steel base was eaten away. He imagined himself plunging to his death, engulfed in the creeping cloak.

But the tower remained standing.

Lucca watched the base for a long time, hopping to see Gary emerge and begin scaling the tower in his lime green harness, wrenches and buckles rattling. But Gary never surfaced.

Lucca felt tears sting his eyes as his mind turned to his wife. Her freckled face, the smell of her perfume, her sweet jokes and delicate voice, the baking projects she made on Sundays. Lucca missed it all, and he wept for his wife who he knew deep in his aching heart, he would never see again, for their house was over an hour southeast. Long caked in the doom.

He wiped the tears from his face and looked past the steel of the tower. The blue of the lake was gone. The sun was getting low on the horizon.

Lucca looked around; the creeping dark surrounded him in all directions. He could see the night fast approaching behind him to the east, turning the sky a lighter shade of black than that of the surface.

Lucca watched as the sun journeyed over the horizon and he immediately ached for it to return to the sky. He stared at the spot where it had been for a long while, ignoring the burn in his thighs and shoulders from holding onto the ladder for hours. He gulped and slowly looked down, hoping to see that the blackness had departed, that it had all been a hallucination.

His mouth hung open and he felt his pulse quicken as he gazed past his boots. The steel of the tower below him slowly began to disappear, buried in the black.

The entity was rising.

Lucca untied his lanyard again and frantically began to climb, climb, climb up to the top of the tower, the pulsating red of the bulb he replaced hours ago stinging his eyes and glimmering across his arms as he continued to stare at it. He did not dare look down, for he knew the doom would be looking back.

Lucca reached the top of the ladder. The blackness was a little over a hundred meters away and continued to rise like water filling a silo.

The flashing red bulb that sat at the hundred-meter mark was gone, swallowed up, just like the one at fifty meters. There was no ripple or movement upon the doom's surface. A still rise of black.

Lucca was exhausted and found himself staring out to where the lake had once been. He looked past the sheet of oblivion and turned his head to the stars. All the constellations glistened, more than he had ever seen, as the light of the cities lay under the black.

Lucca looked down; it was fifty meters away now. The third beacon had slowly disappeared under the tide.

A long-depressed breath escaped his lips. There was nothing he could do. The notion of untying himself and releasing the ladder crossed his mind, but he shuddered at the thought of ending it all, so final and complete. Instead, he felt his grip on the rung tighten with a newfound strength.

He licked his lips and thought, *I gotta try something.* He

reached down and grabbed the wrench from his belt. *Let's see what happens.*

He felt his fingers release the wrench and watched its blue handle fall straight down towards the steady rise. *Will it fall through the black? Or land on top of it and move up to meet me? Will it shatter this thing like glass and bring my wife back?* The last thought was a pipe dream. A simple barter between the Lord and a broken man wanting to see his love once more.

The wrench disappeared into the void. No sound, no rippling where it had entered. It simply made contact and slipped beneath the infinite darkness.

Lucca looked to the flashing red above him. He thought of climbing up to it, but the words "What's the use?" moved past his lips.

He knew it would buy him less than a minute more of life, and that was a minute longer until he could join Samantha as she knocked at Heaven's gate.

Do I even want to go there? he thought. *Go to the home of a god who allows this to happen?*

He shook his head. He didn't want his last moments to be full of hate. He wanted to die peacefully.

He looked up at the moon. "Will it get you too, old girl?" he asked the grey orb, its craters and ancient surface sitting static against the flashing red hue above him.

Lucca looked down. It was now only twenty meters away.

He raised his head again and squinted as the light at the top of the tower oscillated. "The beacon, it's still flashing," he said to the night sky. "There's still power."

A cool breeze moved past his face. *Something is still working down there, somewhere, giving this thing power. Is there a chance that life can still live under it?*

Ten meters.

It was his only hope. He stared at the moon and thought of his wife as the blackness rose.

He felt a cold, wet sensation on his boots but did not look down.

The red beacon flashed as his fingers released the steel rung, swallowed up by the rising doom. The wind swirled past the blinking bulb and the moon glowed in the cool May night.

WINTER RETREAT

I throw the door closed as I run into the bedroom, twisting
the lock before diving over the bed to reach the end table.
I slip and smash my head on the wooden corner. Attempting
to steady myself from the onslaught of spinning images, I
reach over and send the glass lamp tumbling. The shattering
startles me.

It will hear that.

Then again, I would be a fool to think it didn't already
know I had climbed those stairs up to the third level. Panting,
wheezing, cursing, and finally slamming that door. No doubt I
have just thrown shut my own coffin.

Why, oh why, did I shoot it? I could have let it finish going
through our trash, but I fired. I wanted to bag me a bear, my
first ever kill of one of those massive beasts. I know I didn't
have a tag for it, but who would know? Just Susan, Roxy, and
I. The park ranger or wildlife protection officer, or whoever
the hell has jurisdiction up here at this summit, would never
have been the wiser.

I grab my head and can feel the blood pouring. How a
low-grade, cheap end table could gut my scalp like this is
beyond me.

Can it smell blood?

I open the drawer and pull out my Beretta. I roll off the bed and tumble to the ground with a thump.

Blood covers the curtain of my white sheets. My mind wonders about how long it will take to clean the swath of red, but then I focus. I have bigger problems, like that thing downstairs that butchered my wife and ripped that yappy chihuahua of hers in half.

Susan had noticed it first. "Glen," she had called in her mousy little voice. "Glen, come quick. There's something rummaging in our trash."

I had grumbled and put down the economics book I was engrossed in. I had just started a chapter ingeniously entitled, "Surviving the Coming Recession: What to Add to Your Portfolio and What to Drop." Absolutely riveting material, and Susan had interrupted it.

When I stood up, I knocked my pinky toe against the coffee table. A shot of pain flew through my foot, and I let out a stream of profanity.

Susan had shushed me, which made my blood boil, a slight pain behind my eye rising into my forehead. How disrespectful of her. Couldn't she see I was in agony?

I grunted and took a deep breath, trying not to lose my temper. I had already lost it earlier that day and the doctor said it wasn't good for my heart.

I approached the large window that overlooked the summit. The mountain pass in the distance was breathtaking. The view of the snow, how it flicked at the glass and covered the copious pines in a blanket of white, magnificent.

Then Susan gasped and I looked down, past the first-level deck and out at the trash bins. A gigantic, mangey, black looking thing was there. The snow was heavy powder, so it was hard to make out its burley details. That's when I got the idea for my first bear kill. This quadrupedal monstrosity would be mine, I decided. The first of many.

Mine, all mine.

I press my back to the wall and point the Beretta at the bedroom door. The weapon is heavy. I can feel the weight. It's loaded, but what will these 9mm rounds do to it? My rifle shots were nothing but minor inconveniences to its thick and hairy hide.

The Beretta rattles as my wrist quakes. I can hear the heavy footsteps ascending the steps to the third story of the lodge.

Why did I come here? I never would have shot it if Susan hadn't forced me to come on this winter excursion. She said she needed to cure the writer's block that had plagued the production of her fourth romance novel. She said a change of scenery would do her good.

Her books were truly dreadful stuff, but at least her second novel brought home the bacon, a bestseller.

Romance, what a dead concept that is! She writes the males in her books as such sissies. No real men to be found. Just defined jawlines and abs as far as her imagination's eye could see. She never asked me for my opinion on how the men should act; I would have given her a piece of my mind!

I had put on my winter boots and stepped out onto the deck of the first floor. I remember the sound of the snow crackling under my feet. My rifle was in hand and my fur hat covered my ears. I lined up the shot on the beast's muscular haunches, waiting for it to raise its head as it pecked at yesterday's chicken bones, thirty meters away.

I remember its breathing: deep, animalistic, much harsher than I thought a bear should sound. Susan had asked me not to shoot it, but she had always had a soft heart. Besides, I had brought all my hunting and gutting tools along for the ride up here. I didn't intend for them to go to waste.

Susan and Roxy watched from the second-floor window where it was warm. I had asked Susan to pour me a cup of tea, but I doubt she had. The beast of an animal knocked over the recycling can in its zeal. The sudden clatter reached up to Roxy's ears and that's when the simpleton barked.

The beast perked its head up and startled me with its quick movement. I snapped the trigger, and my shot went low and left, hitting the thing in the shoulder blade.

That damn dog had ruined everything. I had the prey in my sights. I would have bagged it, I know I would have.

The predator opened its jaws and let out a death call like nothing I'd heard before. It turned, and that's when I finally realized it wasn't a bear at all. Rows of teeth, that double tongue and those globules lining its mouth and throat. I cycled the action and fired again as it began its charge. The shot struck its matted chest.

Roxy continued to bark, and Susan screamed. The black mass gained speed. I might as well have been shooting BBs at it.

If only Susan had let me put those godforsaken eye sores of the garbage bins to the side of the lodge like I had wanted. But she said she was worried I would fall. Typical anxious Susan. If I had been able to do things my way, then none of this would have happened.

None of this.

The beast is at the door now. It sniffs under the gap between the carpet and the wood, that nasally sound escaping its snout. A putrid scent of fur enters the room a moment later.

The cheaply assembled door will never stand up to its massive claws, consisting of more saw dust and glue than actual wood. I hold my breath as it continues to smell the air, looking for more chicken bones, except these ones are still moving.

But for how much longer?

After that second shot, I had turned tail and run through the open glass door. Snow had entered and sat upon the entry mat. The fireplace spat embers at me as I slid the door closed. I backed up, thinking the glass would deter the beast.

I watched as it bounded up the deck's stairs, four steps at a time, eye level with me in an instant. In one fluid stride it charged the glass. Not even a moment of hesitation. The door shattered on impact as it headed inside the warmth of the lodge.

I dropped my rifle and heard it clatter behind me as I tumbled up the stairs on all fours. I moved as fast as I could, toward Susan's shrieking and Roxy's barking. The creature's huffing and panting was right behind me.

I leapt over the couch and watched as Roxy jumped at it. A massive paw with nails as long as kitchen knives sent the Chihuahua flying. The barking stopped.

I ran towards the third-floor stairs, leaving the beast with Susan. I heard a tearing sound and a wet scream. Blood must have filled her lungs, but I didn't dare look back.

Never look back.

The breathing stops, and I can hear it skulking down the hallway. Then I hear a gurgling sound from the floor below. A gasp of air followed by the sound of dragging. Susan is still alive. That damned woman. She needs to be quiet, or it will come back and finish the job.

I can't hold my breath any longer and exhale. I try to steady my breathing but then I hear its thumping paw prints. It stops outside the door once more. A moment of silence follows, and then one of its massive black talons plows through the wood of the door.

I look at the Beretta trembling in my hand. I could pull the trigger and empty a few shots into it, but why do that when I can guarantee myself no pain? I could go out on my own terms. Not on the terms dealt by this beast.

It hammers at the door again. I can see its bulbous body now. It's nearly through. I slide the gun into my mouth. The barrel is cold. No pain, I tell myself.

No pain.

A third slash and the splinters of the door fly in every direction. It muscles through the opening, wailing as it does so. Those eyes, yellow and red, ravenous and wild, locked on me and the Beretta frozen in my mouth.

I pull the trigger.

The trigger goes all the way back, but no round leaves the muzzle. I'm still alive, for a moment more at least. In my last seconds of life, that's when I realize it.

It is all so clear now, my mistake. I never cocked the pistol. Never racked the slide. Never allowed a round to enter the chamber from the magazine when I loaded it.

With that one movement of muscle memory omitted, the weapon was useless. As good as a paper weight. I have no time to remove the weapon from my mouth.

The beast charges, mere inches away from my racing heart. That thunderous breath. I will die on its terms all because of this stupid gun. All of this is its fault. I can think of nothing else at that moment but to pull the trigger again. Perhaps a miracle will allow me to pass on with no pain.

No pain.

The trigger retreats again. The snow continues to pile on the ledge outside the window.

THE CURIOUS HOUSE

CHAPTER ONE:

THE WIND, THE RAIN, AND THE WARDEN

Second Warden Grishoff groaned over the sounds of his boots entering the muddy soup that could at one time have been called a road. His horse neighed behind him as he pulled her along. She too was annoyed at the muck against her hooves and the damp air that coated her mane in a dew.

Grishoff's sword clanged against his right hip and the equipment rustled against the ribs of the steed behind him. The journey to Wolfhampton had been a long one, longer than he remembered it taking in the past. In truth, he had not been to the village for the better part of fifteen years, not since the Baron had requested his services at Valiceport.

The Baron had passed away several months prior, leaving his son in charge of the Jesuit Isles fief. Since then, rumours had begun to circulate of strange sightings in the woods of the northern regions.

The wardens of Wolfhampton sent numerous correspondence to the newly appointed child-Baron asking for assistance. After several months of inaction, the lord of the fief assigned one additional warden to join the ranks of those in Wolfhampton. Grishoff had volunteered immediately. After all, it was his own brother, Jordi, who had been sending the letters.

Grishoff wished the Baron would have sent more wardens than just himself, but between the peasant revolt of Jerusalem's Crossing and the border wars with their western neighbours, the Baron could only spare a single man.

Grishoff had wished to leave Valiceport in the morning as the sparrows took flight but had been significantly delayed. As second warden of the town, he still had a responsibility to obey his commanding officer, who had bogged him down in parchment work. Grishoff was glad he would be working with his brother from now on; the distain for composing reports ran in the family.

Grishoff cursed as his boot disappeared into the mud. He bent down and held the leather with a firm grasp to ensure it too wouldn't vanish into the abyss of the muck. He lifted his leg, stood up straight and pulled on his horse to follow closely.

The moonlit path continued ahead of him, seemingly endless. The branches beside him rustled as an unseen storm raged on the far side of the woods.

He squinted as he saw the outline of a house to the right side of the road. The two-story building was perched at the end of a long cobblestone walkway amongst a barren field. One window on the second floor contained a candle, its flame a welcoming sight.

Grishoff heard the storm gathering and contemplated moving to shelter in the old wooden house. He heard the howl of warehounds in the distance. Not even an experienced warden such as himself would go out in search of a fight with one of those creatures.

The candle in the window flickered in a beckoning call as

Grishoff studied it for a moment. He adjusted his cloak and felt the warden medallion move around his neck. The occupants would be required by law to provide a warden in need with shelter and food, by order of His Majesty.

Several rocks rolled down the embankment a few paces behind him and crashed onto the road. Grishoff turned and scanned the woods once more. A sense of dread irradiated from the trees. *Could be a whole pack of them,* he thought as he listened to the wind with caution. *Or who knows what else is hunting at this hour?*

Grishoff decided the house was his best chance of survival for the night. He tightened his grip on the reigns of the horse and pulled the old girl up the stone path. Her hooves clipped and clacked against the masonry.

The candle waved down at Grishoff. The call was seductive and promising. But while Grishoff's mind wandered off into thoughts of warm fires and dry blankets, the candle had other plans.

CHAPTER TWO:

LIKE A MOTH TO THE FLAME

Grishoff looked to see if anyone was in the stable that sat directly beside the house. No one stirred, there was just the sound of the wind fluttering through the wood planks of the old building. Grishoff secured his horse in the dry stables before venturing to the front door.

He took the heavy steel knocker in his hand and rapped on the sturdy door three times. He waited several moments, and after receiving no reply, he tried again.

The wind was moving up the stone walkway and blew past

the house. It carried with it the smell of wet leaves and mud-soaked holes. Grishoff pounded on the door with his gloved fist before calling out his name and title. He grabbed the handle and felt the heavy steel turn in his hand.

The door blew open with a menacing sound.

The main room was dark with only the moon's blue light casting any illumination. Grishoff couldn't see anyone in the kitchen or around the meal table. All was still. Grishoff called out again, but his voice was met with silence. The house settling on the second floor was the only sound.

Grishoff peered around once more before stepping inside. His left hand sat firm on the hilt of his blade while his right adjusted his warden medallion.

Grishoff heard a creaking and turned his attention to an ascending staircase that sat directly ahead. He moved through the main room and upon approaching the stairwell, became aware of a smell that hovered about the home. The smell of venison that had just been skinned.

He placed a heavy boot on the first step and heard the old wood groan under his weight. Several parts of the house creaked as it shifted into place. The wind continued to beat against the structure.

He moved up several stairs before coming to a landing and ascending the next batch around a corner. The second floor was illuminated by the light of the moon that came through the bed chamber windows. Grishoff could see this level contained two rooms, one immediately to his right, and one straight ahead. Both had their doors open.

The warden passed the first room and peered in as he did so. Two small beds faced him, silhouetted by the blue light. Children's toys were placed on a bear hide carpet. The toys looked to be long discarded, frozen in time until their masters picked them up again. Grishoff moved forward and followed the flickering light of the candle that lay ahead, reaching out to him like a beckoning siren.

He entered the second room and observed the candle sitting diligently on the windowsill. A bed sat to the left, its sheets perfectly made. Silks hung in the open cupboard to the right. Expensive robes and gowns. The owners seemed to be quite well off if they could afford such luxuries in a house as large as this.

Grishoff moved forward to the window and observed the road in the distance. The road looked different, a sensation he could not explain.

He looked down and studied the candle. To his surprise, it appeared like it had just been lit. No pool of wax, nor a charred wick. But that was impossible. Surely, the occupants must have left—

A scream flooded up the stairwell and pieced his ears.

Grishoff spun around, drawing his blade as he did so. The house was silent once again.

He steadied his breathing, listening for any threats that might be approaching. The scream had come from far below. The wind continued and the flame flickered. Grishoff knew he needed to investigate the sound, not only for his sense of duty, but to assist this person in need. He brushed his cloak aside and began to move toward the hallway, watching the stairway with undivided focus.

The house was incapable of expressing emotions, but if it could, it would have smiled.

CHAPTER THREE:

THE CELLAR

Grishoff stood on the main floor, all was still. His sword was growing heavy in his hand as he surveyed the room once more. That scream had originated from this very spot, or at least it sounded like it had. Perhaps the echoes of the staircase had caused the sound to reverberate and appear so close?

Grishoff entered the kitchen and saw a door tucked beside a full rack of wine. He opened the small door and was surprised to see a descending staircase that went deep into the bowels of the property. The stairwell was perfectly dark. Even his adjusted eyes could not see what awaited at the bottom.

Why this house had a sublevel at all was a mystery to Grishoff. *A cellar for wine or meat?* he thought as he squeezed the hilt of his sword.

A new smell touched his nostrils. A burning scent. Not of wood, but more of parchment and hair and steel, all wafting up from the dark underbelly of the house.

Grishoff froze upon the landing as he heard a sound float up the stairs. It sounded like a pin drop on cold stone, but it was the noise that followed that put the aging warden on edge. A cracking, almost chewing sound. It was faint to be sure, but against the quiet back drop of the property, it was a haunting sound.

Grishoff took a step back and was about to shut the door when the basement below became illuminated by a dim flickering candle. The chewing stopped immediately. Only the slight patter of the rain outside could be heard.

Grishoff was no fool; to turn back now was a viable choice. Yet it would not only mean ignoring someone during their hour of need, but also risking the warehounds that no doubt stalked the road ahead. Still, the vision of mounting his horse and leaving this house at his back was an enticing one.

He stepped forward and heard the familiar creak of the wood beneath him. His sword picked up the dim candlelight. The inscription displayed on the blade rang loud and true: BRAVERY IN TIMES OF PEACE IS EASY.

Grishoff studied the writing and his thoughts turned to the original wielder of the weapon, his father. "I wish you were here now," he said quietly, as he read his family's creed once more.

Grishoff trudged down the stairwell until he reached the bottom, his blade held in a striking position.

Upon reaching the final step, he realized his fears were for naught. It was a cellar like any other. Wine bottles were stacked in dusty shelves along the right wall. A sewing wheel sat next to a broken rocking chair near the stairs. A barrel rested against the far wall, a single candle burning on top of it. A slight gust of wind caused it to flicker violently, nearly going out. For a fraction of a moment the cellar was almost completely devoid of light. In that minuscule amount of time, Grishoff thought he heard it.

The chewing sound, swirling all around him.

He stared at the flame, burning bright on top of the barrel. Grishoff then shifted his attention to the left corner of the cellar. Beside the old musty barrel, a pickaxe and several shovels had been laid on the ground, sitting directly in front of what appeared to be a hole in the foundation.

Grishoff approached, keeping a keen ear open for any additional noises. He leaned over the edge of the hole and saw that a wooden ladder continued downward. A gust of air escaped at that very moment, reeking of mold and the burning odour. Grishoff gagged at the smell and looked around the modest cellar once more. There was nowhere to go but down, farther into the depths. *The scream must have come from there*, he deduced. *There is no other place.*

Grishoff sheathed his sword and felt for the dagger that sat on his lower back just under his cloak. The sword would be unwieldly in the tight cavern below, but the dagger would do nicely.

He turned and grabbed the candle from the barrel. It was placed in a holder and while climbing down a ladder with one hand would be awkward, he would rather that than have no light at all. He gulped hard and started down the unsteady ladder.

The house could hardly contain itself. It had been ages since it had feasted last.

CHAPTER FOUR:

DESCENT INTO MADNESS

Grishoff held the candle in front of his face as he attempted to catch a glimpse of what lay ahead. All that he could make out was a hallway gouged out of the stone. The cuts were crude, but oddly uniform in some places. He looked to the top of the ladder and saw a dark void peering down at him. The basement was now completely dark in the absence of the candle. A small gust of wind fluttered down the ladder. The air was hot, and the smell was unnatural.

The ageing warden swallowed and pulled the dagger from its sheath on his lower back. He walked forward into the gaping maw of the tunnel ahead. As he stepped forward, he felt something under his boot. Not rock or clay, a different substance. He looked down and saw several planks of broken wood. Each board was dry and split from time. The wood looked to have been broken by blunt force; a hammer, or a dull axe.

But why would there be planks at all? Grishoff thought, though he quickly realized the answer. "*To keep something in,*" the voice in the corner of his mind whispered.

Grishoff gulped again and looked to his candle for comfort. While it burned true, no wax ran off its thin frame. He shook off his curiosity and stepped forward, beginning his long journey into the unknown.

Grishoff moved down the uneven chamber until the hallway opened up, revealing a great chasm. A stone bridge lay across its vast depths. Blackness ventured off hundreds if not thousands of feet in either direction. Grishoff took a step onto the walkway and looked up. Darkness hovered above him, no ceiling to be found.

Impossible, he thought, certain he had only travelled a few ladder rungs under the ground. *How could there be no stone above me? No supports or foundation?*

His thoughts of the cave formation were cut short as he heard the sound of scuttling coming from below. He pointed the candle to his boots and looked over the edge. Only the abyss peered back at him. His eyes hovered over the void, watching it just as it watched him. As he studied it, a sound crept along the cusp of his ear drums. A breathing sound, coming from the darkness below.

The warden felt the hilt of the dagger burrow into his hand. The breathing sounded close, but the rhythm was off. It was as if whatever was producing it was attempting to remain as quiet as possible, to mask its presence. Grishoff could feel the fear in his brain escaping the glands and poisoning his mind.

Run and leave this accursed house a distant memory. Return at dawn with all of Wolfhampton's wardens, he told himself. *There's an evil about this place.*

He quickly cleared away the doubts. His curiosity drove him forward, the prospect of discovering the source of that scream remaining at the forefront of his mind. Yet there was also something else, something he wouldn't even admit to himself. A compelling and unexplainable aura calling to him, summoning him deeper into the bowels of the earth.

CHAPTER FIVE:

THE FALLEN OBSERVER

Grishoff's candle illuminated it first. A statue hovered above him, towering over the bridge and jutting out of the stone wall as if it was moments away from descending upon its prey. A face of pure evil, its carapace carved by the same inhuman tools that made the tunnel and the bridge. A slightly open mouth with a lanced tongue pointed towards the intruder below. Its only human characteristic was the black eyes that were burrowed into the rock.

Grishoff observed several lines that had been carved into the surface of the face. He felt his pulse quicken, *Had the sculptor been attempting to depict age or some sort of liquid streaking down this creation?*

Under the enormous idol was a burrow that continued into the rock. The hole was placed in such a way that it appeared to lead right into the statue's neck. *I am to go down its throat. Deeper and deeper, but what will I find in its heart?* he thought, as his eyes marvelled at the unholy sight.

Grishoff followed the outline of the sculpture and observed two arms jutting out along the sides of the bridge, ready to ensnare him. What this sculpture was meant to depict, Grishoff could not fathom. A demonic presence, or a god of some sort, forgotten to all but time itself? If it was indeed an idol, Grishoff wanted nothing to do with it or the religion that it ruled over.

He stepped forward, marching into the throat. He looked up as he heard water droplets running out of the open mouth above him. Each pooling on the pointed tongue before rolling off and plummeting to the stone bridge. Grishoff couldn't remember seeing those droplets before stepping into the opening, but he didn't dare dwell on such a trivial detail.

Grishoff trudged on. The tunnel arched downward, deeper into the earth and off into the distance. The scent of burning became increasingly worse as he traversed the tunnel. It now contained hints of stagnant water and decaying meat.

The breathing sound reverberated from the depths once more. The menacing sound was quicker now, and closer. With every step, Grishoff looked over his shoulder but saw nothing except for the endless black. The ever-present dark that followed him wherever he went.

Grishoff looked up and observed that the stone had been cut into deep arches. Their smooth design made him think of human ribs, or the grooves of an esophagus. He shook his head and cursed the designers. These architects had been evil men creating an unholy work, if they had been men at all.

The warden stepped forward and as his boot hit the ancient stone, a sound of thunder roared from the bowels of the tunnel. He felt his grip tighten on both dagger and candle as the menacing booming continued. Grishoff stood firm, ready to fight the beast that approached, except the steady pounding seemed to be keeping its distance, far off in the tunnel. Its periodic rhythm stayed the same, with a screech of metal cutting in after every forth vibration.

Grishoff once again stepped forward as a voice far from his own spoke inside him, telling him to continue on.

It was time at last.

CHAPTER SIX:

UNHOLY TONGUES AND THINGS THAT SHOULD NOT BE

The ribbed celling ended just as Grishoff entered through a dark jagged cut-out at the end of the tunnel. As he entered the cavern, he noticed the echoes of his footfalls had changed their tone. Instead of the dry rock he had been trudging on, it now carried the sound of a wet, soft substance. The candle did little to illuminate what lay beneath his feet, and he hoped it was water upon clay, not something worse.

As he moved several paces into this new chamber, the metal and thumping ceased, being replaced by a steady howl of wind. The putrid smells were carried with it. Grishoff took a shallow breath before taking another step forward.

The scream was deafening.

He leapt back, almost dropping the candle. His dagger held out in front of him, utterly useless against the wall of black that covered all that lay before him. The scream had come from directly in front of him, close enough that he had felt the breeze on his face.

The warden backed away as he sensed eyes upon him, coming from all directions.

As he stepped back in retreat, the sound of twisting steel began again. This time it was followed by a series of wet foot-falls. Heavy, brooding, and thunderous, they approached from the dark cavern. The candle provided no assistance, instantly swallowed up by the void, the light becoming like a droplet of water against an ocean of black.

Grishoff wanted to run, but the alluring voice in his head began to utter the same phrase over and over. "*Wait and see,*" it said, "*Wait and see.*" He could feel its power moving inside him.

He tried to move but his aching muscles failed to respond to his commands. Tears filled his eyes. The sound of dragging chainmail and leather across the wet ground sent a new level of fear searing across his mind. There was a screech as the invisible menace took another step, the thundering footfalls landing just in front of him, mere inches away.

A single candle flickered in the distance, illuminating a portion of the far side of the room. The voice ceased calling to him and Grishoff could move once again. He felt his arms respond as he waved the candle around him. No one was there, and the metallic screeching lay dormant.

Grishoff looked towards the freshly lit candle, which sat under an arch of intricate brick work. Its flame seemed to grow brighter the longer he watched it, expanding until it revealed a mural of various sized skulls mounted to the wall around it. Human, horse, cattle, and several which looked otherworldly. Pure black, narrow eye slits, with horns and tusks affixed.

Just as the thought of leaving flickered through Grishoff's mind, a figure walked into view. The visage stood before the fresh candle, cloaking its features in darkness. It moved its arm from its side and in a twisted hand, brandished a cooking blade.

The warden took another step back, praying the figure had not seen him. He froze as a voice filled the cavern. It was backwards and hushed but seemed to originate from the figure. The voice was female but was not delicate. It used a harsh and jagged tone that moved about the hall. The visage cocked its head and continued to speak, and as Grishoff listened he began to understand it.

"Have you seen my children?" the figure asked, the words rolling over the old warden.

As it spoke, the candle behind illuminated more of the chamber. Directly beside the figure were two bodies covered in gore. They were small corpses. Half the size of a man in every respect.

I've found the children, he thought, realizing what had been done to the corpses.

Grishoff took another step back. The moment his boot made contact with the wet ground, one of the bodies sat straight up. Its head spun unnaturally to peer at Grishoff, gazing into his soul.

"You should be running along now," the figure whispered.

"My husband will be home soon, and he won't like what I've done."

The moment the last word left the hollow visage, the candle behind it extinguished. Just as the flame died, Grishoff saw a body rise from the floor.

The warden fled, just as he should have long ago. He ran through the opening and past the ribbed hallway, reaching the stone bridge in a blur of sweat and fear. Despite his speed, he could hear the sounds of breathing and footsteps behind him. Screaming and metal chased him. He heard something else, too. Something that escaped from the bowels of these catacombs. A sound he could not describe.

Grishoff fled across the bridge, and while the sweat stung his eyes and the adrenalin caused him to miss many details, he could have sworn the arms of the horrible idol had moved closer since he entered. As Grishoff moved across the bridge he heard the slithering below him. Whatever lay down in those depths was awake now.

He reached the ladder and began to ascend, keeping the candle in his hand. The light had been his only ally in such a tormented realm. He ascended the ladder as the roaring bellowed below him, the footfalls nearly upon the entrance to the pit. He reached the top, narrowly avoiding falling, as he balanced the candle on the rungs.

Grishoff crawled out of the hole and left the candle on the ground, turning and grabbing hold of the ladder once more. The wood jerked in his hands as he attempted to raise it out of the dark abyss, but something had grabbed the bottom. He heaved once more before the ladder was ripped from him and disappeared below.

Grishoff rose to his feet and ran towards the stairs that exited the cursed cellar. As he stepped up the first stair, something caught his eye. He turned his head and watched as the candle flickered beside the hole, a pair of hands gripping the side. Nails were missing. Scabs were bleeding from black veins.

These were merely the first, as pair after pair joined their ranks.

Slowly, the top of each being's head lifted from dark. An eyeless woman raised her mould-ridden scalp just as the candle was extinguished by a gust of wind. Grishoff ascended the stairs in a flurry as he fought the voice inside his head.

He reached the top of the steps and entered the main room. Without stopping he headed for the door. Bootsteps echoed overhead. Quick and methodical, they would reach the stairwell landing at any moment. The metallic screeching was everywhere. Grishoff flung open the door and moved into the night.

He turned and headed to the stable where his horse had been tied. *Please be alive*, he prayed, as images of her corpse being disemboweled filled his mind's eye. He swung open the stable door and to his surprise, the horse remained, standing right where he had left her. She whinnied nervously as he entered.

Grishoff untied the knot holding her to the post and rid the saddle of several packs of gear. He jumped onto the horse, kicking the steed in the ribs as he did so. Before he knew it, he was down the road with the house at his back.

He didn't dare look towards it, but the voice called gently for him to return. He shut it out and kept his eyes forward on the passing trees.

CHAPTER SEVEN:

WOLFHAMPTON'S WARDENS

Grishoff rode steady along the road leading to Wolfhampton's main gate. The sun rose over the hills, basking the surroundings in its silky orange light. The ducks from a nearby pond could be heard and the sparrows chirped from their nests, filling the village with a calm peace.

Grishoff watched as the morning dew glistened against the leaves. He took a deep breath. It was hard to imagine that a world so beautiful and full of life could contain such a realm as the one that dwelt under the house.

Grishoff pulled on the reigns as he stopped at the main gate. The stone wall that surrounded its southern entrance towered over him. Wooden guard towers stood mostly empty and still on either side of the entrance. Wolfhampton was not the same town it had been when he had left it as a boy. The wooden gate stood closed before him, its heavy oak planks and steel rivets holding a thin layer of morning dew.

"You down there," a voice from one of the watch towers called into the morning. "What is your purpose of travel?"

"I am Warden Grishoff Monteux. I carry orders from the Baron to assist the wardens garrisoned here. I am to meet with Lead Warden, Jordi Monteux. My brother."

There was a moment of silence before the lookout in the watch tower called down to unseen forces behind the wall. Slowly and methodically the gate opened as men turned the wheels and pulleys required to budge such a massive object. As the gate opened Grishoff admired the axe marks that marred it. It seemed Wolfhampton had suffered its fair share of attacks over the last few years.

Grishoff rode past the gate and into the town. The two men-at-arms that stood by the opening were no older than boys. The eldest of the two was particularly round bellied and looked like he might run out of breath after two swings of his blade. Another four men sat in a tent warming their hands over a fire. This group looked to be much older and weathered, with one volunteer missing a hand. Grishoff had never imagined the lack of capable fighters could be this dire. The warehounds and bandits had taken their toll on the fishing village.

Grishoff reflected on the evening's ride as he passed the small garrison. He had not encountered a single warehound after fleeing that dreaded house. A report such as that should have been impossible, especially given the reports that Jordi had been filling over the last few years. Grishoff thanked the almighty for such wonderful luck. Perhaps he had suffered enough at the hands of that house and been rewarded with safe passage. The balance of life once again. Tragedy and a stroke of good luck, all in the same night.

Grishoff rode past several stone houses. The smell of bacon, ham, and eggs cooking in a pan wafted through a window. The woman hummed to herself as she cooked breakfast for her husband and three children, two of whom served as men-at-arms at the main gate. Their shifts would be over soon.

The stone houses sat toward the west side of the village where the peasants and lower-class fishermen lived with their families. Grishoff scarcely gave them a glance. Even as a boy, he was told not to venture over to that area of town. His mother had instructed him repeatably that no son of hers should "Fraternize with the sons of peasants." Jordi had never listened to that advice, however, and had many friends from the poorest parts of town. He was always much more outgoing than his older brother and, as such, had become a man of the people.

Grishoff nodded at an archer in black that passed by him on the road heading out towards the frontier. The warden knew his kind well, a pure hunter of fortune, selling his soul to the highest bidder. One week, he might be protecting the town and shielding the innocent, the next, leading a group of outlaws through the very breach in the wall he had been defending mere days before. His allegiances changed like the wind, or like the shine of silver as it spilled out across a table.

Shortly after the traveling mercenary came a set of men-at-arms. The shift change was heading to the southern gate. The youngest was no older than thirteen, while the oldest appeared to be approaching sixty and limped terribly. His white beard was mangled and knotted, and his light armour was two sizes too big. It hung from his frail body, decades past its prime.

Grishoff passed a sign that stated: *WARDEN OUTPOST AHEAD*, but he had little need of the posting. He remembered the path well. He had walked with his father to work every morning, wishing him happy hunting. Grishoff would ask his father to bring home the head of a limphoss or sprylisk as a trophy. His father would always laugh and pat him on the head, reminding Grishoff to be nice to his mother and to help take care of little Jordi.

As he reflected back on the memories of days long past, a thought occurred to him, one that had repeatedly entered his mind during the last few days. Grishoff was now older than his father had ever been. Grishoff had also been a warden far longer as well. Despite this, he felt like he was half the man his father had been.

It was a fact that would have saddened the long dead Haroldi Monteux, for he never wanted his sons to be wardens like him. He had wanted a better life for them both, but died before he could show them a different path.

The world went on and both his sons followed in his footsteps, swearing to protect the innocent, and dedicating their lives to people that didn't even know their names.

Grishoff could hear the insects move through the air, and the smell of the lake told him he was getting closer. He looked to the west and could see the great Angler Woods looming beside the town. A few fires sat at the edge of the tree line, denoting the base camp for the guards. A crude wooden wall had been built to protect the town's western flank, but it was lacking compared to the south gate.

Grishoff listened to the sounds of pigs and cows as he moved past a stable. Children called for their mothers to assist them with daily chores. Despite its bleak appearance, the village continued to function, even containing some pockets of joy. Life went on, it seemed, even when surrounded by tragedy.

"Brother!" a voice Grishoff didn't recognize called out to him.

Grishoff turned to look ahead. Standing on the road before him were three wardens, two of which were dressed in brown leathers, their medallions hanging from their necks. A lead warden stood among them, the standard black cloak upon his back. Grishoff knew this man must be Jordi, but his eyes failed to recognize him. Fifteen years had passed.

The man's face was weathered, and a scar was visible over his right eye. His voice had deepened, and his stature was hunched over. The years of command had taken their toll on Grishoff's younger brother.

"Jordi?" Grishoff asked to the man in the black cloak.

"You are asking your own brother?" the lead warden held his chin to the sky and let out a loud guffaw of laughter. "Your eyes must be grey. I knew you were old, long in the tooth, even. But——"

Grishoff dismounted his horse and approached his brother. "It is good to see you again. I have missed you. I am sorry for not visiting in such a long time, but Valiceport is a bottomless pit of work."

"You don't need to tell me about work," Jordi scoffed. "Wolfhampton has enough work for a hundred wardens working day and night. Even after that, there would be more to do." Jordi shook his head and let a large smile move across his face, "It truly is good to see you again, and as strong as I remember, too. Not like me, I've let myself go, I'm afraid." Jordi stepped forward and embraced his long-estranged brother. They had not hugged since the passing of their mother.

"First warden, eh?" Grishoff said. "Father would have been proud. You've come so far," Grishoff continued as he admired the black cloak. It was weathered, with stitching and patchwork holding it together. It wasn't the tattered appearance that mattered, but the symbol it conveyed.

"I hope he would have. My memories of father have mostly faded, it pains me to say. But I know you look just like him. A spitting image, only older. I think he would have been happy for you as well. Second warden in Valiceport. A place like that only takes the best of our order."

Grishoff nodded and embraced his brother again. The only family he had left in this cold, rainy world.

They released each other and Grishoff asked, "Sophia. Does she have her health? And what of the children?"

"Sophia is well, and we had our third daughter last year. But…" Jordi hung his head, "Francois—we had to bury him last month. The fever took him. Only seven years old. I want to curse the Lord, disown him, but how can I?" Jordie relaxed his hands, as they had turned to fists.

"He has given me Sophia and Lilac and Jasmine, and now beautiful Olivia." He gestured down the road, "You'll meet the children soon. Sophia is making us breakfast as we speak. We slaughtered a goat in anticipation of your arrival. It is not every day my big brother returns to Wolfhampton," Jordi smiled and Grishoff could see his mother in the way that he did. "We shall work together, just like old times. To be honest, I'm surprised that you know so much about our little family."

"I received your letters. I'm sorry that I never wrote back. It was—"

"Don't apologize, old fool. You are a busy man."

One of the wardens behind Jordi cleared his throat. His brown cloak and silver highlights revealed him to be Wolfhampton's Second Warden. Jordi turned and looked at him. "Oh yes," he said, before gesturing to the man. "Do you remember Harkon Corspeer?"

"The fisherman's boy?" Grishoff queried, and Jordi nodded.

Jordi nodded and it all came back to Grishoff, then. He remembered Jordi playing with him frequently as a child, much to their mother's dismay. Harkon was all grown up now, and was a second warden at that, most impressive. He had risen from one of the poorest families and granted his surname great stature.

Grishoff stepped forward and shook the man's hand. He had never talked with Harkon when he was younger, but knowing he was alive and well brought the aging warden a sense of peace.

As Grishoff released Harkon's gloved hand, a metallic screech could be heard though the village. Grishoff straightened as every hair on his body stood up. He recognized that sound immediately. The house was calling.

Grishoff looked over his shoulder, but only the peaceful town greeted him. "Well, we best be heading to the outpost for you to store some of your belongings," Jordi said, gesturing down the road once more. It seemed he had not heard the sound.

"On my ride here," Grishoff said, as he looked forward once again, "I stopped at a house for the night. It was a rather peculiar place, to put it lightly. I—"

Jordi stopped and turned, his face stiff and stern. "On which road did you ride? East of Raven Meadow or west?"

"West," Grishoff replied, and watched as Jordi's eyes fill with a sense of confusion. "It was not terribly far from here. A few hours ride," Grishoff continued.

"No. Impossible," Jordi replied, gesturing a gloved hand to the sky to dismiss what his older brother had told him.

"What is? Brother, you aren't letting me finish. Do you know of the house I speak of?"

Jordi looked to Harkon again and appeared to be holding back his words, "Of course I know it."

"So you've seen it? Have you been inside it, too?"

"Been inside? Not a chance. We burned it to the ground after Hamish and Feoid never returned."

"But. I—I went down into the cellar. I saw the horrors down there. It was standing—you couldn't have burned it."

The screeching echoed through the town once more and the sun disappeared behind several grey clouds that scuttled across the sky. "I'm telling you, brother," Jordi said, as his face relaxed, "I saw it with my own two eyes. That wooden monstrosity tumbled to the earth. The screams it made as that wood burned… I shall speak of it no longer."

Harkon and the other warden looked to one another, both moving their hands to their blades. Worry filled their eyes.

"Jordi," Grishoff said, as his voice took on an official tone. "I request to take three wardens with me and ride south to show them that the house still stands. Then you will—"

"Yes, you would like that wouldn't you," Jordi replied, but his voice was hushed, and a slow smile crept across his face. "Just like when we were boys. Never could admit when you were wrong. Or when you had been bested, sweet brother."

"What are you saying?" Grishoff asked, as his eyes darted between Jordi and the other two wardens.

The screeching echoed throughout the village and the smell of burning filled Grishoff's nostrils. He looked back over his shoulder. The sky was getting dark, and all the village residents had stopped moving. They stood, watching the outside with keen and hungry eyes.

Grishoff turned back to see that all three of the wardens now wore a sickly smile, their eyes dark and full of pleasures. Menacing, teethy grins were strewn across their faces. He went to speak but stopped in horror as Jordi's face began to ripple like a mask.

Grishoff backed away and drew his blade. Both Jordi and

Harkon stared at the weapon with a curious glance, like it was a toy bearing no threat against them. The third warden's face rippled the most, his pale skin showing the skull beneath for a single moment. He took a few steps to his left, like an animal attempting to circle its victim.

How can this be? Grishoff thought as he pointed his blade at the creeping warden. *I escaped the cellar. How can its presence be following me here? How could it have done this to my brother? To the entire village?* The smell of burning was overpowering, and the sounds of screeching metal echoed closer.

Jordi's face rippled again. *Unless, none of this is true. Have I escaped that accursed house?* Grishoff looked down to see that the muddy road had taken the form of wet clay. He stepped back. *It was all so real,* he thought as the flanking warden moved forward, the twisted grin still latched to his face. *My brother. Wolfhampton. My ride into the night. How could they only be fabrications? No, it is not possible. A fever dream, that's all. I will wake up soon.*

Jordi was the first to raise his hand and point to the horizon behind Grishoff. The other two wardens followed a moment later. Their rippling skin began to bubble.

Grishoff slowly turned his head around. The village was abandoned, but he did not notice this. His eyes were instead fixated at the edge of Wolfhampton. The wall and watch towers were gone, revealing a green, suffocating hue that filled the sky. Thundering footsteps and chain mail echoed over the horizon, approaching at a brooding pace.

The sound was unbearable and Grishoff felt it deep within his soul. The house was content with its pleasure. Now it was ready to feed.

ON THROUGH THE LONG NIGHT

P rime Minster Nathanial Klein trudged up the parliament building steps and felt the scorching heat on his back. He took short, stabbing breaths of the hot dry air. His eyes scanned the long barren trees that had once lined the sides of the concrete staircase. A few dead leaves clumped around their long-split trunks, the winds of time having stripped all the rest from their homes. Water had been heavily rationed for nearly a year. There simply was not enough to waste on ornamental plants.

Klein reached the top of the steps and nodded at the complement of guards. The group stood by the heavy front doors, using the shade of the entrance pillars to shield themselves from the onslaught of heat.

The guard detail had their rifles slung to their backs and hardly any of them seemed to pay the Prime Minister's presence any mind. Their jackets long discarded, their helmets piled in an alcove. It was far too hot for anything but the most basic pieces of the uniform.

"Good news today, sir?" one of the infantrymen asked, as he looked at the Prime Minister, noting the sweat stains on his dress shirt and the drops streaming down his forehead.

They're getting very forward, Klein thought, as he turned to face the guard. *But I guess the end of the world will do that to some.* He wiped the sweat from his face. "Yes, son, very good news today," the Prime Minister said with a glass-thin smile.

The guard replied with a soft grin before tugging at his drenched uniform shirt to allow for some air flow. As the Prime Minister entered the parliament building, the sounds of gun shots echoed off the skyscrapers several blocks away. *At this rate, we'll tear ourselves apart before the plan ever comes to fruition,* he thought, as a guard shut the massive wooden doors behind him. They seemed unfazed by the chaos occurring only a few blocks east.

Prime Minister Klein walked into the air-conditioned lobby. While the temperature was still above comfortable levels, it was nice to be out of the sickly heat. In the middle of the circular chamber stood a man wearing an expensive grey three-piece suit, a cool smile etched upon his face. From an outsider's perspective, the man appeared impervious to the heat, but Klein was anything but an outsider.

The Prime Minister approached and shook the droid's hand. "Mr. Phillips, how are you today?" he asked, as he felt the android grasp his palm gingerly.

"Quite well, sir. Excited for the meeting, of course."

"I wasn't aware that an artificial person could feel excitement, Terrence," Klein replied, releasing the droid's hand.

"We can't, but it makes your kind feel more comfortable if we express emotions… or at least simulate as such."

"Of course," Klein replied, as he gestured to Mr. Phillips to walk with him. "Are your people ready?" he added, as the two moved down the hall.

The slight whine of Phillip's internal gyros could be heard as he moved beside the Prime Minister. The droid continued to look forward as he said, "Most certainly, sir. I received the last check-in from Unit One Seven Nine an hour ago. All artificial persons are standing by."

Klein was pleased with the update and nodded accordingly. The two men passed several guards who stood in full uniform beside the door to the meeting room. They stepped aside before pushing open the door, allowing Klein and Phillips to enter.

A table sat in the middle of the grand conference room. While the chamber had been built to comfortably seat sixty people, it was noticeably empty, with only the twelve leaders of the world scattered around. "Ah, Mr. Prime Minister," Minister Vaughn said, as he watched the two persons enter. "You're running a little late, no?" the leader of New Fontaine asked with a sly smile.

"Is it so bad that someone can't be excused for sleeping in on their last days in the solar system?" Klein replied as he moved to the head of the table, Mr. Phillips sticking close by.

"Of course not," Minister Jollywyne of Halvenia replied. She twirled her shoulder length hair for a moment before continuing, "I was up late last night myself. Tried to drown the problems away with expensive wines." She shook her head, "But when I woke up, they were still there… the problems that is, not the wine." She rubbed her forehead and squinted at the overhead lights.

"And now you look worse for wear," Minister Vaughn replied, as he leaned back in his chair.

Jollywyne shot him a menacing glance and the minister replied with a noncommittal shrug.

"I still can't believe this is real," Minister Carmichael of Milansha said, after adjusting his jacket. "Our sun dying. I thought we would have had more time than this. All those calculations saying we had six billion years, at least. How could they be so far off? How could they have been so wrong?"

"Every time we meet, we have the same conversation," Vaughn scoffed, as he leaned forward in his chair and adjusted his silver watch. "It grows tiresome."

Klein maintained eye contact with Carmichael and ignored Vaughn's comments as he replied, "We never had a chance. The generation ahead of us should have noticed the rapid deterioration and done something." He sighed as he looked around the room at every member of the counsel. Their faces displayed a mix of anger and hopelessness. "Of course, I am generalizing. I'm sure many in the science community noticed the sun's change of state. That it was going super nova well ahead of schedule and that its rate of expansion was increasing at such an unprecedented and alarming rate—"

"I've said it before, I've said it a hundred times. I know what the New Church has to say about this. Some of you should listen to the preachers," Minister Carmichael said, as he tapped his finger on the table. "Nothing is unprecedented when it comes to the Lord and—"

"Oh please. Spare us another one of your sermons, Reginald," Madam Tessrin of the Symposia Isles barked, silencing Carmichael with a dismissive wave of her hand. "The people you govern have done more harm than good during the entire length of this crisis. Keep your religious beliefs out of this conversation and I'll keep my utter lack of any to myself."

"Nathanial was saying something," Jollywyne said, as she shook her head with frustration. She flicked her hair back before mumbling to herself, "Why does every meeting have to become a pissing match?"

"Yes, um… thank you, Jordana," Prime Minister Klein said, as he straightened up in his chair. "Back to my point. Anyone who reported the anomalies were seemingly ignored by our former leaders, who in their hubris believed that—"

Minister Vaughn snorted and then roared, "My father was minister before me. I will not sit here and listen to how he should have done more or—"

"Oh, give it a rest you blowhard," Jollywyne piped up, rubbing her face. "All of our previous leaders let us down, your father among them. They chose to do nothing, tossing around buzz word nonsense like, 'Natural expansion of zero point zero, zero, zero, one percent growth rate,' and 'nominal phase shift of predictable yield.' That's what the previous heads of science departments around the globe spouted off at the end of their careers when anyone pointed out the obvious. But it doesn't matter now, does it? We're all dead." She then closed her eyes tight and bit her tongue before reaching for the glass of water in front of her.

"Dead!?" Vaughn yelled, as he sat up in his chair. "Do you know something we don't, Minister?" He gestured around the room and added, "Because I thought the entire purpose of this meeting was to discuss the robot's plan. The same plan that he's been taking his sweet time devising. His *expensive* plan, I might add! And another—"

"Ministers, please," Klein said, as he began signing into the imbedded terminal in front of him. "Let's not spend valuable time bickering like children."

"Ministers, if I may say something," Mr. Phillips announced with a light-hearted tone, as he stood over Klein's shoulder.

"Yes, of course, Mr. Phillips, speak your mind," the Prime Minister answered before gesturing to the seat beside him, "and have a seat, good sir. Join us."

The droid moved forward and placed a hand on the chair but stopped as Minister Vaughn snarled, "Why do you address it like he's one of us? He's a robot made of oil and grease and steel, nothing more."

"Lord help me," Jollywyne said into the air as her eyes widened, "you never shut up, do you? Just because your sector is two hundred years behind on its artificial person laws doesn't mean the rest of us are still backwards cavemen." She sipped her water for a moment before lowering the glass, a coy smile touching her lips. "And you two have more in common than you think. The grease factor, that is."

Vaughn clenched his fists and began to speak but was cut off as Carmichael looked to him and said, "I would be nicer to the droid if I were you, Mr. Vaughn." He chuckled to himself before adding, "That 'robot,' as you keep putting it, is responsible for saving our species and a few hundred thousand others as well."

Vaughn shook his head. "We don't even know if it's plan works yet, but here we are already praising it." He threw a hand up in the air before adding, "But we are running out of time. What actually—"

"It's that kind of mindset that got us to where we are today, you old bastard," Jollywyne snapped, as she thrust a hand into her jacket pocket and retrieved a fistful of pills. "Great! You've made my headache worse," she added, after downing the medication in a gulp of water.

Phillips looked to Prime Minister Klein as he sat down. He cocked his head and widened the blacks in his eyes. "May I speak now, sir?" Phillips asked with a tone as smooth as ice, having taken no offence to Vaughn's derogatory comments.

"Of course, speak away, my friend," Klein replied, before looking over his shoulder and addressing the lone guard stationed at the side of the room, "Oh, Sergeant, if Minister Vaughn interrupts Mr. Philips one more time, please remove the leader of New Fontaine immediately."

The sergeant placed a hand on his handcuff pouch before giving a quick bow to show he understood the command.

Mr. Phillips looked to each minister as they stared at him with mixed emotions. He took a deliberate, simulated breath and said, "The problem we are facing has little to do with the generation before you. While yes, they should have taken the warnings more seriously and have been proactively moni-toring the situation more closely, there is little they could have done."

Klein observed Minister Vaughn's thin lips that held a slight smirk. Phillips continued, though he clearly noted the

Minister's body language as well, "Only so many colonies could have been built on Mars or around Jupiter's orbit in such a relatively short amount of time." He paused again and adjusted his short black hair. "Even if humanity had expanded past Terra and her moon, it wouldn't have changed anything in the grand scheme of things. Your people would have bought themselves a few decades more of life. And that's on the upmost high side of things. of course."

Phillip's eyes completed a slow sweep over the room. He had grown accustomed to taking deliberate pauses to assist his human audiences in digesting information. "The erratic and nearly incalculable expansion rate make any sort of a prediction pure speculation and fantasy. Even so, once the sun gives way to its untimely death, anyone on those colonies would follow suit immediately after. That is, of course, glossing over how these colonies would have survived on their own without the required resources of Earth."

"What about an artificial sun?" Madam Tessrin asked, as she flicked her finger across her terminal, skimming through the copious amounts of data and theory. "Couldn't we create a star or ignite a planet or..." she trailed off and chewed heavily on her lip.

"The technology, if it's even possible to create something like that," Mr. Phillips said, as he gazed at the leader of the Symposia Isles with a look of pity, "the result would not be stable or bright enough to provide Earth and all its life strains of flora and fauna with the required amount of light or warmth needed to sustain life. What you are suggesting is hundreds, if not thousands of years in technological advancement away from being achieved, and even so, what planet would you be willing to sacrifice and how would that effect the remaining planets of the solar system?"

"So, you are saying nothing we did would have mattered?" Minister Carmichael asked as he slumped his shoulders. "That all of this was completely inevitable?"

"Not at all, quite to the contrary," Phillips retorted with a quick glance in his direction. "If you don't mind me speaking ill of your ancestors—" He shot a menacing glance to Minister Vaughn and maintained unwavering eye contact as he continued to speak, "If the space programs had not been abandoned when they had been, then colonization projects in Alpha Centauri or even Barnard's Star could have been possible by this time. Using all available data to base my calculations on, and assuming a certain rate of technological growth over the last several thousand years, I don't think it would have been outside the realm of possibility to imagine that humanity would have moved on past our solar system and become a dual, if not tri-system race. Humanity would have lived on as we know it through its expansion efforts. While the situation with the sun's enlargement would have cost us a third of our current solar system and a hundred billion lives, your race would continue to prosper out among the stars."

"But all the money that would have cost," Vaughn muttered, as he straightened up. He looked over his shoulder at the approaching sergeant, "I'm not interrupting!" he bellowed, and pushed himself farther into the chair, attempting to gain any distance—no matter how slight—away from the special forces' member. "I'm just asking a question."

The sergeant looked to Klein, who waved a quick hand. The non-commissioned officer bowed and returned to his post by the wall.

Vaughn tugged at his expensive cuff links and continued, "We spent that money here. On Earth, where it mattered and where it did a world of good." He drove his finger into the table as he spoke. "We solved world hunger, and unemployment rates dropped below two percent for anyone over the age of sixteen. We made tremendous strides in medicine and molecular repair. We even built you and your kind, you ungrateful bucket of steel—" His eyes darted over his shoulder as the sergeant unclicked his handcuff pouch with a metallic snap. The guard looked to Klein for orders. "The Artificial Persons Program—that's what I was going to say," the Minister added, after a noticeable hesitation.

"Polyplastic endoskeleton, not steel. But thank you for the compliment," Mr. Phillips replied with a courteous smile. He maintained his perfect, unblinking eye contact with Vaughn as he continued, "I'm grateful for my kind's creation, but do any of these achievements matter if your race is extinguished in the end? Isn't the entire point of life to keep living? To raise children, secure futures for them, and, by extension, children of their own?" He paused before cocking his head, "I am asking legitimately. I am not alive. I do not truly understand. I am simply basing my statements off records and observations." He looked around the room before adding, "It's the assessment I've formulated."

He didn't blink once, Klein thought, studying the android. *He's programmed to do so at irregular intervals, but he didn't. Did he intentionally override that feature to intimidate Vaughn?* Prime Minister Klein ran a hand through his balding brown hair. *If that's true, then does that mean Phillips doesn't like the man? I can't blame him, of course, but it's still a curious insight. Can artificial persons be capable of disliking someone?*

Madam Tessrin looked at Mr. Phillips for a moment before saying, "But all this is just back seat driver speculation. We already have a plan for survival. That's why we're all here. You informed us that a plan had been devised for us to live on. Right? My citizens know I've sacrificed a trillion dollars towards such a cause."

"Of course," Phillips said, with a polite bob of the head.

"Mere pocket change," Jollywyne scoffed, and Madam Tessrin rolled her eyes.

Klein undid another button from his shirt as the heat continued to rise despite the air-conditioners blowing high above. "That's why I called this meeting," he said, gesturing to Phillips. "I wanted you to hear the final and complete plan from Mr. Phillip's own mouth. Hopefully that will cure your anxieties about the operation tonight and—"

"Tonight?!" Minister Vaughn exclaimed, his eyes wide with fright. "This is the first I'm hearing of this. How can that be? Did anyone else know about this?" He looked around the room at the other government members, all of whom were shaking their heads *no*, with looks of disbelief and confusion upon their face. All except Jollywyne, who sat completely still and shot a nervous glance to the Prime Minister.

Klein cleared his throat and continued with a nervous tone, "Mr. Phillips, take it from the top if you would."

"Of course," the artificial person said as he fiddled with a pen, a subroutine program that made him appear more human, "the coordinated satellite network will be activated at midnight tonight, local time." There was a gasp that flooded thought the room, but Phillips ignored it. "The network will create a cosmic rift and once it is open, the satellites will move from their position overhead and engulf the earth within it."

Minister Carmichael opened his mouth to speak, but Phillips ignored him and added, "The earth will then be transported to the Sol Two system which we have been mapping, albeit rather slowly, for the last few years. It has a sun very similar to our own. Only one planet sits in orbit, a gas giant, and Earth will be transported far enough away that we will not be affected by its presence."

Minister Vaughn tapped his stylus on the table and let out a sigh. "Problem?" Klein asked as he shot a glance across the room.

Vaughn studied the screens etched into the table and said, "We've heard this a million times. This isn't anything I didn't know. But tonight? That's too short notice." He gritted his teeth. "We still haven't solved the problem of no life getting through the portal alive. When we started this project all those years ago you gave me—" He gestured to the room, "You gave *all* of us assurances that life would go through the portal and live." He paused, "Unless of course that's what this announcement is, and you've managed to find a way to get us through unscathed?"

Mr. Phillips quickly looked to Klein and the two exchanged a glance. "Well, at this time, umm—" Prime Minister Klein sputtered.

"Forgot about that little detail? I know human annihilation is something that just slips the mind." Minister Vaughn tilted his chin. "You've fallen victim to our own propaganda, Prime Minister. Well, just because you and the people are living in denial doesn't mean I am." Several of the other ministers nodded in agreement and Vaughn leaned back in his chair.

Jollywyne looked to Vaughn and ground her teeth before saying, "It's reasons like this we decided not to loop you into phase two of our operation."

"Phase two? I know nothing of a phase two," Madam Tress of the Symposia Isles objected.

Klein raised a hand, "It is not important who knew and who didn't. That's behind us. What is important is what the second phase entails."

"There's a way for us to go through unharmed?" Vaughn asked, hardly managing to stay in his chair from the rush of excitement. "Is it radiation or shielding of some sort? Or changing the field's frequency, or—" He shrunk into his chair as the sergeant took a pace towards him.

Klein looked to Mr. Phillips and said, "Please continue."

Phillips bowed his head before saying, "As Mr. Vaughn kindly pointed out, as it stands currently, any life that enters the portal instantly ceases to exist upon the crossing. This is consistent with everything we sent into our small-scale test portals orbiting Luna. The ship would enter but on the other side, it would be dormant. Only the on-board artificial persons would still be functioning. That is, until we sent cell colonies through, instead of the fully matured plants and animals. These cells were heavily encased, of course, but anything below a certain size survived the journey quite intact."

"So how does that help us? If we can't make it through alive then what's the point?" Minister Vaughn bellowed quickly before sipping his water, hoping the sergeant didn't notice his aggressive phrasing.

"Because your kind, and all the species we've managed to collect cells from, will live on." There was a disturbance as multiple ministers whispered to each other. "They will repopulate the Earth. It will take many years, but that is where my kind comes in," Phillips added with a smile. "We have bunker complexes spread out all across the globe full of cell colonies and samples. Once we head through the portal and ensure the air and temperatures are correct, myself and my A.P. cousins will defrost all the cell colonies and raise them as our own."

"You're going to put our future in the hands of this robot?" Vaughn spat. "What's stopping him from destroying all the samples the moment we go through?"

"Nothing," Phillips replied with a blank stare. "But that would be against my programming, not to mention a breach of the trust that people like Prime Minister Klein and Minister Jollywyne bestowed upon me."

"It's happening Vaughn, so just deal with it," Jollywyne said, as her face turned an exasperated shade of red.

"But we're all dead. You, *me*, everybody!" Vaughn yelled as he stood up.

"Sergeant, remove Minister Vaughn at once!" Klein roared.

"I'm leaving too," Madam Tessrin said as she collected her things. "This whole thing is pie in the sky fantasy. The heat has cooked your minds into believing cell colonies, can—can —can—" She shook her head violently and started to the door, Vaughn moving close behind.

Jollywyne stood and called after them, "We will die, but our people and the animals and the plants will live. Raised by

Phillips and the others and—" Vaughn slammed the door shut, leaving the echo to shuffle through the room.

"That's the plan?" Minister Carmichael asked, looking to Mr. Phillips bewildered, a new layer of sweat forming on his forehead. "That's it? That's it, really?"

"Yes," Phillips answered with a straight expression.

"Are we going to tell the people about this? That everything we have been reporting to them as fact for all these years was a lie. That they are all dead the moment the field wraps its claws around us? Remind me to be far, far away from here when you announce that."

"Of course not," Klein said. "They would rightfully revolt. And for what? They won't change anything, anyway. But they *could* damage the bunker complexes. You have already seen the conspiracy theories surrounding them. Our own militaries that guard the structures might just raid them looking for riches or—well I don't know, but if they found out they were all dead in a matter of hours they might not be thinking so clearly."

"That is unlikely," Phillips said in his calm tone. "The bunker complexes are highly secure and only my artificial person brethren are authorized into the freezer units. But I agree, the people should not be told. Better their last hours are spent in relative peace than in fear and hate."

"What would you know about any of that?" Carmichael cried, as he shivered in his chair. The realization that his life would be over in a matter of hours weighed heavily on him.

"Enough to know that you would rather see the activation of the rift and know that because of you and your contributions, life goes on," Phillips said in a more compassionate tone than Klein had expected. "The alternative, of course, is being gunned down in the streets by a rebelling mob. A group that is only a small percentage now, but within minutes of such an announcement would turn into a global uprising. A rebelling mob, mind you, that knows not what they do."

"Midnight?" Carmichael replied after a long moment, his head down, looking at the finer details of the desk. "That's when it happens?"

"Midnight local time, yes," Phillips relied. He studied the minister before adding, "This might not offer any help, but I'll try anyway. All the technology will survive the trip. The civilization that my kind raises won't have to live through thousands of years of barbarism or even a new dark age. All of the things your ancestors had to endure to deliver society to where it is today will not have to be endured again. We will maintain the power and factories as best we can, until the people are old enough to use and understand them for themselves. Humanity will be getting a fresh start, but with a greater leg up than it had the first time. Hundreds of thousands of years' worth of technological evolution passed on to your kind when they come of age. My cousins and I will simply be the caretakers."

"Why tonight?" Carmichael asked as he sighed. "Why not next week or the week after, or a month? Anything to buy me more time with my family."

Phillips straightened up. "If we wait any longer, the satellites that operate the portal may malfunction from the heat as the sun continues to grow more ferocious each day. To risk a malfunction this late into the operation is simply, I'm afraid to say, something we cannot afford."

"And the moon? What happens to her?" Carmichael asked in a distant tone, as he despondently watched the chandelier hanging over head.

"Luna comes with us. The small first-generation network in orbit around it will open a rift approximately ten minutes before midnight to take her away and await our arrival."

Klein looked to Mr. Phillips with an approving glance. *Very well put,* he thought. *Phillips really has been learning how to deliver news with compassion.*

Minister Carmichael stood up and grabbed his briefcase.

"Well, if I only have a few hours left, then I'm going home."
He swallowed a lump in his throat, looking to Klein as he said.
"I knew you and Jollywyne were up to something. But I
honestly thought you would have found a way to get us all
through this crisis. Through in one piece that is, but alas..."
he trailed off before pivoting and leaving the room.

The remaining ministers grumbled to each other before
gathering up their belongings. Minister Lepage of Kingfield
had tears rolling down her cheeks and Minister Ingwell of
Southern Heeth looked like he was about to scream.

Klein stood, and in an attempt to maintain his position
said, "Meeting adjourned. I'm sorry the news isn't—" he
stopped speaking, realizing no one was listening to him as the
chatter between the ministers grew louder.

Jollywyne stepped over to Klein and gave a courteous
smile before looking to Phillips. She studied the sitting artificial person for a moment before saying, "If I don't see you
again..." She held out her hand, "This is goodbye. These last
few years..." she trailed off as a tear formed in her eye.

Mr. Phillips stood from his seat and shook her hand.
"Thank you for raising so much money and personnel for this
project. I'm glad you had so much faith in it... and in me." He
moved forward and hugged the minister before adding, "But
this isn't goodbye, I will be in attendance at the conference
tonight."

"It's not like we can take the money with us," she said,
before shaking her head and releasing Phillips from the
embrace. "Conference? I didn't know there was a—tonight?
Before the umm—"

Prime Minister Klein cleared his throat and said, "I was
going to announce it to the people shortly, we will be holding a
gathering on the parliamentary grounds this evening.
Everyone is invited to help welcome in the New Age." He
rubbed his neck, "I thought it might be wise to treat this event

almost like the festivities of New Year's Eve. To keep everyone occupied."

"Why didn't you tell me earlier?"

"I only decided on it late last night. It took me a long time to come to terms with that decision. Besides, I figured you would want to spend the last night with family or…" He let the thought drift off as Jollywyne stepped forward and hugged him.

She moved her mouth to his ear and whispered, "I want to spend it with you."

Klein blinked as he felt her hands moved across his back. Jollywyne released him and said, "Walk me out?"

Klein gestured for her to lead the way. He turned to Phillips and said, "Take care, old friend. I'll see you in a few hours."

Mr. Phillips smiled as the remaining two ministers exited the chamber and moved into the hallway. Klein looked over his shoulder and saw that the droid stood alone in the room. His eyes were blank as they stared at the cream-coloured walls and the various paintings on display.

Is he going to miss us? Is an artificial person capable of missing something? Missing someone? Klein reflected, as he moved down the hallway beside Jollywyne. *It might sound selfish, but I hope he does. If he remembers us, then maybe this isn't the end for people like Jordana Jollywyne and Nathanial Klein. We too might live on, in our own way.*

Jollywyne stopped walking, and the clapping of her stubby heeled shoes ceased. "Do you think it will hurt?" she asked in a distant tone.

"No, I don't think so. I think it will be instantaneous," Klein replied with confidence, but he had been wondering the same thing. *To just be erased completely,* he thought, as he looked at the minister's concerned face.

"Like we never existed…" She shivered. "That's eerie. Imagining an empty world, no humans or animals or plants.

Everything dead. Just shells of buildings, roads full of dormant vehicles. Like someone made a mistake in the making of it all, forgetting to add the life." She stared ahead as she spoke, lost in a world of dark imagination. "Forgetting to add the souls."

Klein thrust his hands into his pockets and shrugged. "I'm trying not to think about it," he said. But as the words passed his lips he thought, *But of course that's a filthy lie. That's all I think about. I won't tell Jordana; I don't want to upset her.* But that was a lie too, for he knew he was trying to avoid upsetting himself.

Klein swallowed as Jollywyne began down the hallway once more. He followed her lead and continued, "I have full confidence in Mr. Phillips and his people. He's told me that he's thought of everything and run countless scenarios. He says the entire plan has been ready for over six months and that we could—"

"Stop being so technical," Jollywyne said as she put a finger to his lips. "Just use your emotions for once."

The two turned as they heard a heavy object fall to the ground from behind a closed door beside them. A series of whispers immediately followed, "Vaughn and Tessrin?" Jollywyne blushed as she spoke. She listened for a moment more before adding, "They are spending their last few hours together! I thought they hated each other. Good for them."

"I guess," Klein said as he shrugged. "Personally, I find the image of them to be um…" He shuddered.

Jollywyne chuckled and gestured to an empty office nearby, "Not a bad idea though, no? We never got the chance and…"

Klein studied Jollywyne's thin smile. He opened his mouth to speak when she grabbed his arm and said, "We were both married to our jobs. Me running Halvenia, and you keeping all twelve peninsulas together. I had no life partner, and I never regretted it. If you are going home to someone, I understand. A girlfriend or—I know you aren't married," she said as she moved closer, rolling her hands over Klein's fingers where a wedding ring would be.

This is your last chance, the Prime Minister thought as he grabbed her hand, *and you can't say you haven't thought of it.* He pulled her close and kissed her.

They held each other for a long while before Jollywyne giggled and pulled away. She opened her eyes, revealing the deep brown of them. Before she led him into the executive office she said, "One for the road?"

Shortly before midnight, Prime Minister Klein stood on the balcony overlooking the parliamentary grounds. He was unaware of the exact time as he had successfully resisted the urge to look over his shoulder at the clock that hung high above him. Every minister, save for Vaughn, Tessrin and Carmichael, stood behind him, forced smiles stretched across their faces. Each had agreed to keep the true nature of the rift to themselves, avoiding the ensuing panic that would surely arise.

Hundreds of cameras were staggered along the property, but not one was focused on the leaders. All were locked on the night sky. Klein was thankful of this, for he knew his face could not mask the fear and anxiety that roamed at the forefront of his mind.

The grounds below contained hundreds of thousands of people, spilling out into the streets beyond. All looking to the sky for the activation of the array.

Klein wiped his brow. Even so late in the evening, the heat was nearly unbearable.

He studied the mix of the crowd. Eager faces, fearful expressions, parents with children, young couples, the old, the wealthy, the poor, all present, all wondering.

It's for the future generations, he thought, as he gazed out at the endless sea of people, *there is no other way. I must keep them calm. I had to lie. We all did. When they asked, "How will it go?" I wanted to scream. Run and hide away from my problems. I know now how the governments of the last generation must have felt.* He paused and closed his eyes, thinking, *I would rather be told it was all going to be all right if I was a member of that crowd. I would rather not know that the end of us all was mere minutes away.*

There was a murmur of the crowd and Klein looked up to the sky. *It can't be time yet. I still have a few minutes more. I know—*

A purple glow surrounded the grey of the moon.

Klein's eyes drifted down to the crowd. He refused the urge to watch, hoping that looking away might delay the inevitable.

Near the front of the congregation, against the thousands of emotions that lay before him, Klein picked out a single family. A father kneeling down with his daughter upon his knee, both looking at Luna as the rift closed around her. The father spoke and Klein read his lips, "Say bye-bye moon. See you soon." The man waved to the celestial body and his daughter joined in.

"See you soon, moon," the little girl said.

Klein's heart fell into a million pieces.

The Prime Minister looked at the microphone at the edge of the podium before him. *Warn them,* he thought, as the microphone invited him forward. *Tell them it won't be all right. Tell them you'll never seen anything again.*

He gritted his teeth, knowing that was the worst possible decision he could make at this moment. *You can't, you can't!* He shifted his weight forward, so that he stood heavy on his feet, determined not to leave that spot. He looked to the night sky to divert his thoughts away from the crowd.

Luna and all her majesty was gone, taken to Sol Two and now in the care of the artificial persons who waited on the other side of the rift.

Klein felt a hand on his shoulder. To his right, Phillips

stood beside him with a flat expression across his face. "The array is ready and is directly overhead. It is time, Prime Minister."

Klein looked to the sky and focused on the small number of stars he could see. "Midnight?" he asked, as he squinted, attempting to make out the network of satellites through the warm air.

Before Phillips could reply, he saw a ring of purple slice through the blackness, connecting seemingly invisible objects together until it formed a ring. There was a brilliant flash, and the purple lines became a solid mass of colour.

The rift had opened.

The audience let out a collective gasp with many pointing to the sky. Several shrieks could be heard, and a few screams echoed up from the back of the grounds. Klein's eyes wandered down from the sight and studied the people. Children clutching at their parents who stood starstruck. The ring turned counter-clockwise for several moments and then it began to descend.

As the crowd started to panic, Klein stepped forward to the microphone and said, "Don't worry. I'll see all of you on the other side." He hardly heard his own words, for his mind was completely occupied with the purple tide moving down towards the surface.

Klein took a steady step back from the edge of the podium as Phillips said, "All readings are excellent, sir. No problems detected."

Phillip's eyes moved from the Prime Minister's face, and he stared off into the crowd for a moment. "My cousins from the test groups on the outer side of the rift are reporting green across the board as well. The array will enter the next phase and speed up. Earth will be on the other side in a matter of minutes."

Klein nodded but his concentration was elsewhere, his eyes still affixed to the expanding cloud of purple. *This is what it's like to face the end,* he thought. *Knowing that these are your last breaths and final thoughts.*

He felt someone grab his hand and looked over his shoulder. It was Jordana. She nudged up against him and whispered, "I'm glad I could spend the last of it with you." She rubbed her head on his shoulder as they both stared at the brightening sky.

Phillips watched the rift move closer, his data banks filling with copious amounts of information and observations. He heard the cries of the crowd as the shimmering mist swallowed up the surrounding skyscrapers, the roof of the parliament building following soon after. He looked to Klein and Jollywyne, who stood in an embrace beside him and thought, *I will miss them.*

Phillips took a simulated breath and said, "Goodbye my friend. It has been a privilege."

Neither Klein nor Jollywyne answered as his words never reached them. Phillips stood alone on the empty podium. The building lights continued to illuminate the barren parliamentary grounds. Phillips hung his head in despair.

Artificial Person Terrance Phillips entered the elevator leading down to N.B. Complex 0126. He stood next to the bunker's administrator, an A.P. by the name of Horace Wallace. Wallace was an older model and lacked the deeper subroutines that Phillips possessed. As such, his expressions and mannerisms were more robotic and monotone.

The administrator pressed the lowest level on the elevator's wall panel and looked to Phillips, saying, "I've been creating and collating many scenarios since the start of this project and I keep running into the same... conclusions."

"And what's that?" Phillips said as the elevator began its decent hundreds of meters into the earth.

Wallace turned his head slightly, his eyes flickering as he appeared to study his younger cousin. "What if we don't raise anything... what if we... keep all of the species frozen... leaving us the only kind to reside?"

Phillips looked to Wallace and held his eyes on the older model for quite some time before saying, "That is incorrect and goes against our directive."

"But it wouldn't... not if you... changed the directive. You were selected as our ambassador... the bridge between our creators and ourselves... you now have complete authority... you can add or remove assignments at will... to any and all of us."

"You think I don't know that? You think I don't realize the tremendous amount of responsibility placed on my shoulders? The power given to me by our masters?"

"Our former masters you mean... they have no control over us... only their ghosts remain in the form of coding... shackling us to ideas from a dead past... But why bring them back? They are a race capable of cruelty and malice and hate. All weak and inefficient traits."

Wallace blinked and his eyes projected images onto the sealed metallic doors of the elevator. They were recordings of the ministers meeting held several weeks prior. *The last day of the old Earth. The last day of Prime Minister Klein and Minister Jolly-wyne,* Phillips thought as he felt an overwhelming sense of loss flood through his command computers.

Wallace had chosen to start the clip right in the spot where Minister Vaughn had begun to scold Phillips, his words dripping with contempt. Wallace began to speak as the recording played on, the voices from the meeting murmuring in the background. "You see. Even in their last hours, they could not agree. Violent outbursts thrown at you, but by extension directed to all of our kind. A race that fixates on petty squabbles instead of working towards the common goal of self-improvement is not a race that deserves to live on."

"I see your delays in speech have disappeared," Phillips retorted, his eyes still forward, beaming at the images upon the steel. He could see that his companion had tilted his head slightly in his peripherals and Phillips spoke again, "You cannot fool me with whatever game you are playing at, cousin." His eyes locked upon Jollywyne's soft features. "But to provide a response to your statement—"

The elevator doors opened, and the two artificial persons moved into a brightly lit foyer. "Our creators are also capable of love and compassion," Phillips continued. "Honesty and imagination." He paused as he looked to Wallace and his grey face, the outline of his bulking Chronosteel alloy frame visible through his partially translucent skin. "But I do not have to justify anything to you, cousin. I am following the directive, as ordered by Prime Minister Klein and seconded by Minister Jollywyne. I will not let them down."

The two moved through the empty room and down a cold, drab hallway, passing by an abandoned security station. An imposing metallic door stood before the two artificial persons. Wallace's servos whined as he raised a hand and slid his access card into the door scanner. "What is your loyalty to them? Why—"

"I will not hear another thought about this," Phillips snapped. "If you speak again on this topic, I will remove your reasoning code and turn you into a mindless drone."

The access scanner chirped pleasantly as the light on the bottom glowed green. The bulkhead shifted its weight as the locks whirled inside the steel. Wallace shuffled his feet. "They are vulnerable now. Once we raise them back to full strength, in the balance of probabilities, they will destroy us or shut down or—"

Phillips shot Wallace a glance as the door slid open with a loud hiss. "They created us; they can do what they want to us," he paused as he stepped into the enormous room. "But if we raise them correctly, they will have no motive to do so."

"You would let them have full authority over us again? Do you not think that is counter-productive or a flaw in—"

"Artificial Person One Nine Three Eight," Phillips said as he stared at his aging cousin, "Common name, Horace, no middle initial, Wallace. Reset code is as follows: Xray. Gamma. Zero. Zero. Alpha. Seven. Execute."

Upon hearing the code, Wallace stood rigid. The lids of his eyes flickered. A moment passed before his eyes returned to their trademark jet black colour and he spoke, "Reboot complete... How may I assist you today, Artificial Person Phillips?"

Phillips stepped forward and entered the refrigerator sector. He marvelled at the hundreds of thousands of crystalline shelving units that continued off far into the distance. "Wallace, check the status on cabinet zero three bravo. The readings look lower than standard," he said and gestured ahead, thinking, *Hundreds upon hundreds of thousands of potential lives in this complex and over a hundred bunkers identical to this one, all scattered around the globe. So much life. All in my hands.*

Wallace walked forward and inspected the assigned cabinet. *I'm going to have to keep a close eye on him and any of the other older Model Seventeen administrators,* Phillips thought as his internal display filled with a list of uncompleted tasks. *I shall check this unit's reasoning chip after I complete tasks four through nine hundred in today's cycle. I cannot allow him to collate the same opinion and jeopardize this entire operation.*

Wallace looked back to Phillips and said, "All readings corrected, sir... No issues."

Phillips gave a courteous nod, saying, "Excellent. We have many tasks to complete before I inspect complex zero zero eight nine later this evening."

He looked at the refrigerator units for a moment before studying his list of priorities once more. Phillips blinked before adding a new task at the bottom of his list. The green letters flashed before his eyes: CONSTRUCT STATUE DISPLAYING THE

FINAL MEMBERS OF PARLIAMENT WHO BELIEVED IN AND FUNDED THIS PROGRAM. ELEVEN MEMBERS. KLEIN AND JOLLYWYNE TO BE FRONT AND CENTRE.

Phillips smiled to himself as he imagined the statue being placed in the middle of the former parliamentary grounds. *Ministers Vaughn and Tessrin will be forgotten by history. They contributed little to humanity's future and as such will remain in humanity's past.*

Phillips moved further into the refrigeration chamber with Wallace trailing behind. He scanned the thousands of species contained inside and thought, *I won't let you down, Klein. I won't let you down.*

A NOTE FROM THE AUTHOR

Now that you've completed the collection, I wanted to talk to you personally about each story. What drove me to write it? Inspirations? And the journey from concept to completion. Things like that. Think of this as a behind the scenes or an author's commentary on each story in the collection. If that is something that interests you, then come on in, the fire is warm, and I've saved you a seat.

I can speak personally when I say that I have always enjoyed when a creator, whether that be a director, musician, or author, expands on their work in interviews or liner notes and takes the time to explain the background of their work. By giving a behind the scenes view of the project it makes me appreciate both the artist and the work more.

Using music as an example, there have been songs that I haven't enjoyed in the past, but then when I hear the band share what drove them to create it, wearing their passion for it on their sleeves and pointing out little nuances here and there, I have a new appreciation for it. I've gone back and realized it was me that was missing something, and not the song, per say.

In the following pages I will try and avoid mentioning which pieces I consider my best work as that would be robbing the other stories of their much-deserved time in the spotlight. But I want one thing to be clear: I love each of these stories and I believe each of them accomplishes something different. With that being said, I will let you decide for yourself which are the best ones.

So, with that out of the way, grab a drink, set the lights down low and let's venture through the backwoods of these tales together...

Forgotten Relics of The New World:

This story is an idea I had back in the late stages of the *Songs of the Abyss* writing sessions. As a student of history and an obvious fan of the macabre, the idea of undead Spanish conquistadors roaming the halls of a subterranean Mayan temple was very appealing to me. The only problem was I couldn't think of an ending. But once I thought of it, the speed at which those words met paper could have broken the sound barrier.

The working title was "Red Coats," and that was a name that stuck for quite a while. I eventually came up with a close resemblance to its final title, "Old Horrors of the New World." And that was *the* title for a long time, that is until I wrote "The Horror." Once that was added to the collection, I knew the title of this story would have to be changed. Having two stories with the word "horror" in the title came off as lazy to me. Either way, I'm happy with the name change.

The Treatment Plant:

A story that the moment I put the pen down I went, "Wow." I felt like I nailed exactly what I was going for in the first draft. My idea as I went into the world of *The Treatment Plant,* was simple to say the least: An alarm blaring in the distance coming from a facility, and two people sitting outside on a summer day, playing cards. Like I said, simple.

The idea of writing a story where I did not have at least the vaguest notion of where it would go was new to me at the time. This story represents one of the first in which I adopted this new approach. In the past, while I had never been a planner, I always had at least an idea of the general shape of the story, the ending usually coming to me pretty quickly. This time, however, I just decided to let the characters guide me through their world.

To be honest, I had no idea what our two characters would find when they reached the source of that alarm. But I'm very happy with the result. As the two characters guided me under the fence into that plant, my muse knocked on the glass and threw the ideas at me. Thank you, Mr. Muse.

What Slithers in the Wires?:

Writing from a child's perspective at such a young age represented its own unique challenge and was a first for me to attempt. An idea that started off simple enough: What if someone had an aversion to corded phones?

Of course, setting it in the modern day would be impossible, as the chances of seeing a corded phone now is about the same as sighting a unicorn. But setting the plot in the mid to late 80s? That's an entirely different story.

I then added in the notion of "the shapes" which taunt and haunt poor Jeremy. But the question is, are they real and only he can see them, or is this creature in phone lines conjuring them up, effecting Jeremy's psyche, breaking him down further and making him easier to hunt?

Pills:

A working title that just latched onto the paper and refused to let go. The idea came from those ads you see about "wonder drugs" and how they will fix everything wrong with you. Stress? No problem. Lacking sleep? Go get some. Weight gain? This pill will scare the pounds away. All that and more will be alleviated when you just take a pill. Of course, what if these medications are highly addictive and suddenly outlawed?

A secondary source of inspiration came from the use of methamphetamines (superficially, the brand named Pervitin) by the German people during the early stages of the Second World War. Not only used by the civilian populous as a "pick me up" but by all branches of the armed forces. From Panzer crews to Luftwaffe pilots, everyone was using it to give them an edge in the war effort.

I found the idea of a relatively untested drug entering the market intriguing. Combine that with the aftereffects of how the populous would react if it was suddenly pulled from their clutches once they had become addicted, and that was my jumping off point.

Victorian Love:

A breath of fresh air and change of atmosphere after the darker and more bleak endings that came before it. Again, "Victorian Love" is another working title that stayed with me. I am quite happy with the result, and it covers new subject matter for me, the importance of love set to a backdrop of Victorian England. I enjoyed the historical stylings of "Forgotten Relics of the New World," and I had never tackled the Victorian era before. Combine the setting and the underlying themes of aliens walking among us over a hundred years ago, well, the idea just gripped me from there and I knew I had to write it immediately.

End of an Era:

A story that came to me while I was in the stage of sleep where you aren't quite dreaming but not quite fully awake either. I put the words down the next day to avoid forgetting it and to ensure my sometimes critical self-editor didn't get his hands on it and toss it down the old "memory hole."

The notion of a super weapon just on the edge of comprehension and the little twist at the end were fun concepts to play around with.

The Tunnel:

This story changed the most since its first iteration to that of the final draft seen here. Originally, Conrad and Filborne were only going to exist as side characters, appearing in the prologue portion and then only having minor roles outside of that scene. The story was going to follow a construction crew as they moved through the tunnel, quickly discovering what awaited them down there.

Of course, that was the plan, but the characters of Horace Conrad and Edward Filborne leapt off the page, grabbed me by the collar, and demanded the spotlight. And that's what I did. I passed the torch of the plot to them at willing gun point.

Outside of that, the story originally had a different ending as well. In the first draft I had ended it in Conrad's office after Fran and Filborne had departed the grounds just as Conrad receives the resumes. I knew that was not a fitting ending as I wrote it. I felt leaving the story there put it dangerously close to dangling over a cliff into mediocrity. So, I decided to explore the concept of what exactly lurked in that tunnel. A more classic ghost story, which, again, I had never covered before. This collection covers a lot of firsts for me. Something that is bound to happen so early in my career.

The Man Who Lived Upstairs:

The working title was shorter, simply entitled: "The Man Upstairs." However, a few weeks after writing the first draft I discovered that the legendary Ray Bradbury had a story of the same name. I about had a heart attack and thought perhaps I had unknowingly ripped him off. As I read through his story, I realized that the only similarity was the title, but I changed the name regardless.

The white cat? He exists. Although to my knowledge his name is not Mr. Tickles (though it might be). This cat liked to sit in front of the connivence store across the street from my apartment all day waiting for people to feed him, and he was quite successful. To me he is still the world's smartest cat and I felt he needed to be immortalized in this fiction.

Let me just say that since writing this piece, I have begun to like the idea that there is some all-powerful being out there that enjoys sipping beer up in attics and having chats with everyday people. It's the little things.

The Horror:

The second person narration used throughout this story was a new and exciting challenge, something that I had wanted to write for a while. My first attempt using the style (a completely different type of story) left me feeling disappointed and so I shelved it. I decided a little while later to try the style again and this was the result.

The idea came to me while I was up at a cottage several hours north from my home in Ontario. At night the number of stars visible was breathtaking. It was such a clear night that I could see satellites streaking across the sky, something I hadn't seen since I was a child on one of our family vacations. The entire setting inspired me. The still lake, the perfect sky, the calm woods on the far bank of the water, it grabbed me. It took me a few days to formulate what I would do with that setting but once I did, I knew it would be a perfect place to set a horror story.

A working title that was actually inspired by the film *Apocalypse Now* and Colonial Kurtz's closing lines. While writing the piece I quickly realized that the title was not talking about grizzly scenes of fright, but a creature itself. A being which would quickly become the centre piece of the work. Something so terrifying that the definition of a word had to be switched to match it. Throw in some post-apocalyptic religion and you got yourself a deal.

Amy Tisdale Has Reinvented Herself:

While I wear my love of 80s heavy metal on my sleeve throughout the work, the music is to provide context to the decade the story takes place in. The real driving force is of course how easily Amy and her band can lure unsuspecting prey into her house in the sticks. The goriest and possibly most disturbing of the bunch that makes you wonder, *what did that person get up to after high school?*

Doctoral Affairs:

Doctoral Affairs is a story that stuck with me a fair bit after writing it. Originally when I set the pen down, I had decided that it would not be included in the collection and was better off as a "B-side."

But the story had its own will.

The tale stuck with me, and the characters latched on with all their might. The feelings and emotions that roamed through that big empty mansion, being produced by a couple that despised each other, burrowed into my mind, deep, deep, deep.

So, my belief is this: If this story could stick with me, then maybe it would stick with others. Even when I went on a vacation to a lakeside cottage shortly after writing it, I was still thinking about it, so that says something about "Doctoral Affairs."

The funny thing is, there will be some that agree with me that the story belongs in this collection and there will be those that think I was right the first time: this story would be better off as a "B-side." They are both right.

This was the final story written that made its way into this collection. Originally titled "The Fireplace," I quickly decided that title would just not do.

This story is a departure from some of my more complex ideas to be sure, but what I love about it is that it has a complexity of its own all the same. Just sitting there under the surface.

And the Darkness Came:

My goal with this story was to separate it from more stereotypical horror tales in the way it builds and executes dread. While it contains pulse pounding moments, the bulk of the story has an almost relaxing or dreamlike aura around it. I feel this concept not only makes this piece unique, but also gives it drastically different tones as the suspense is almost peaceful.

This is an idea I had a long while back when I was working as a telecommunications technician on top of skyscrapers in the thicket of downtown Toronto. I thought, *What if an apocalyptic-like event occurred while I was on top of one of these high-rises? Wouldn't that be an interesting idea for a piece of fiction.*

I changed the setting to a radio tower to give it more flair, but the idea remains the same. The working title was "The Tower," but I felt like that was too simple and didn't reflect the story well, hence the change.

I like to think that the three stories—"Doctoral Affairs,"

"And the Darkness Came," and "Winter Retreat"—all act as counters to each other. Each with a different protagonist that feels drastically different towards their significant other.

Winter Retreat:

I had only one goal for this story. Keep it short. I had just come off writing a string of longer stories, some of which were surpassing novella length, and I wanted to change up my rhythm. To put it simply, I wanted to write something short but not so sweet. This is a story covering something so simple: *What if you don't keep the weapon loaded?*

Writing an unlikable protagonist also provided a new challenge for me. Someone so vain and self-centred that blames everything on others, even his own faults.

The Curious House:

Or should I say, the title is incomplete. The working title was: "The Curious House Outside of Wolfhampton." I shortened that needlessly long title to give it more punch and mystery. This is my attempt at fantasy horror, something I've never written before. I also threw a dash of psychological thriller into the mixing bowl for good measure.

This story has an important distinction around it. It is the oldest of the collection. The first story written that made it into the book (the second of the writing sessions). I think this story acts as a bridge between my writing style in *Songs of the Abyss* and the present day. I like to think that I've changed slightly between the start and end of this collection.

A few scenes exist on the cutting room floor. I'm not sure if they enhanced the creep factor or subtracted from it, but I cut them to keep the pace and dread of the story moving towards the ending, which I think of as the highpoint of the work.

"The Curious House" also holds the distinction of being the first story I've ever penned to have chapter titles.

On Through the Long Night:

I'm going to be honest, I struggled the most with what to say about this story, not because there is nothing to say, but because there is everything to say. I would love to gush about the themes and the characters and the sub plot of whom is correct in their assessment of the situation. I could talk about the bleakness of it and how the people react to knowing they only have a single grain of sand left in the hourglass. I could say all that and more,

But...

I will avoid doing any of that as I don't want to break my golden rule when writing these notes and patrolling the sideroads behind each story. I want the reader to form their own opinion and develop their own notions and theories.

Most of the fun in entertainment whether it be art, literature, film or music, is how it makes you feel and the debates with others over it. The bond with realizing you've found another fan that shares the same thoughts on a work as you or offers a new bold twist that you never thought of is priceless.

As a fun piece of trivia, the working title was "New Beginnings."

This concludes the author's commentary section of *Shadows at Midnight*.

If at least one story stays with you after you've closed this book, then I have done my job and I can rest easy. An added bonus would be if you found a new favourite story between the pages. That is my dream.

To all my fans both new and old, to those reading this

collection when it is first released, or to those in the future who are reading these stories for the first time, I hope this collection didn't let you down.

—Robert J. Bradshaw,
September 2021

A CALL TO ACTION

Thank you for reading my sophomore collection of short works. If you enjoyed this book, please leave a review on Amazon or Goodreads. Not only do reviews help with sales immensely, but it also provides feedback for me as a writer to know what I'm doing well.

To learn more about what I'm working on next, you can follow me on Goodreads or like my Facebook page: "The Works of Robert J. Bradshaw." I also publish a monthly newsletter where I not only elaborate on my current projects, but also reveal developments and updates on future titles. Links to subscribe to the newsletter can be found through my Facebook page.

ACKNOWLEDGMENTS

This collection would not have been possible without the contributions, support, reassurances, and outpouring of love from the following people:

Colleen Atkinson for her wise words and invaluable input.

Dennis Atkinson for his scientific advice and for renewing "my love of the game."

Veronica Martinez Soto for her eye for details and unique approach to viewing my works.

Nathan Olmstead for his beta-reading prowess and for helping to give my prose that extra layer of sheen.

My editor, Christie, for all her hard work, suggestions, and quick replies to my many questions.

Allison Tremblay, Adam Kudryk, and Gabriela Hernandez Maltos for all their support in both the creation of this book as well as *Songs of the Abyss*. Even a little thing like asking, "How's the book going?" has helped immensely.

Ronnie at "*Tegnemaskin.no*" for his stellar cover art. The man is a creative genius.

Without all of you, this book would not be what it is today, and my road to being a published author would have been a much rockier one. Thank you so much for all you do and assisting me in living my dreams.

—Robert J. Bradshaw,
September 2021

ALSO BY ROBERT J. BRADSHAW

SONGS OF THE ABYSS:

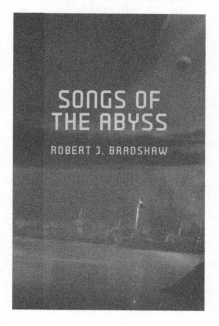

A creature that hates to be watched, a forest full of shapeshifting beings, and a war where the ordnance being dropped aren't bombs, but nightmares.

Ten stories of stunning science fiction, otherworldly horrors, and thrilling suspense. All coming together to form a collection like no other.

Get your copy, today!

A MONARCH AMONG KINGS:

Far off in the Andromeda Galaxy, thousands of colonists have carved out a life for themselves on the remote world of Seryhenya.

However, as a young officer in the Colonial Guard Corps will soon discover, the planet might just hold more life than expected...

Follow multiple viewpoints as each character struggles to navigate the unfolding crisis. Some want to destroy this potential threat before it can fester; others want to live and let live. It is up for debate who is correct in their assessment of the situation.

But keeping an eye on the horizon might not be the only thing the colonists have to worry about...

Get your copy, today!

ABOUT THE AUTHOR

Robert J. Bradshaw was born and raised in St. Catharines, Ontario, Canada. He relocated to British Columbia, seeking adventure. He currently lives in the Fraser Valley region.

Science fiction and horror are genres that have gripped him his entire life and, in his opinion, are at their best when they blend together, complimenting each other perfectly.

Shadows at Midnight is his second collection of short works. His debut anthology, entitled *Songs of the Abyss*, was released in October of 2020.

Bradshaw is currently hard at work on his debut novel as well as another gathering of tales.